COLTON
CHRISTMAS
PROTECTOR

BY
BETH CORNELISON

MILLS
BOON

First Published in Great Britain 2016
By Mills & Boon, an imprint of HarperCollins*Publishers*
1 London Bridge Street, London, SE1 9GF

© 2016 Harlequin Books S.A.

Special thanks and acknowledgement are given to Beth Cornelison
for her contribution to The Coltons of Texas series.

ISBN: 978-0-263-91949-3

18-1216

Our policy is to use papers that are natural, renewable and recyclable products and made from wood grown in sustainable forests. The logging and manufacturing processes conform to the legal environmental regulations of the country of origin.

Printed and bound in Spain
by CPI, Barcelona

Beth Cornelison began working in public relations before pursuing her love of writing romance. She has won numerous honors for her work, including a nomination for the RWA RITA® Award for *The Christmas Stranger*. She enjoys featuring her cats (or friends' pets) in her stories and always has another book in the pipeline! She currently lives in Louisiana with her husband, one son and three spoiled cats. Contact her via her website, www.bethcornelison.com.

This book is dedicated to YOU, dear reader!
Thank you for your years of support and sharing
my stories with me. Long live romance!

Chapter 1

Andrew's funeral was well attended, the burial full of the pomp and ceremonial rites traditionally on display for a fallen police officer. His brothers and sisters in blue packed the church and lined the street as the funeral procession made its way to the cemetery.

Through it all, Reid Colton tried to stay in the background. He knew his presence could prove a distraction from the send-off Andrew deserved, and he refused to be responsible for any disruption to the service. Seeing all the dress uniforms, the military-like formality of the service, made Reid glad he'd never made formal allegations that his partner was mixed up in something bad.

Whatever Andrew had gotten involved with in recent weeks didn't negate the years of loyal service and heroism Andrew Clark had shown the community and the police force. Andrew had been a good friend, a great partner and a decorated police detective. Reid's purpose in investigating Andrew, in making his quiet allegations of theft and drug use, was only an effort to rein in his partner, to bring him to his senses before he got in over his head. Before Andrew got addicted, got arrested, got thrown off the force in disgrace.

For his efforts to save his partner's career, save Andrew's life, Reid had become the one under investigation, the one whose career had been sacrificed due to innuendo and unsubstantiated claims of wrongdoing.

Hugh Barrington, the Colton family's lawyer and Andrew's father-in-law, had tried to salvage Reid's reputation and position with the police department, but in the end, Reid had walked away in disgust. He'd given too many years, too much of his heart and soul to his post as a Dallas police detective to continue working under the shadow of suspicion. He wouldn't put himself through the indignity of skeptical side glances, sneers of disrespect and walls of silence from his fellow officers. He'd rather leave on his own terms than wait to be cleared of the trumped-up charges or let half-truths end his career. He had his pride. He was a Colton, after all, and he deserved some modicum of respect for all his family had done for the community, if not for his years of service, loyalty and sweat.

Yet even knowing he was *persona non grata*, he'd needed to come today. He had unfinished business. And so, after the interment ended and the crowd of well-wishers had largely dispersed, he made his way toward Andrew's wife, wanting only to extend his sympathies. Penelope Barrington Clark dabbed at her eyes as the chief of police spoke to her and gave her hand a consoling pat. Pen, as Andrew and her close friends called her, flashed a strained smile, the corners of her mouth quivering with the effort to be polite. Once the chief walked away and while Pen greeted an older couple, Reid stepped out of the shadow of the big oak tree where he'd lingered, waiting, and approached his partner's widow.

He'd spent numerous Sunday afternoons in the Clarks' home, watching the Cowboys with Andrew. He'd driven Andrew from a stakeout to the hospital when Pen had gone into labor a week early, and he'd been one of the first to hold their son, Nicholas, when he was born a few short hours later. He'd been to cookouts, birthday parties and the celebration following Nicholas's baptism. He'd come to count Penelope Barrington Clark as one of his closest friends. After all, she was Hugh Barrington's daughter. As the daughter of the Colton family's lawyer, he'd known *of* Penelope even before he'd gotten to *know* her. He'd admired her from afar as a randy teenager and been the one to introduce her to Andrew at a police-department fundraising event seven years ago.

He never regretted that Penelope had chosen to marry Andrew. They'd been happy together, and he'd been happy for them. But he'd been a tad jealous of his partner. While Reid had his back turned and his womanizing interests focused elsewhere, Pen had grown from a shy but attractive teenager into a tall and willowy bombshell. More important, Pen and Andrew had built the kind of domestic partnership and loving home he secretly longed for. They may have been solidly middle class, living solely on Andrew's detective's salary after Pen's falling-out with her wealthy father, but all of the Coltons' billions hadn't made his home life as harmonious and satisfying as what the Clarks had shared. Which, he knew, meant Andrew's death was all the harder for Pen.

Reid kept a steady gaze on her as he approached, waiting for that moment when she first saw him. After years of studying people, their body language and emotional tells, he knew her first reaction to seeing him would be her most honest one. Penelope had always had a certain grace bred into her by her society parents. But today, with her silky auburn hair twisted up in a severe knot at her nape, her ivory skin blotchy from crying and her hazel eyes luminous with tears as she grieved her husband, she looked fragile. Vulnerable. Yet still as beautiful as a cherished china doll. Reid's gut twisted seeing her so wrecked by her grief, so torn. Though she was surrounded by mourners offering condolences and had her father standing just behind her in a theatrical show of solidarity, Reid knew from the bleak look in her eyes, the wooden formality of her expression, she felt completely alone in her loss.

He wished he could simply push his way to the front of the crowd and pull her into a bear hug. But how would that impulse be received? Did she buy into the hype and lies that had been told about him since Andrew's death? Was there any of the old respect and friendship left?

That instant moment of truth came as she dropped the hand of the older man, turned toward the last woman in the line of well-wishers…and her eyes met Reid's. For one second, that first startled heartbeat, her one unguarded moment of recognition, she stared at him. He saw the raw emotion, the heartache and her longing for the refuge and support she knew he'd give her. And he prayed his eyes said all that was in his heart, because that one brief moment was all he had before her hazel eyes grew glacial.

Her shoulders stiffened and her back drew up straighter. Despite the hostile ice in her glare, he approached her. "Pen, I'm so sorry for—"

"You have a lot of nerve showing up here," she spat at him, spots of color rising in her cheeks.

"Pen, I only wanted—"

"No!" She raised a trembling hand to ward him off. Then aiming her index finger at him like a gun, she snarled, "I don't ever want to see you or your lying face again! Leave me the hell alone, Reid."

Her warning hit him in the gut, as painful and final as if she had fired bullets at him instead of icy words. "If you'd just hear me out, Pen, I only wanted—"

"You heard her, Reid." A firm hand closed on his shoulder and pulled him away from Penelope. "I think you should go."

Reid turned to meet the cool blue gaze of Hugh Barrington. Behind his silver-framed glasses, Hugh's eyes narrowed. The man's squinty-eyed glare reminded Reid of the teasing way he and his brothers had referred to the man as The Weasel as kids, because of Hugh's narrow eyes and ferret-like swath of dark hair.

"I can handle him on my own, Father," Pen grated, turning her chilly stare on Hugh. "I don't need a keeper. And if I did, it certainly would not be *you*. Not after you defended a *Colton*, took his side over Andrew's. I'll never forgive you for standing behind a Colton instead of my husband!"

If Reid had wondered whether the strained relationship between Hugh Barrington and his daughter had been set aside during this family crisis, he had his answer. A resounding *no*.

Pen whirled away from the men and stalked off, her chin high and her mouth pressed in a taut line of fury. She made a beeline to the waiting black Cadillac, where the funeral director stood with the back door open. A woman Reid thought he recognized from one of the Clarks' barbecues—a neighbor or college friend of Pen's maybe?—stood next to the Cadillac, as well, holding Pen's six-month-old son, Nicholas. Penelope took her son from the woman, kissing his forehead and cradling him close. She took a moment to hug the baby, her eyes closed and cheek against his hair. Reid could see her body visibly relax as she held Nicholas, her baby's presence clearly calming her frayed nerves. Finally, she raised her head and sent one last backward glance to her husband's casket. Where Reid still stood. Watching her.

Her chest heaved with a deep sigh or a sob that she'd tried to choke down, then she spun away and slid into the backseat of the Cadillac. The funeral director closed the door, climbed in the front passenger side and the black vehicle pulled away.

A hollow pang assailed Reid's chest as the car carried Pen away. As inappropriate as it was, especially here at his former partner's graveside, he couldn't ignore the facts. Pen hated him, blamed him for Andrew's death. And he still harbored an undeniable lust for Penelope Barrington Clark.

Eighteen months later

The bitter tones of a woman sobbing set off alarm bells for Reid as he left his suite one morning in December the following year. His family had endured no shortage of tragedy, danger and suspicion of late, and the fact that a woman was crying somewhere on the first floor of the mansion didn't bode well. On the other hand, his mother, Whitney, was known for her theatrics and over-reactions, and the voice sounded like hers. He'd never been close to either of his parents, and for the last several years, he'd demonstrated as much by addressing them by their first names.

"Now what?" he mumbled to himself as he closed the door of his upstairs suite and headed toward the kitchen to find a late breakfast. He hated the prickle of dread that bad news waited downstairs. Was it his father, Eldridge? Was there bad news on his whereabouts?

Early this summer, his elderly father had gone missing from his bedroom in the main house of the ranch. Foul play was suspected, and speculation and suspicion had been thrown about within the family for the last six months with little real progress other than to eliminate several of his siblings as suspects. Reid had dabbled at finding his father, kept abreast of the investigation, but he still had a bad taste in his mouth for the police and their crime investigations based on the way his own case had been handled. Frustration over how the search for his missing father had stalled ate at him most days, but he knew what local law enforcement would say if he tried to intervene. *Leave it alone, Reid. You're not a cop anymore.*

But that didn't mean he didn't still itch to take over the investigation and show the incompetents handling the case how effective detective work was done.

The glimmer of winter sun streaking through the foyer windows told him how late in the morning it had gotten while he lolled in bed and took his lingering hot shower. He used to be an early riser. He used to religiously get up before the ranch hands and head out for a run before the sun was up. But then he used to have a job to get up for, stay fit for, start his mornings early for. In the last eighteen months, he'd begun sleeping later, skipping days at the gym and generally hating the tedium of spending his days at the ranch with little to occupy his time.

To pass a few hours in recent weeks, he'd chased a few rabbits concerning Eldridge's case to no avail and worked with his siblings on a few matters where his expertise was useful. He'd spent some time this fall riding his horse, fishing and reading some of the dusty books in the ranch library. But for the most part these days, he was at loose ends.

He trotted down the grand staircase in his family's mansion, the crown jewel sitting at the heart of their working ranch, Colton Valley Ranch. Although he'd invested in an apartment in Austin, a lake house that he used as a secret getaway and a condo in Aspen for weekends when he wanted to ski, he still spent most of his time at the family ranch.

Truth be told, he didn't want to move out. The daily histrionics and chaos of the family mansion were better than any British TV drama or American reality show. And despite all their nutty, backstabbing, snobbish ways, he knew he'd miss his family if he moved out. How could he live alone after growing up in this twisted version of the Brady Bunch? He'd really be bored then. And lonely.

Seeing his siblings pairing off with their soul mates and moving on with their lives in recent months had sharpened his sense of being alone, even in the midst of the hustle, bustle and drama of Colton Valley Ranch. The coming Christmas holiday only emphasized his feelings of idleness and solitude. Reid didn't do bored well. His restlessness was building, and he knew he needed an outlet for his frustrations over his stalled life and the stagnant investigation concerning Eldridge. Something had to give, or he'd lose it.

*Speaking of losing it...*he thought as he strolled into the kitchen in search of coffee and found his mother dabbing at her eyes and bawling into a napkin at the breakfast-nook table.

"Mother?" he said warily, not really wanting to get caught up in one of her tedious emotional rants, but unable to completely ignore her tears. "What's wrong?"

Whitney raised her head and gave him a bleary glance

from green eyes rimmed with smeared mascara. "What do you think is wrong? I miss my Dridgey-pooh."

Reid clenched his back teeth. "I've asked you not to call him that around me. It's a little too nauseating, especially at this hour of the morning."

She lifted her chin and gave a haughty sniff. "Well, you certainly got up on the wrong side of the bed."

Reid ignored her rebuttal and lifted the coffee carafe to examine the sludge that remained in the pot. "Bettina?" he called and the family cook scuttled out from the prep room adjoining the kitchen.

"Yes, sir? Would you like me to fix you some eggs or sausage?"

He shook his head. "Just some fresh coffee, please. I'm not hungry."

Bettina got busy brewing a new pot of coffee, and Reid strolled over to the table where his mother sat with the newspaper.

"Was there something in the paper about Eldridge?" He nodded to the folded *Dallas Morning News* by her tea mug.

"No," Whitney answered with a pout, still wiping her eyes and sniffling. "Everyone seems to have forgotten he's still missing except me!"

"No one's forgotten, Mother. We just haven't had any new leads to follow up in a few days. Instead of crying, you should be happy the burned body they found wasn't Eldridge."

The previous month, thanks to a tip from Hugh Barrington, a body was recovered from a car wreck and was believed to be the Colton patriarch's corpse...long enough for Eldridge's will to be read. But further inquiries proved the body's ID had been faked, putting the search for Reid's father back to square one.

"I am glad the body wasn't his," Whitney replied, squaring her shoulders. "And don't tell me how to feel!" She narrowed her eyes at him. "You could stand to be a little more upset over Dridgey—over Eldridge's disappearance. He's you father, after all. Don't you care—"

"Save it!" he said holding up a hand. "I'm in no mood for a lecture."

"Reid! Don't you think—"

"Pardon me, ma'am."

Reid silently thanked the butler, Aaron Manfred, for his interruption and sneaked back over to the counter to hover by the coffeepot. He shouldn't have had Bettina brew a new pot just for him. He could have made a Starbucks run. It wasn't like he had anything else on his calendar today.

"I was hoping I might be able to take the evening off tonight."

"Again?" Whitney snapped.

"Yes, ma'am." Aaron gave a quick nod, clearly unrattled by Whitney's waspishness. But then, Aaron had been dealing with the moody and snobbish Coltons for as long as Reid could remember. "Moira will be here and will be happy to help you with anything that should arise."

"But why? What do you—" Whitney clamped her lips together and flapped a hand at the man. "Oh, go ahead. It's not like my husband is here to need you."

And with that statement, she ducked her head and began sobbing again. "Oh, Dridgey-pooh!"

With an impatient grunt, Reid snatched the coffeepot from the maker before it finished brewing and poured himself a steaming mugful. "I'm going out."

He didn't know where, but he had to get out of the claustrophobic atmosphere of the mansion. Maybe as a favor to his mother, to the whole family really, he'd check up on the progress of the search for Eldridge. Or better yet, he'd do some searching of his own. The case was growing as cold as their frost-dusted ranch pastures. No more procrastinating. The time had come for someone to break this case. If the police were going to drag their feet, then Reid would find his father by himself.

Chapter 2

Penelope Barrington Clark stood in the threshold of Andrew's office/man cave and gathered her courage. She'd procrastinated cleaning out the room as long as she could. Immediately after his death, well-meaning friends had offered to help her with the painful task, but she'd put them off. How could she possibly throw out or give away all the things Andrew had owned, touched, cherished? Wasn't it bad enough he was gone? Losing all of the possessions that cluttered his home office would have added salt to her wounds.

But the house had sold more quickly than she'd anticipated it would. She and Nicholas were downsizing, moving to a more affordable home. Ironic that she, a Barrington, needed to worry about finances, but she refused to take a dime from her wealthy father, and Andrew's death benefit from the police department didn't cover the mortgage and all her expenses. She knew she'd have to get a job, was all right with the idea, but she'd put it off. She'd wanted to dedicate as much time to Nicholas while he was young as she could. He would only be a toddler once, and she couldn't stand the idea of missing any of his baby days.

The new house needed work, but it was in an out-lying area with good schools and plenty of parks with playgrounds where Nicholas could run and climb as he grew older.

Andrew will never see Nicholas start kindergarten or jump out of a swing. The kamikaze thought shot straight to her heart with a sharp, piercing ache. She squeezed her eyes shut and balled her hands at her sides as she forced the stray thought down, tucked it away. If only she could pack up the random painful reminders and reflections like shards of a broken mirror to be discarded forever. Time was supposed to heal her wounds, but eighteen months after Andrew's death, she still groped her way through the morass of memories and unexpected flashes of insight that dragged her down like quicksand.

She shook her head and steeled herself with a deep breath. *Just do this. Get it over with.*

Rolling the tension from her shoulders, Penelope strode into the man cave/office and moved an empty box to the top of Andrew's desk for easier packing. She could start with the ugly stuff, the tacky things, the dear-God-what-were-you-thinking items. They would be the easiest to get rid of, she figured. From there, she could work her way up to sorting through the commendation awards for heroism from the police department, the family pictures, the personal papers and sentimental items that screamed *Andrew*.

She took the woman's leg lamp, á la *A Christmas Story*, from the top of the bookcase and groaned, re-membering when he'd brought the gag gift home from a Christmas party.

"It's a major award!" Andrew had joked when she'd

sneered at his party gift and tried to usher it straight out to the trash. Now that she had her chance to throw it away, she hesitated. Maybe one of the guys at the police station would like to have the lamp as a memento of Andrew's quirky sense of humor.

"Oh, Lord. If I second-guess every item in this room, I'll be here until Christmas." She chucked the leg lamp into a box for charity and moved on to the trophies he'd won with the community softball league. She couldn't bring herself to toss those, so she put them aside to go into storage.

The taxidermy-preserved fish was a no-brainer. Trash!

"Dead animals are not home decor," she'd argued when Andrew had brought home the prize bass mounted on a plaque and intending to hang it on the living-room wall.

"Do you know how much I paid to have this mounted?" he'd countered, as if that made the bass any less hideous to her.

His office wall had been their compromise, so long as he didn't put it on the wall opposite the door, where she'd see it when she walked down the hall.

She shuddered as she lifted the dusty bass down from the wall now, surprised by how heavy the ugly thing was. As she struggled with it, the trophy fish flopped backward and thunked against the wood-paneled wall.

Trying not to get dust in her nose, Penelope carried the bass to the discard box. The inscribed metal plate under the fish's belly read Caddo Lake Largemouth Bass, 20 inches, 4.88 pounds, July 5, 2013. Andrew had been so proud of that catch. He'd bragged about it at cookouts for the rest of that summer and on occasion afterward, when the topic of fishing came up. Maybe she should...

No! Get rid of it. The new house would not have room for all of Andrew's valuable things, much less his junk.

As she strolled back across the room to continue the packing, she noticed a dent in the wall where the fish plaque had banged the paneling. Great. Something else to repair before the new owners took possession. Penelope lifted a hand to rub her fingers over the indentation, and as she stroked the wood paneling she found that the wall had unexpected give. When she pushed a little harder, a section of the paneling came loose and fell back into a recess behind the wall.

"Lovely," she grumbled under her breath. "Now instead of a dent you have to replace a whole—" She stopped mid-gripe and furrowed her brow. Behind the section of paneling that had come loose, a thick file folder and a small box rested on a horizontal two-by-four inside the wall. A hidden file? What could that be about? Had Andrew put this file and box there or had the house's previous owner?

Before removing the hidden items, Penelope wiped her hand on her yoga pants and mentally tried to quell the nervous jumble in her gut. Probably an old case file and piece of evidence. No reason to think Andrew was keeping secrets from her. Maybe it wasn't even Andrew's. Maybe it was a rare jewel or coin collection with papers of authenticity worth thousands of dollars.

"And your financial worries will be over." She gave a wry chuckle. "Dreamer. And maybe the moon is made of cheese."

With a trembling hand, she lifted the file folder and box out of the secret cubbyhole and read the inscription on the file's tab. *Hugh Barrington.*

Penelope drew her eyebrows together in a frown. What in the world? She walked over to Andrew's desk and set the small box aside as she sank into his office chair and opened the file. Heart pounding, she paged through the documents and photocopies of receipts. The pages all looked pretty routine. Copies of billing statements for her father's time working for his clients, receipts for business lunches and hotels. Tax returns.

Penelope examined the tax return more closely and whistled. Her father still earned a boatload of money, most of it from his wealthiest clients. The Colton family topped that list, she noted, seeing how many billable hours he'd charged them.

"Suckers," she grumbled, setting that document aside when a strange gnawing sensation bit her gut. Thoughts of the Coltons invariably led her back to memories of how Andrew had died. Reid Colton's part in it. Reid's appearance at Andrew's funeral.

If you'd just hear me out, Pen, I only wanted—

But she'd shut him down, shut him out, walked away without listening. What could he possibly say to change things? He'd admitted he'd been the one to deliver the tainted shot that killed Andrew. He'd injected Andrew with potassium chloride, one of the chemicals used by states to administer the death penalty by lethal injection. He'd admitted to arguing with Andrew the morning her husband died. He'd confessed to making allegations against Andrew, claims he couldn't prove, statements that tarnished her husband's good name and reputation. What Reid had done was indefensible. What more could he have to say that would make a difference now?

You'll never know if you don't give him a chance to explain.

A chill raced through Penelope, and she quickly silenced the nagging voice that still unsettled her. The uneasiness inside her that wouldn't let her close that chapter of her life and move on. *Damn you, Reid Colton, for causing these doubts!*

She'd once considered Reid a friend via his relationship with Andrew. Growing up, she'd thought Reid, the son of her father's best client, was handsome, if rather spoiled and overbearing. She'd written off his snobbery as a sense of entitlement earned through his life of privilege. But his bossy and driven personality had proven to be assets as a police detective. Reid was smart, decisive and commanding, and he'd used those qualities to his advantage to rise quickly through the ranks at the Dallas PD. Andrew had often said he was lucky to be partnered with Reid. They complemented each other's skills and had a good time together even outside of duty. All of which made Reid's betrayal more difficult to swallow.

Penelope forced thoughts of Reid's dastardly accusations and suspect actions out of her head. Clearing out Andrew's office would be hard enough to endure without constantly dredging up the questions, heartaches and bitterness surrounding his death.

Rubbing her eyes with the pads of her fingers, she bent her head over the file again and studied the papers Andrew had collected about her father. At first glance, the file seemed innocent enough. But why would Andrew have hidden these papers in the secret compartment behind that hideous fish? She flipped faster through the pages of printouts and photocopies. What did it mean? Why—?

She stopped when she reached a spreadsheet Andrew had complied. God love him, Andrew had a thing about spreadsheets. They appealed to his sense of order, his nerdy perfectionism and love for analysis. She gave a sad chuckle as she scanned the grid of information, then froze when what she was reading penetrated the haze of her walk down memory lane.

The headings on the columns of data read: Evidence, Date, Research, Corroboration, Exclusions, Conclusions.

"Evidence? Corroboration? Andrew, what were you doing?" But the further she read, the more obvious the answer became. Her husband had been building a case against her father. Andrew had been keeping a secret file of evidence that pointed toward malpractice, tax evasion and other crimes against his clients. Double billing. Padded expense reports. Extortion.

A chill crept through Penelope. Was her father really guilty of all the wrongdoing laid out in Andrew's file? Did Andrew have proof or were these just allegations he was investigating?

She slapped the file closed and rocked back in the swivel chair. Dear Lord! She'd never had a good relationship with her father, especially after the cold way he'd treated her mother before her death.

Hugh had acted as if his wife had gotten cancer merely to annoy him. He'd treated her as if he saw her as a burden and financial drain rather than the loving spouse, mother of his child and woman in physical and emotional pain that she was. Many other times through the years, Hugh had made it clear that he put the needs and wishes of his hoity-toity clients over the needs of his family. Sometimes Penelope couldn't believe she'd survived the superficial and warped-priority world of Hugh Barrington and his cronies. Her life with her blue-collar husband had shocked her father, but she'd found a happiness and rootedness high society had never offered. Andrew had never been a fan of her father's, either, but this...

She lifted the file and frowned. If Andrew was investigating her father, that was enough for her. She trusted he had probable cause, sufficient evidence to suspect Hugh. But what exactly had set off the warning bells for him? What should she do with the file Andrew had collected?

She couldn't ignore it. If Hugh was doing something illegal, didn't she have a responsibility to turn in the information to the authorities?

She chewed her bottom lip and sighed. If, just *if* Andrew was wrong, she didn't want to be responsible for tarnishing her father's name, no matter how bad her relationship with him was. And if Andrew did have a strong case against Hugh, why hadn't he exposed his crimes? Did Andrew's silence mean he hadn't proven anything yet? Did he—

Her cell phone buzzed with an incoming text, interrupting her ponderous thoughts. The message was from her dry cleaner. Her clothes were ready to be picked up. She huffed another sigh of frustration. She'd taken her dresses and pantsuits in to be refreshed and ironed, knowing she couldn't live off Andrew's life insurance money forever. She either had to get a job...or suck up to her father for the money to pay her mortgage. She grunted. *Never!*

Begging her father for money would be admitting defeat, in her view. And if Andrew's suspicions were on target...

She had to know. Surely Andrew had confided his suspicions about Hugh to someone. But who?

The obvious answer made her gut roll, and she balled her hands in irritation. How could she call the one man she wanted to avoid even more than her father? She couldn't! She wouldn't!

She...had no real choice if she wanted answers.

Growling in defeat, she raised her cell phone and scrolled through her contacts for his number. Why hadn't she deleted him months ago? His sandy brown hair, deep blue eyes and charismatic smile popped up on her screen when she tapped his contact icon. She tried to deny the swirl of feminine appreciation for his chiseled good looks that tickled her belly, but the sensation was as undeniable now as it had been when she was a teenager. The man was flat-out hot. Which also annoyed her. Why couldn't he be an ogre?

Her finger hovered over the green phone. *Just call him. Ask what he knows and be done with him. Then delete him from your contacts and your life for good.*

She tapped the screen, held her breath and raised the phone to her ear.

After two rings he answered, "Reid Colton."

Chapter 3

Just hearing Reid's voice rattled her. Penelope had to purposefully draw a calming, centering breath.

"Pen? That you? Is something wrong?"

She startled a little when he said her name. Damn caller ID. Now she had no choice but to talk to him or look foolish. "Hello, Reid. Do...do you have a minute?"

"For you? Always. Is everything all right?" His baritone voice was like a rich dark-chocolate liqueur, sweet and sultry with just a little bite. Sneakily intoxicating.

"I'm fine," she said automatically, hearing the defensive edge in her voice.

"Okaaay," he drawled. His tone told her he'd heard her snappishness, too. "So then this is a social call?"

"No. I—I just have a question for you."

His grunt sounded disappointed. "Ask away."

"Did Andrew mention anything to you about a file he was keeping on my father?" A brief silence answered her. "Reid? Did you hear me?"

"Yeah, I... Andrew was keeping a file on Hugh Barrington?"

Now it was her turn to grunt. "Hugh Barrington is

my father. Yes," she said sarcastically, as if her tongue had a mind of its own. *Stop it! No reason to be so snarly.* "Shall I take your surprise as a *no*? That he didn't tell you about his suspicions?"

He was silent a beat. "What sort of suspicions?"

She pinched the bridge of her nose. Tension coiled behind her eyes, and her temples gave an achy throb. "I don't know for certain. I only just found the file and haven't read it in depth but—"

"Where was this file? What does it say?"

"He'd hidden it in his office, and—wait. Just answer my question. Did he ever mention suspecting my father of any wrongdoing? Did you know he was keeping a file on him?"

"No," Reid said flatly. "Now answer my question. What is in this file?"

"I told you I haven't read it carefully. It may be nothing. I just… It surprised me and…" *Damn it!* What had she done? Had she stirred up trouble over nothing? "Oh, never mind. Forget I said anything."

"I want to see it."

"Reid, no. I shouldn't have called you. Can we please just forget—"

"If Andrew was keeping a secret file on Hugh, he had a good reason."

She agreed. Andrew had been a good cop, and he wouldn't have undertaken something as serious as an investigation of her father without cause. But Reid's concurrence settled the issue. She should have been relieved to have been vindicated, but Reid's assessment left a hollow pit in her stomach. The truth hit her like a rock to her skull. Andrew believed her father was corrupt.

Cold, snobbish and unloving toward her—she knew already, but…corrupt?

She muttered an unladylike curse as a tremble started at her core.

"I want to see that file. Your father has far too much influence and knowledge of my family's business for me to ignore any suspicions Andrew had."

She rolled her eyes. How typical of Coltons to think first of how any revelation affected *them*. Their bottom line. Their secrets. Their precious reputation. "Oh, of course! The Colton family must be protected from scandal at all costs!"

"Really?" Reid said dryly. "Is that what you think?"

She didn't reply. The file sat on the desk before her, mocking her. She could almost hear the alarm bells, the blaring computer voice. *"Danger, Will Robinson!"* She knew with a certainty that whatever Andrew suspected her father was guilty of was enough to rock her sheltered life. She did not want to expose the skeletons in Hugh Barrington's closet. And yet...

"Pen, the last thing I want to do is cause you any more pain," Reid said, bringing her attention back to the phone call. "But if Andrew was working on something..." He paused. "I need to see that file. I can be there in ten minutes."

She stiffened her spine and blinked rapidly. "Come here? But—"

When she'd called Reid, she hadn't considered the idea that he'd want to review the documents. That she'd have to *see* him.

"Is that a problem?" he asked.

Yes! her head screamed, while she stammered, "Uh, I... No. But..."

"All right. Good. Ten minutes, then." Reid hung up before she could think of an out.

* * *

Reid pulled his truck to the curb in front of his late ex-partner's ranch-style house and huffed out a breath. In months gone by, he'd parked in this same spot and headed into Andrew's modest but comfortable home to spend hours watching football, or discussing cases, or sharing meals with the family. Andrew had joked that because Reid was a bachelor, Penelope seemed to think that meant he always needed a home-cooked meal. Forget the fact that he lived at the family ranch where Bettina Morely, the Colton's full-time cook, was at his beck and call and elaborate dinners were prepared most evenings for him and the rest of the Colton clan.

But Pen was something of a mother hen, even before she had Nicholas, and loved nothing more than to have people gathered around her table for a big dinner. Her nurturing extended to animals, as well, and the Clarks always seemed to have at least one foster dog and a few stray cats they were caring for in addition to their own elderly beagle, Allie.

Reid had always suspected her love of such domestic events as family dinners and cookouts on football afternoons stemmed from a lack of such familial events as a child. Penelope's father, Hugh Barrington, had never struck Reid as the home-and-hearth type, and on his few visits to the Barrington estate through the years, Reid had found the mansion cold, more of a showcase than an inviting home. Not the kind of place he thought Pen would have felt comfortable or warmly loved. Especially after her mother died when Pen was a young teenager.

Andrew's few comments on the matter had confirmed as much. Pen had shaken the metaphorical dust of the Barrington estate from her sandals as soon as she could.

Nor was there any love lost between Penelope and her father.

Was that the reason behind this mysterious file Pen had found? Andrew's attempt to keep tabs on the man who'd been such a disappointment to his wife? Or was Andrew onto something more?

Reid climbed from his truck and walked up the front sidewalk, admitting to himself he had a few nerves about this meeting. He hadn't seen or heard from Pen since Andrew's funeral, even though she'd crossed his mind many times in the intervening months.

The front door opened before he could ring the doorbell, and he met Penelope's stormy expression. "Hey, Pen. How are—"

"Don't 'Hey, Pen' me." She braced her hands on her hips, lips taut in classic ticked-off-woman mode. "Just because I called to ask you a question doesn't mean you can invite yourself over or think I've forgotten or forgiven what you did."

Reid drew a slow breath and released it. He'd had to deal with plenty of bad moods in his life, from his own pissy and entitled family members to suspects high on any range of chemicals. He raised a conciliatory hand. "But you did call, and the best way for me to make sense of the file and why Andrew may have kept it, and *hidden* it, is for me to take a look at it."

He hoped once she'd had a chance to voice her spleen, they could set the ill will aside long enough to get to the bottom of this mysterious file on Hugh Barrington. She held his stare for several silent seconds, returning his petitioning look with unmoved hostility. Not that he expected anything else.

Reid was too realistic to fool himself into believing he could magically change her opinion of him. Not in one day. Maybe not even if given weeks to plead his case and counter the false information and supposition fed to her by the police department and media following Andrew's death. True—he had been overheard in a loud altercation with Andrew the day his partner died. And he *had* administered the injection that proved fatal to Andrew. But there was so much more to the story...

Then her expression seemed to crack. Her pert nose flared, and her sculpted eyebrows dipped as if she were fighting tears. Her chin wobbled and she turned her face away just as moisture sparkled in her hazel eyes. That brief flash of vulnerability and grief sucker punched Reid in the gut. He was prepared to deal with her anger, but a widow's multilayered emotional quagmire was beyond his skill set. Especially the fragile emotions of a woman he cared about.

Without comment, she spun on her heel and marched into the house, leaving him to follow. He caught the door before it closed and stepped out of the chill December air. The house looked much the way he remembered it, but different, too. Instead of Andrew's sports magazines and accent pieces reflecting Penelope's feminine taste, the living room was littered with toddler toys and piles of tiny-sized laundry featuring dogs, giraffes and trains in primary colors.

Penelope had disappeared down the hall toward the bedrooms, and Reid considered whether he should follow or wait there. Playing it safe—he didn't want to cause more strife than his presence already did—he took a seat on the couch next to the folded clothes.

When Pen returned with a fat manila folder in her hand, he stood again and held out his hand for the file. "Is Nicholas asleep?"

She shrugged and replied curtly, "Don't know. He's not here." She jabbed the folder toward him, scowling.

Taking the file, Reid frowned his confusion. "Where is he?"

"Mother's Day Out."

He arched an eyebrow. "Come again?"

She rolled her eyes as she sat, smoothing the seat of her yoga pants with her hand as if they were fine linen pants. She perched on the edge of the nearest wingback chair, sitting primly, with her back straight and her ankles crossed, as if she were at etiquette class instead of in her own home. Apparently the social training from her youth kicked in when she was stressed. Or else she was purposely refusing to let herself relax around Reid, a choice wholly contradictory to her yoga pants, oversize sweatshirt, sock feet and sloppy ponytail. "He's at Mother's Day Out, a program the Methodist church down the road offers three times a week," she explained. "They watch young children from ten o'clock to three so that mothers can run errands or do…whatever. I needed time without Nicholas clinging to my leg to get Andrew's office sorted out."

Reid balanced the folder on his lap. "Oh." He nodded as he opened the folder cover. "Okay."

As he glanced over the top sheet in the file, he realized another oddity. No dog had barked when he came in, and no beagle was sniffing around him asking for a head scratch even now. He glanced toward Pen. "And where's Allie?"

A shadow crossed her face and he regretted the question instantly. After all, the dog had been quite old and suffering from arthritis when he'd last visited the Clarks' house eighteen-plus months ago.

"Never mind. I can guess," he hurried to say as her eyes brightened with tears. He made no comment on the fact that there didn't seem to be foster animals around at present. Clearly that was a scab that needed to be left alone.

Schooling her face, she shifted on the seat and flicked a hand toward the file. "So...what do you think?"

Returning to his reading, he gave her a wry grin. "I think I'm still on the first page and need a minute to see what's here."

She rubbed her forehead and snorted. "Sorry. Of course. I'm just..."

"Antsy. I understand." Reid dropped his gaze to the first document again and tried to focus his attention on what he was reading—which was difficult with Pen watching him. For the next several minutes, he paged through the folder. He gave each document a cursory look at first, then went back to study the information more closely once he had an impression of what Andrew might have been trying to establish with his file. Finally a pattern emerged, though Andrew had marked spots with sticky notes where there were gaps in the data.

Reid drew a slow, deep breath, clenching his teeth in anger and disgust as he lifted his gaze to Penelope.

"Well?" she asked, perched on the edge of her seat. "What do you make of it?"

"I think what we have here—" he held up the file and tapped it with his index finger "—is not enough to make a case."

"But?" She turned up both palms. "You see something incriminating there. Don't you? I can see it in your face."

"If these records are real, not fabricated, then yes. They point to a long history of theft and deceit. There are two sets of records for every client, including my family. I see evidence of overbilling, falsified records, probable tax evasion—"

"Now, wait just a minute!" Penelope shot to her feet and glared at him, hands balled at her sides.

Reid set the file aside, prepared to defend his conclusions. He'd known she wouldn't like what he had to say—implicating her father in felony crimes—but she'd asked his honest opinion and—

"What do you mean, 'if these records are real'? You think Andrew made up those documents? Some of what's there is on my father's official office stationery! If you think I'm going to let you use this as an excuse to deride Andrew—"

"Penelope."

"—and throw more mud on his good name—"

"Penelope!" Reid stood and moved around the coffee table toward her.

"—then you can get the hell out of my house, right now! I only asked your opinion because—"

"Pen!" He had to raise his volume to match hers, but he kept his tone nonconfrontational.

Taking her by the shoulders, he gave her a quick, interrupting shake. Beneath his hands, Pen felt fragile. Her willowy limbs were surprisingly thin under his large hands, and he felt the tremor that raced through her. "Time out!"

She blinked at him, her expression wounded, offended, then shrugged roughly from his grasp. "That's what you said. *'If* these records are real, not fabricated.' As if you think Andrew was trying to frame my father for something!"

"Yes. *If.* I said all that about fabrication as a qualifier of my assessment, not as an accusation against Andrew." He stepped back and wiped his hands on the seat of his jeans. "The fact of the matter is, I believe Andrew was onto something. I think…" He hesitated, not wanting to set her off again and not finding any way to soften the blow for her. He respected Pen too much to sugarcoat what he suspected. "Pen, it looks like your father was stealing from his clients. *Is* stealing from his clients. He's hiding income from the government. Falsifying records. God knows what else, but…"

He stopped as she sank slowly back onto her chair, her eyes wide and her mouth slack with shock. "You really think my father is doing all this? What I mean is, you think he *knows* about it? Couldn't it be someone who works for him? Or…" She let her voice trail off, as if she knew the truth without him answering.

He said nothing, taking his seat again and giving her a moment to process the stunning bomb he'd dropped. He knew well enough that Pen had never had a good relationship with her father, but learning Hugh was likely guilty of criminal activity was another matter.

"So…now what?" She sounded as stunned as she looked, her voice an almost breathless whisper. "What do I do…" she motioned weakly toward the papers in his lap "…with those files? What do you think *Andrew* planned to do with them?"

"Andrew was a good cop. He wouldn't have sat on incriminating evidence like this long. Chances are he was waiting for the case to come together to spare you the strain of a drawn-out investigation." Noticing her befuddled look, he asked, "What?"

"So *now* you think Andrew is a good cop?"

He clenched his teeth, measuring his words. "Pen, I've always thought he was good at his job."

Her mouth pinched, and one thin eyebrow lifted in

skepticism. "That didn't stop you from trying to sully his name before he died."

He exhaled slowly, struggling to keep his frustration in check. "I wasn't trying to sully his name. I was trying to intervene, bring him to his senses, before *he* sullied it!"

"Fine way of showing—"

"Pen, stop!" He raised both hands, palms toward her. His voice was louder than he'd intended. "This is a conversation for later. I will explain to you everything that happened eighteen months ago, if you're willing to listen."

She firmed her mouth and folded her arms over her chest. Classic body language saying she was closing herself off to what he was saying. He knew better than to press on with the topic if she wasn't ready to hear him out.

"Later..." He tapped his finger on the files. "We need to address this, right now."

He didn't tell her this insight into Barrington cast a new light on issues involving his father's disappearance. Hugh Barrington had been very vocal of late, claiming to have seen Eldridge being kidnapped, claiming a burned body must be the missing Colton patriarch—which it wasn't. And, not the least of which, pushing forward a reading of Eldridge's will, in which Hugh Barrington was named the heir of a controlling interest in Colton Inc. As a detective with the Dallas PD, Reid had learned not to believe in coincidence. If it looked like a dirty rat, smelled like a dirty rat and squeaked like a dirty rat, he didn't need an exterminator to tell him he was dealing with a dirty rat.

If Hugh Barrington was as corrupt as Andrew's files seemed to indicate, Reid had to wonder what role the family's lawyer may have played in his father's disappearance. Had Eldridge gotten wind of his lawyer's disloyalty and theft? Had the senior Colton threatened to expose Hugh?

Or, Reid thought with a twist of dread in his gut, had Eldridge been mixed up in his lawyer's illegal practices and crossed the wrong person?

She glared at him silently, stubbornly, for several moments, and he used the time to formulate a plan.

"Are you with me on this, Pen? For Andrew's sake? Because I'm going to need your help if we're going to get the proof we need to either finish building this case or disprove it."

She blinked slowly, turning her gaze away. "How?"

Gathering together the papers he'd spread out on the floor to review, he tapped the stack into order and stood. "We need to look at your father's personal files. We need to see what's saved on his computer, what's locked in his safe."

Penelope scowled her disagreement. "He's hardly going to just stand aside and let us search his office—especially if he has something to hide."

"So we don't ask." He jammed a hand in his pocket and shifted his weight uncomfortably. He was crossing a line, and he knew it. They'd have to tread carefully.

Her expression was incredulous. "You want to break into his office and steal his files?"

"I doubt he'd keep the incriminating stuff at his office where his staff could come across it. We'll start at his house. *Your* old home." She opened her mouth as if to argue, and he added quickly, "If we are freely admitted to the house, then it's not breaking and entering. If we only snoop around and don't take anything, it's not stealing."

"I don't know." She bit her bottom lip and rubbed her hands on her pants. "You're playing rather fast and loose with the definition of *legal*, Colton."

He flashed her a wry grin. "Hey, that's what my family does best."

* * *

They'd laid out a plan and were in Reid's truck ten minutes later.

"You've been to my father's house before, right?" she asked in a tone that said she knew he had.

Reid dipped his head once in reply.

"Then you don't need my directions?"

He lifted a corner of his mouth. "No. But thanks." He pulled away from the curb and drove toward the highway that would take them out of the Dallas city limits and toward the affluent area where Hugh Barrington lived.

A stilted silence filled the cab of his truck, but Reid resisted the urge to turn on the radio. If Pen decided she did want to talk, he didn't want anything to interfere with an open communication between them.

In fact, he really ought to be the one to broach the topic of what happened to Andrew. She should know why he'd started his investigation of his partner and his theories about what really happened that fateful date last year. He might not get another chance like this one to explain his side of events to her.

Penelope's body language didn't invite conversation, however. She sat as far away from him as her seat belt would allow, and with her body stiff, she kept her head turned toward the passenger window.

He cleared his throat and started, "Pen, about what hap—"

"We need to be through with this junket by three p.m." She cut him off so deliberately and sent him such a quelling glare, her intention was obvious. "That's when I have to pick up Nicholas at the church."

He held her stare for a moment, waffling between pushing his agenda and letting her have her way. Since they still had the task of searching her father's home office and anywhere else in the house she thought might prove worthy of attention, he backed off. For now.

"Three p.m. Got it." He glanced at the digits glowing from the dashboard. 11:14. That left plenty of time to conduct a search, keep Pen with him long enough to have the conversation he wanted to have and still get her to the church to pick up her kid.

His heart drubbed a slow, heavy beat. He rather hoped he had an excuse to go with her to pick up Nicholas. He was curious to see how big Andrew's son was now and reconnect with the boy. Not that he expected the kid to remember him. Nicholas was still a baby last time Reid had seen him.

"Nicholas must be talking pretty well by now. Does he—"

"Why are you turning here?" Another quick change of subject and determined look. "The turnoff to my dad's street isn't for another mile."

"Fewer traffic lights this way."

She shrugged and turned back to the window.

"So, Nicholas…" This time he let his words trail off, allowing her to fill in the blank. Or not.

"Is none of your business."

He frowned and scoffed a laugh. "Ouch."

She drew a breath and faced him with narrowed eyes and a dented brow. "This is not a social outing. You lost the right to personal information and any relationship with my son when you killed my husband." He opened his mouth to defend himself, but she raised a silencing hand. "Correction. You lost that right when you accused Andrew of being corrupt. Of stealing drugs from the evidence room or whatever cockamamy bull you dreamed up!"

"It wasn't bull. At least I had good reason to believe

what I said at the time." Reid braked for a stop sign at a busy intersection and had to give his attention to traffic. Once he'd pulled onto the crossroad, he shook his head and gave Pen a pleading look. "Listen, this is a conversation we need to have. But we're almost to your father's place. Can we put a pin in it and—"

"It's the next turn on the right. Where the brick entry gate is," she said unnecessarily, but again effectively cutting him off.

He sighed and let the matter drop. For now.

Because they were at Hugh Barrington's estate, he would need to stay on his toes and not raise any red flags as to why he was there with Hugh's estranged daughter.

Reid pulled in the long driveway to the redbrick mansion, and when he would have parked on the section that circled near the front door, she directed him to the back. At his querying look, she offered, "I'd rather not call attention to the fact that we're here."

From the front, everything about the Barrington estate was symmetrical, formal and unimaginative. The house was little more than a large brick box with an equal number of windows on either side of the main ground-level entrance. Boxy shrubs framed the entry, and black shutters were the only relief to the three-story brick edifice.

Reid glanced around the backyard. The swimming pool was still crystal clear and free of leaves despite the December chill. He knew the detached four-car garage contained at least one antique Rolls-Royce—a status symbol Hugh liked to show off at high-society events. But Reid was unfamiliar with the cottage sitting behind the main house. In all the years Hugh Barrington had been Eldridge's lawyer, Reid had only been to this house a few times, and then always through the front door for dinner parties that kept him in the formal guest areas.

As he studied the smaller house, deciding if it was a pool house or something else, one of the venetian blinds swayed and a shadow crossed the window.

He nodded his head toward the cottage. "What's that building?"

"That's where Stanley lives."

The name rang a bell, and Reid searched his memory. "Stanley?"

"Father's butler."

"He lives on-site?" That shouldn't surprise Reid. After all, Aaron Manfred, the Colton family butler, and his wife, Moira, lived in the staff wing of the mansion at Colton Valley Ranch. He'd simply not realized Barrington had any of his house staff living on the grounds.

"Of course he does. Where else would my father's right-hand man live?"

He heard more than a little sarcasm in her tone. Maybe even some hurt. And he had to admit, he was a tad surprised by the idea behind her sentiment. "Your father is especially close to Stanley?"

She cut a startled look toward him. "I just mean he trusts Stanley like no other person in his life. If my father weren't such a snob, he might even call Stanley his best friend. He depends on him. Heavily. And having his butler living right behind his house seemed a no-brainer to my father."

But he could tell from the tension in her body and her tone that she wasn't nearly as unconcerned about her father's reliance on his butler as she pretended. Perhaps what he sensed was jealousy? Was she upset that the butler had the trust and closeness she'd never had with Hugh? Or that Hugh had never had with her mother?

Turning to the gym bag he kept in the backseat of his truck, Reid unzipped a side pocket and fished out a flash drive, a small flashlight and a screwdriver. Just in case. Jamming all three in his pockets, he followed Pen to the back door where she punched in a code on the security system, receiving a quiet beep from the door pad signaling admittance.

"You've been gone from this house for how many years? And your father hasn't changed the security code?"

She gave another one-shoulder shrug. "He did change it once a few years ago. But he couldn't remember the new code after years of the same one, and he kept setting off the alarm when he put in the wrong numbers. He gave up and went back to the old code after three months."

"And you know this how? I thought you weren't on good terms with your dad."

"With my dad, no. His maid, yes. After my mother got sick, Helen and I became closer. We still talk every now and then."

Reid glanced back out to the butler's cottage. Had the blinds moved again? He couldn't shake the prickling sense that they were being watched. As a detective with the Dallas PD, he'd learned to trust his gut instincts. More often than not, that sixth sense was correct. He may not be with the police department anymore, but he still had his training, his experience and the instincts from his years on the job. "You had me park in the back to avoid attention, but we've been seen nonetheless."

Chapter 4

"Seen?" Pen jerked up her head, sending him a look of dismay, then shot a glance around the backyard. "By who—"

Reid put a hand on her shoulder and moved to block her view. "No, don't look. You'll only look more suspicious. Carry yourself in a manner that says you have every right to be here, that you don't care who sees you."

She straightened her back. "I do have a right to be here. It's my childhood home. I—" She stopped, pitching her voice lower, and twisted her mouth as if rethinking her assessment. "Well, if I'm not welcome to come as I please, he could take away my key. But he hasn't, so…"

Before she could unlock the back door, the knob rattled, and the door swung open. A woman in her late fifties with graying brown hair and a black maid's uniform gave them a curious look. "May I help…? Oh, Miss Penelope! I thought I heard someone back here."

"Helen." Pen sounded breathless and nervous, but squared her shoulders. "Hello. I didn't want to bother you, but I just needed…"

Reid tensed when Pen hesitated. It seemed they were about to test Penelope's welcome at her father's estate.

"Um…to look for something from my old room. Something of my mother's."

Reid hid his relief over Pen's smooth lie. He hoped Helen hadn't heard the same flutter of nerves in her voice that he had.

"Of course. Is it something I can help with?" Helen waved a hand down the back hall as she stood aside to admit them.

Reid mentally scratched *B and E* off the list of crimes they were flirting with.

"No. No, I don't want to bother you. Reid can help me look." Pen smiled at the maid and waited for Helen to return to whatever she'd been doing before heading down the long dark hall. He followed her as she moved quietly through the house, bypassing the kitchen where the clank of dishes and a woman's humming could be heard. She led him up a back staircase not nearly as grand as the wide marble one with polished wood banisters he remembered from past visits to the house. Their footsteps were muted on the thick white carpet, and he could imagine Penelope as a teenager, sneaking up these quiet and more hidden stairs after her curfew.

Pen led him down the upstairs hall, past numerous closed doors, and she paused, casting a surveying glance around before crossing the landing at the top of the grand staircase in the foyer. Reid looked over the balustrade to the cold marble entryway he remembered from previous trips to his family lawyer's house. A sparkling crystal chandelier hung over the foyer and replicas of Greek statutes in white stone and Italian urns in hues of gray and black were positioned around the walls. For all its opulence, the foyer lacked color and gave visitors no sense of warmth or welcome. Much like the other rooms Reid had visited. Much like the man who owned the home. In Reid's opinion, Hugh Barrington loved the idea of being respected, admired, even envied for his position and wealth, but did little to earn it on a personal level.

The man might have been one of Eldridge's closest advisers and confidants, he might have come to Reid's defense when suspicion was thrown at him following Andrew's death, but Hugh Barrington was a hard person to feel any affection or warmth for. Appreciation, maybe. Polite friendliness out of respect for his alliance with and assistance concerning Eldridge, but hardly the sort of Hallmark greeting-card feelings that engendered real esteem. Hugh's priorities simply seemed oddly skewed. Case in point, his disregard for Penelope, while he fawned—rather obsequiously, in Reid's opinion—over the Colton family.

"Is there a problem?" Penelope asked in a hushed tone.

He shook himself from his thoughts and caught up to her. "No. Why?"

"You seemed preoccupied and so…serious." She waved a dismissive hand and gave her head a brisk shake. "Never mind. Come on. That's his home office." She aimed her finger down the hall to a door that stood ajar. "The second room on the left."

He nodded. "After you."

She balked, and he lifted a corner of his mouth in a wry grin.

"Are you scared to go in there?"

Penelope scowled. "No." Then after a beat, "Not… *really.*" But she still made no move to enter Hugh's study.

"You said you had a right to be here," he teased.

"I do!" She squared her shoulders, then glared at him. "It was your idea to come here and search!"

"Hey, you called me when you found that file." He folded his arms over his chest. "Do you really want to stand out here and waste time arguing over who is more responsible for us being here? Or do you want to get in, find the evidence we need to incriminate—"

"Or clear!"

"Or clear him," he conceded, though he was skeptical. "We should get busy."

She glanced guiltily at her father's office door, but straightened her spine and, wiping her hands on her yoga pants, marched into the room.

Reid paused at the threshold of Hugh's office, taken aback by the contrast of the man's study to the other parts of the house. As stark and colorless as the entry and living room were, Barrington's private study was dark with deep browns, crimsons and polished brass. The room reeked of masculinity, right down to the lingering musky scent of Hugh's overpowering aftershave. The walls were wood paneled and the matching desk, bookcases and file cabinets were made of darkly stained hardwoods. The couch and desk chair were a rich burgundy leather. A slight patina of age dimmed the brass of the grommets on the seat coverings, the furniture hardware and the lampstands. He drew two pairs of latex gloves from his pocket and held one out to her. "Here. Wear these. You may feel you have a legal right to be here, but let's not leave fingerprints, just in case."

She eyed the gloves he handed her, then with a furrow of worry denting her brow, she worked her fingers into the latex encasement.

"Look at all this. This could take forever," she said pulling out a drawer of his filing cabinet.

Reid closed the office door behind him. "If there is information here somewhere that incriminates him, my guess is it won't be anywhere obvious like a file cabinet or desk drawer."

She gave him a dubious look. "We're talking about a man who hasn't changed his home security code in twenty-five years. He's smugly overconfident about his security. Andrew tried to talk to him numerous times about safety issues, but he insisted his status quo was good enough."

Reid nodded. "His hubris may work in our favor. Just the same, check for out-of-the-way cubbyholes. Even an overconfident old-schooler probably has hiding places for sensitive stuff."

Pen slid closed the file drawer she'd opened and quirked a moue of agreement. "Why not? Andrew had a secret hiding place in our wall I didn't know about. Why not my father, too?"

Reid's first task was to boot up Hugh's desktop computer. He plugged the flash drive into a USB port and rolled the mouse to wake the screen. The computer started up and asked for a password in order to continue. "Any guess what his computer password might be?"

"Try 12-18-46. That's the house security code."

Reid arched an eyebrow. "Let me guess. Also his birthday?"

She shot him a deprecating, can-you-believe-it smile.

He tried the numbers. "No dice."

"Maybe…*MavericksFan*? No spaces. I think that was the password on the parental-control blocker on our television when I was in high school." She put a finger to her lips and whispered, "Shh. Don't tell him I knew it. That's how I learned he had a Playboy TV subscription."

"My lips are sealed," he replied with a chuckle, and typed in *MavericksFan*. Nothing. *Mavericksfan* and *mavericksfan* also failed. So not an issue of capitalization.

"Nada." Next, he tried *Penelope* and hit enter.

From behind him, she scoffed. When the error message popped up again, she strolled back to the bookshelves. "I coulda told you that wouldn't work. Aren't passwords usually something *important* to a person?"

The hurt and resentment was back in her voice. He'd never realized how deep her wounds were, how wide the gulf in her estrangement with her father.

Reid scrubbed his face and thought. "Any other suggestions? We're losing time here."

"Sorry. No. Not unless it's something stupid like *password* or *1234ABCD*."

For good measure, Reid tried both. To Hugh's credit, neither of those obvious codes worked, but when he tried *MavericksFan1*, the computer continued to start up and took him to the home screen. "I'm in." He started opening files and sending documents, internet history and financial data to the flash drive. It was too easy. Reid shook his head and mumbled, "Jeez, and this guy is our family lawyer?"

When they found Eldridge, he'd need to have a talk with father about trusting Hugh with family business. If they found Eldridge.

He pinched the bridge of his nose. No. He couldn't think that way. He would see to it his father was located and brought home, one way or another.

Pushing back from the desk, he turned his attention to a physical search while Hugh's computer dumped information onto the flash drive.

He opened a file drawer and felt the underside, scanned the labels of the drawer contents. Across the room, Penelope pulled a painting down from the wall and pushed at the wood paneling behind it. When she found nothing, she rehung the picture and moved on to the next.

Reid watched her for a moment, mesmerized by the way the soft stream of sunlight from the office window made her auburn hair shine with coppery highlights. Her Dallas Cowboys sweatshirt was unflattering, too big for her—probably one of Andrew's—but her blue yoga pants fit snugly and showed off her shapely bottom and long legs. She moved down the wall to the next painting, checking for a hidden safe, a spot of color in the otherwise darkly masculine room.

A niggling guilt bit him. What right did he have to be ogling his late partner's wife? Especially when, intentional or not, he'd had a hand in Andrew's death.

She glanced his way, caught him staring and tilted her head. "What? Did you find something?"

Scrubbing a sobering hand over his face, he turned back to the file cabinet. "No. Just…thinking."

"Anything you want to share?"

"Not at the moment." He moved to the next file drawer, found nothing suspicious, and repeated the process, being careful to replace any file he pulled out in the exact manner he found it.

Finding nothing behind the pictures, Penelope moved on to the bookcase, pulling books from the shelves and flipping open the covers of larger books. "I heard about your father, that he's missing, presumed dead. I'm so sorry."

Reid paused and jerked his gaze back to her. "So you heard, huh? Guess I shouldn't be surprised. We've tried to keep it out of the news but…"

"Actually, Helen mentioned it when we talked last time. She said they found a burned body in a car they think is your father. She said the house staff has been all abuzz about it and the reports that my father thought he'd seen him before the body was found."

"Yeah, well, thanks. He is missing, but the burned body they found proved not to be him."

"Oh!" She flashed an awkward smile. "Good. That's... I'm glad."

"Yeah, that was a relief." Reid didn't really want to talk about the disappearance of his elderly father. The five months of crazy twists and unexpected turns to his father's case would take more time than he and Pen had and would only renew his simmering frustration. Still... if it opened a line of communication with Pen, he'd indulge her with the abridged version. "Needless to say, it's been a stressful few months, and we don't seem any closer to finding him."

"The police have no leads?" Pen crossed the floor toward him, her arms folded loosely over her chest. "You'd think, as high profile as his case must be, that there'd be pressure on the cops to find him. To do more. To leave no stone unturned."

"You'd think. There's been no shortage of suspects, but nothing that's been substantiated. A few clues, and numerous theories, but nothing that's been proven helpful."

"My father's sighting—"

"Hasn't panned out yet. But it's worth further investigation." Reid turned to Hugh's massive desk and began sliding open drawers, searching for a key that might indicate there was a safe in the house or any other indication he'd secreted information somewhere.

She strolled to a window seat and knelt to lift the pillows and the lid of a storage space. "Well, you have my sympathies and prayers that he'll be found soon and well."

"Do I?" He paused to study her again, wishing he

could get past the distance she'd put between them in the past year.

She sat back on her heels and sent him a puzzled look. "Of course. I may be angry with *you*, not trust *you*, feel betrayed by *you*, but I'm not so uncaring as to wish you or your family ill. I have no grudge against your father." She dropped her gaze to her lap and frowned. "Not much of one, anyway." She huffed softly, then added, "But then, my father's preference of you Coltons over me isn't your fault, I guess. Coltons are wealthy and powerful clients." She gave him a bitter smile and waved a dismissive hand. "I'm just family."

Reid sighed. "Pen—"

More hand waving as she pushed back up on her knees and dug into the window-seat storage again. "No, no. Don't start. I shouldn't have mentioned it. My troubles with my father aren't for you to worry about."

But he couldn't write off her feelings of disappointment and jealousy so easily. When Andrew was alive, she'd managed to set aside her feelings toward Reid's family and enjoy his company at face value. This return of her hostility toward the Coltons showed him just how high the wall she'd built had become. He didn't want any barriers between them. Especially something he had no control over, like the family he belonged to.

Having the name Colton was a mixed blessing. Along with the prestige, the wealth and the opened doors, his family connection carried a lot of baggage. The Coltons had made enemies in a variety of ways, unintentionally rubbed some people in the community the wrong way, while some folks disliked them simply because of what they represented. They were a part of the infamous 1 percent. The .01 percent even. Not a popular distinction with the other 99.99 percent these days.

"Thank you," he said quietly, "for your prayers and well wishes. I still have hope he'll be found. A man like Eldridge Colton doesn't just disappear without *someone* knowing *something*. We just haven't found that someone yet." He rubbed a thumb along the beveled edge of Hugh's desk as he pondered the circumstances surrounding his missing father. "Or we haven't provided the right incentive to make that someone talk." He opened a desk drawer and rifled through the files, felt the bottom of the drawer for anything suspicious.

They worked silently for another minute before Pen glanced in his direction. "Do you suspect foul play, or is it possible he left on his own terms, that maybe he doesn't want to be found?"

Reid twitched a grin. "Yes."

She frowned at his evasive answer, then shook her head and continued her searching.

"Anything is possible. The truth is we really don't know."

Reid looked on the underside of the desk for a file taped to the unfinished wood. Nothing. He gritted his teeth. Hugh Barrington didn't strike him as the cleverest man. Devious, perhaps. Intelligent, yes. But the man had a twenty-five-year-old passcode on his house security system. Surely Reid could figure out where Hugh might have stashed incriminating information. If there was any to find.

And he believed there was. Because despite how things had gone down in the last months of his time on the police force with Andrew, he trusted his partner's intuition and insights.

Pen climbed to her feet, abandoning the window seat, and moved down the wall to another bookcase. "But you're a cop, Reid. Surely you have some gut feeling about what happened to your father. Haven't you done any investigating on your own?"

He snorted. "I *was* a cop. I'm not privy to all the details of the case. The family knows some, but not all of what the detectives have learned. They have to keep a few tricks up their sleeve to stay a step ahead." He moved on to a bottom drawer, big enough for hanging files. The drawer rattled but wouldn't open. A locked drawer. Not uncommon, all things considered, but...

He felt the underside and checked the smaller top drawers for a key. Nothing. The matching file drawer on the opposite side of the desk slid open easily, and Reid walked his fingers through the contents of the drawer, scanning tab labels. "All that said, I—"

His gaze snagged on a file with the heading Penelope. He stilled, his line of thought forgotten. Furrowing his brow, he pulled out the file and flipped it open. The file was full of legal documents. A few medical records. A picture or two.

The last document was a petition for adoption. Hugh and his wife had signed as the adoptive parents and two names were scribbled on the lines for the birth parents. He blinked and reread the opening lines.

We the undersigned do permanently relinquish all claim and parental rights for our biological child, Lisa Umberton, to Hugh and Constance Barrington of Dallas, Texas...

His breath snagged in his chest, and the thump of his pulse grew in his ears. With fumbling fingers he flipped back to the front of the file to the first documents. A court order to legally change Lisa Umberton's name to Penelope Lisa Barrington.

"You what?" Penelope prompted, dragging his attention away from the file. Her expression shifted when she glanced at him. "Reid, what's wrong? Did you find something?"

Uncertainty and shock fisted around his lungs. He swallowed hard and scrubbed his cheek with his palm before stammering, "Uh, no. N-nothing…relevant."

Did Pen *know* she was adopted? He thought back through the many meals he'd shared with Andrew and his wife through the years, game-day parties and birthday celebrations. Had she ever mentioned being adopted? She'd talked about how hard her mother's death had been on her, how distant she felt from Hugh, how alone and out of place she'd felt in the large, sterile home growing up. She talked about her envy of Reid's large family, how she'd hated being an only child.

But she'd never mentioned adoption.

"Reid," Pen said, a note of excitement in her tone. "I found a safe."

Chapter 5

Reid hurried over to where Pen stood, anxiety lining her brow.

Sure enough, behind the row of law manuals, she'd discovered a false wall panel that when opened revealed a safe.

"Do you think you can get in it?" he asked.

"I'm sure gonna try." She rubbed her hands together and twisted her mouth in deep thought. "We'll start with birthdays."

While she began testing different combinations, Reid stuffed the file on Pen's adoption into the waist of his jeans at his back and pulled his shirt over it to hide it. He moved over to where Pen stood, his gaze riveted on her slim fingers delicately adjusting the safe dial.

He held his breath, as much from anticipation as so he could listen in the near perfect silence for the snick of the lock's tumbler.

When the telltale click came, he touched her arm. "Stop. Did you hear that clink?"

She cast a quick side glance, then narrowed her eyes

on the dial. "Twenty-one. The first number is twenty-one."

"Can you think of any significance for that number?" he asked. "Maybe you can come up with the other numbers, if you can think of any relevance for twenty-one."

She drew her bottom lip into her teeth and furrowed her brow. "It's not his birthday or anniversary. Nor my birthday. Or Nicholas's."

"Well, try turning the dial slowly the other way and let's see if we hear the next tumbler click."

She nodded and leaned close to the safe as she turned the combination dial slowly to the left. The dial went completely around without another giveaway snick.

He gave her shoulder an encouraging squeeze. "Keep trying."

She angled her gaze to his hand, then raised a dubious look to him. "Back up. You're crowding me."

He raised both hands, palms out and took a step back. "Sorry."

Then, while she worked, he had an inspiration. Turning his back to her, he pulled out the adoption file and cracked it open. With his gaze, he scanned the document on top until he found the date her adoption was finalized. The date she came to live with the Barringtons. *August 21, 1987.*

One month and a few days after she was born.

He hid the file under his shirt again and faced her. "Try eight with the twenty-one. Before or after. Then…" The dial had no eighty-seven. The numbers stopped at 50. "Then eight again and seven."

She faced him, her head cocked to the side. "Why? What do you know about those numbers?"

That the digits meant nothing to her was more evidence she didn't know about her adoption. He'd have to think long and hard about whether he would tell her about his find. For now he downplayed his suggestion. "Just a hunch. May be nothing."

When she continued to question him with her dubious glare, he flicked a hand at the safe. "Let's go. We need to hurry and get out of here before someone finds us."

She huffed her acquiescence and spun the dial slowly to the combination he offered. Nothing happened when she tested the door, and she gave him a so-much-for-your-idea look.

He returned to her side, nudging her out of the way with his hip. "Let me try."

He tested the combination again, turning the dial the opposite direction to start. And heard encouraging clicks as he progressed through the pattern. When he tugged on the safe door, it swung open.

She made a little grunt of surprise, then moved forward to peer into the hidden lockbox. "You *will* be telling me the significance of those numbers later."

At the front of the deep compartment were the expected jewelry boxes. When they opened the first box they found a diamond and sapphire choker necklace.

Pen sighed sadly. "That was my mother's. I remember her wearing it out to big fundraisers and parties with my dad."

"It's stunning." He passed the jewelry box to Pen, and she swiped gentle fingers over the stones.

He took out the rest of the jewelry boxes stacked at the front of the safe and set them on a shelf of the bookcase. The back of the safe was dark, but he could clearly see stacks of something. He reached in and drew out bundled cash. He gave a low whistle. "Pen, look."

She blinked. "Money? Good gravy! Those are hundred-dollar bills. That's got to be in the thousands of dollars!"

"There's more." He reached in and withdrew another bundle of cash, an envelope with municipal bonds, more cash in Euro bills and two bank-record booklets of off-shore accounts.

When he turned to Penelope, she was pale and trembling.

"I don't understand. Why…" She paused to swallow. "There's a fortune here. Why wouldn't he put this in the bank? What—"

"A getaway fund?" Reid suggested.

"But getaway from what? Why?"

"My guess is he didn't declare any of this to the IRS. Remember the tax records Andrew had?"

"Tax evasion? A getaway fund?" She shook her head, clearly in shock and trying to process their find. She flipped through the stack of money, then the bonds, with damp eyes and shaking hands.

Reid reached back into the safe and pulled out a dusty ledger, a file folder with old tax returns and a flash drive. When Pen saw what he had found, her face crumpled in further distress.

He longed to pull her into his arms and comfort her. Bad relationship or not, learning your father might be breaking the law and cheating people would be hard for anyone to accept. The nail in Hugh's coffin was the passport with his picture under the name Samuel Morris Griffin. He held the fake passport up for her to see and Pen blanched. "He's prepared to flee the country at a moment's notice. But…why?"

"Good question." Reid spread the evidence on the shelf, pulled out his phone to snap a picture, then returned the money, files, bank books, passport and bonds in neat stacks to the safe. He slipped the flash drive into his pocket to delve into later.

"Do you think…" She seemed to be having a hard time breathing. "Andrew knew about this? Is that why he was keeping the…" she paused again to rub her hand on her sternum "…the secret file on him? That he was going to turn my father in for…whatever made my dad think he needed a getaway plan?"

Reid shrugged. "I don't know, Pen. Andrew was a good cop. If he suspected foul play—"

"What is the meaning of this?"

Reid and Pen turned quickly toward the office door, where an older gentleman in a suit and dark tie scowled at them from the hall. Beside him, Pen gave a soft, guilty-sounding gasp.

"Who let you—" The older man paused, his expression growing more startled and confused than hostile. "Oh, Ms. Penelope. I wasn't told to expect you."

"Stanley!" She fixed a stiff grin on her face and moved to block the butler's view of the bank books and cash still sitting on a lower shelf. "Gracious! You nearly gave me a heart attack!"

"I apologize, ma'am." The butler's face remained stern and suspicious. "But I'm equally surprised to see you in your father's office." His tone was heavy with judgment and castigation. "Is there something I can do for you?" He raised his chin and narrowed his eyes. "Or would you like me to call your father for his assistance with something?"

The threat was clear, though delivered in a thinly ingratiating manner.

Reid tensed, mentally searching for a way to defend their presence when Pen said, "Not necessary, Stanley. I've simply come to retrieve my mother's necklace."

She reached behind her without turning and groped for the black velvet jewelry box. Reid surreptitiously nudged it toward her fingers. She grasped it and held it out for Stanley to see.

With a calmness in her tone that Reid would bet belied butterflies in her gut, she explained, "Daddy has been keeping these here for me, but Mama left it to me. I was thinking I'd wear it next week to a fundraiser for the Fallen Law Enforcement Officers Memorial ball."

A muscle in the butler's jaw twitched, and his suspicious gaze shifted from Penelope to Reid. "And he is with you, because…?"

Penelope jerked her chin higher and gave a delicate grunt of disgust. "Stanley, really!"

"I insisted on coming with Penelope for her security. The necklace is clearly quite valuable, and I didn't want anything to happen to her or the jewels as she took them to her bank lockbox." Reid ad-libbed, giving a deferential smile. "Can't be too careful these days. Right?"

"Stanley, you've met Reid Colton, haven't you? He was Andrew's partner." She paused, then added as she tipped her head, "And the son of one of father's best clients. Don't be so inhospitable."

The man's face hardened for having been chastened. "My apologies, Ms. Penelope, Mr. Colton. I simply meant to look out for your father's interests. You are in his private office, after all. I believe he'd consider this an invasion of his privacy."

"Understood." Reid gave a brief nod of agreement and put the other jewel boxes back in the safe. "We have what we came for, so…we'll be off. Pen?"

"Right." Penelope clutched the jewelry box to her chest and moved toward the door.

Reid restored the safe and bookshelf to order as best

he could and took several large strides to catch up with her. As he passed the desk and computer, he pretended to hit his leg on the desk chair. Grunting, he bent to rub his knee and stealthily unplugged the flash drive and hit the power button on the desktop tower on the floor. Palming the flash drive, he winced as if in pain as he hobbled to catch up with Penelope in the hall. He'd have loved to get a peek in that locked desk drawer but clearly that wasn't going to happen. Today.

If only he could come back without Pen and get in that drawer. If he were still a cop, he could get a warrant. He had cause based on the documents Andrew had left hidden in his wall. But unless he wanted to be nabbed for breaking and entering or turn the case over to the authorities before he knew what was truly going on with Pen's father—which he didn't—he'd have to sit tight. For now.

In the meantime, he had a flash drive full of files and browsing history to review, and that could prove quite interesting.

As Reid drove away from her father's mansion, Penelope stroked the velvet-covered jewelry box in her lap and exhaled the stress knotted in her chest. "Well, that didn't go so well."

He rolled his shoulders and cocked his head side to side, stretching his neck. "I don't know. We found some evidence that backs up what Andrew seems to have been onto, and I copied a lot of his computer files to look into."

She leaned back against the headrest and closed her eyes. "Maybe. But…isn't it possible the money and bank accounts are legit? I mean, there's nothing illegal about keeping money in your safe or having offshore accounts."

"Not in theory. But it is illegal to fake a passport. In my experience, if it hides in an office safe like a duck and supports a reasonable suspicion like a duck, it's not an innocent puppy."

She angled her head to stare at him and frowned. "That is…the most tortured and convoluted analogy I've heard in…ever."

"But you get my point."

She sighed. "I do."

"And there is no good explanation for the fake passport."

"No." Turning to gaze at the frozen north Texas landscape that flew by, she acknowledged the hollowness, the sinking sensation that gnawed inside her.

"Please tell me that your mother really did leave those jewels to you and that we didn't just steal a necklace worth thousands of dollars."

She cracked open the box and peeked at the shimmering stones. She'd have to take the jewels to her bank lockbox on the way to pick up Nicholas today. "She really did. I just never had a reason to wear it, so I left it in my father's keeping." She huffed a sigh. "Guess I should be glad he hadn't sold it for getaway cash, huh?"

Reid didn't bother to answer, but he sent her a sympathetic glance.

"So now what do we do? Call the police? Turn him in to the IRS?"

Reid didn't answer, and she shifted on the seat to study his profile. Truth be told, she'd always considered him an unfairly handsome guy. While Andrew had been her first love—a sweet, honest, loyal man—he'd been only average in looks. Her husband had started putting on a bit of a belly when he hit thirty and she'd gotten better at cooking and baking. But along with his family's wealth and power, Reid Colton had inherited uncommonly good looks. From his square-cut jaw and straight nose to his thick sandy-brown hair and deep blue eyes, he had turned her head from day one.

She recalled that first day she'd met Reid Colton at the exclusive private school they'd both attended as preteens. He'd had little more than a cursory glance and polite smile for the daughter of his family's lawyer, who was not only too tall for her age, but also cursed with both freckles and braces. Her mother had barely finished the introduction on the front steps of the school that first day of sixth grade before Reid had been trotting away to join the cool kids across the crowded lawn. She'd never entirely shaken the crush she had on him in junior high. Even after she met Andrew and had been charmed by his boyish grin and gentlemanly ways.

"Reid?" she repeated when he remained silent. "What are you thinking? What do I do with this information?"

He cut a quick side glance to her and flexed his hands against the steering wheel. "Nothing."

"What!"

"*You* will do nothing. Let me handle this. I'll do some more digging, see what I captured on the flash drive, go over the files Andrew kept more closely and maybe make a few quiet inquiries to see if I can put together a case that will stand up."

"*You*? By yourself?" She sent him a dark look.

"Yeah." He scratched his slightly stubbled chin as he nodded. "I think that's the best move. If we make accusations too early, show our hand before we have hard proof, your dad could get rid of evidence, cover his tracks…" He paused to send her a meaningful glance. "Leave the country…and we'd never make a case. An important part of managing a case is to not tip off your suspect to what you're doing too soon."

Penelope tightened her mouth and shook her head in

disbelief. Was he deliberately ignoring her disgruntled tone or was he that obtuse?

"I don't think so."

"Hmm?" He sent her a frown with his puzzled look.

"One, I won't be shut out." She bent to stash the jewelry box in the main compartment of her purse. "I didn't call you today to have you bulldoze in and take over. I get a say in how we handle this."

"Pen—"

"Two," she continued, poking his shoulder with her finger and cutting him off. "You are not on the force anymore. You don't have the authority to investigate this and arrest my father if he is, in fact, breaking the law. *Remember*? You were dismissed for *killing my husband*."

And yeah, she allowed her tone to reflect the bitterness she'd been nursing toward Reid for months. She felt tears rise and wondered why she'd brought him into this mess. She really didn't want to be involved with him in any way, shape or form.

He didn't respond for several tense seconds. His expression said her comments had hit their mark. "I may not be on the force anymore, but I haven't forgotten how to investigate a crime," he said in a low tone. "And until I have a more complete picture of what's going on, what Andrew was thinking, I'm not going to involve the authorities. As far as you being involved…"

His jaw tightened, and a muscle in his cheek flexed as he gritted his teeth. "I'd rather you stepped back. You're too close to this. Let me see where it goes. If I need anything from you, I'll let you know. But you don't need the worry added to your plate."

She pinched the bridge of her nose and chuckled without humor. "Very smoothly put, Reid. All that was missing was patting me on the head and sending me back to the kitchen with my apron and high heels."

He cringed. "Aw, come on, Pen. You know I'm not a chauvinist. I just want to protect you from as much of the fallout from this as I can. You've had a tough enough time without adding—"

"Don't tell me how hard my life has been," she interrupted, bristling, "when you're the reason my husband—" She gasped and grabbed the dashboard as Reid abruptly took a sharp and unexpected turn onto a side road. "What are you doing? This isn't the way to my house!"

"I'm not going to your house…yet."

"Not going…?" She studied the buildings and parking lots they passed, trying to decide where he was going. Not the Colton estate where he lived with his large, extended family. "Reid, take me home. I don't have time for this." She angled her body toward his on the front seat and balled her hands in her lap, itching to slug him in the shoulder. "I have to pick up Nicholas from the church soon."

"I'll take you to the church for Nicholas if we run late."

"Reid!" She tightened her fists, her frustration and dismay over the events of the day building inside her. If she did haul off and slug Reid Colton in the arm, who could blame her? Taking a calming breath, she said instead, "You don't have a car seat for Nicholas, and I will not let my baby ride anywhere unrestrained."

"Point taken. Just…give me a little leeway, a few minutes. Okay?" The look he sent her said he knew how hard that would be for her in light of Andrew's death.

Her answering stare voiced her skepticism, impatience and irritation. But she swallowed a verbal reply. She didn't trust her voice not to crack or sound harpy-shrill. She was wound too tight, had too many emotions churning inside her.

Her father's duplicity. Andrew's death. And her complicated feelings toward Reid. Anger and hurt and... attraction. Her stomach jumped and swooped crazily with the private admission. Admitting her continued physical interest in Reid was a big step. She had successfully quashed those feelings while she'd been married to Andrew. Had put them aside all those times her late husband's partner had been in her home, sat at her dinner table and given her friendly hugs or shoulder squeezes. Shaking herself from her unsettling thoughts about Reid, she noticed a familiar sight out the window and sat straighter in the seat. "The park? Your urgent errand is the local playground?"

"You don't like the park?" he asked, furrowing his brow. "I thought I remembered this place was one of your favorite places to unwind and blow off steam, even before Nicholas was born."

Amazingly, her nerves seem to calm just seeing the tranquil pond and grassy fields of her favorite park. "I love this place. But I'm hardly in the mood to play on the swings or feed the ducks."

He parked his truck near a boat ramp at the edge of the sparkling lake and cut the engine. "We're not here to feed the ducks. I just couldn't waste the opportunity of having you as a captive audience. We need to set the record straight."

Reid saw Penelope stiffen, her jaw grow tight, and he raised a hand forestalling her arguments. "Before you say anything, I know I'm the last person you want to talk to and this is the topic you most want to avoid, but you need to know the truth. You need to know what really happened the day Andrew died and not the innuendo and half truths the media chose to disclose."

"I've based my opinion of what happened on the police report and trusted witnesses within the department, not the news reports. Give me some credit!" she snapped, her eyes blazing.

"I'll give you credit if you'll do the same for me. Give me credit for being his friend, for being *your* friend." She huffed her disagreement, but he didn't let her dissuade him from his purpose. "Give me the benefit of just a moment's doubt based on what you know about me. Based on the man you know I am. I'm not a murderer, Pen!"

She opened her mouth to speak, but he plowed on, cutting her off. "I loved Andrew like a brother. He was my partner, and that means something. We had each other's backs. Because of the volatile situations we faced regularly together, we had a level of respect and trust most people can't understand."

He paused for a breath, and she only glared at him, arms crossed over her chest. Closed off. Resentful. Hurting. As much as he regretted losing his partner, he hated most the pain Pen had suffered since Andrew's death. The circumstances of Andrew's death made the loss all the more difficult for her. The questions and loose ends. The doubts and anger. He would do his part to put an end to all of that today.

He turned his attention to their surroundings, taking in the skeletal hardwoods and empty park benches. The rusted swings that swayed in the cold wind. A lone woman, bundled in a scarf and knit hat, walked her pug on the pathway near the lake. Otherwise the park was deserted. His law-enforcement training put him in the habit of paying attention to such details, be it a restaurant, a park or neighborhood street. Even after all these months off the force, he still kept a keen eye on his environment.

He drew a slow breath. "I know you've heard from others in the police department that Andrew and I argued that morning."

Pen arched an eyebrow, her expression beyond peeved. "They said you nearly came to blows. That you made awful, ungrounded accusations against Andrew that could have ruined his career. Hell, ruined his reputation and his life!"

"We did argue," he said, curling his hand around the steering wheel and battling down the sickness in his gut the memory stirred. "But we weren't on the verge of a brawl. Our discussion got heated, got loud. He slammed a mug on the counter too hard, and it broke. But we weren't about to throw punches. That was just bystanders projecting their interpretations on a discussion they didn't understand."

"Isn't that a moot point now?" She grunted her disgust as she turned her gaze out the side window. "You're splitting hairs over irrelevant details."

"It's not irrelevant, seeing as that argument was used as evidence to try to establish a motive for me to kill him. It was grossly mischaracterized and misinterpreted. And the fact of the matter is, I confronted him because I did have evidence he'd taken drugs from the evidence room. I wanted him to explain what I'd learned, if he could. Instead of clearing up any misunderstanding, he blew up at me."

Her lips tightened, and if he hadn't seen her nostrils flare slightly, the bridge of her nose crinkle in distress, he'd have believed he'd angered her further with his explanation. But those telltale details told him the battle she was having with her emotions. He'd known this conversation would upset her, but he wanted to make it as easy for her as possible.

He touched her arm and whispered, "Pen, I don't want to upset you, but if you'd—"

She shook off his hand and glared. "Oh, really? You actually thought we could have this conversation without upsetting me?" She scoffed. "Take me home, Reid. Now."

"Give me just a minute to—"

"Fine." She turned to the passenger door and shouldered it open. "I'll walk."

Reid sighed. "Pen, wait." When she didn't stop, he popped open his door and trotted after her, jockeying to block her path. "I swear to you on Andrew's grave, I didn't know there was anything in that syringe besides insulin. I was trying to save his life, not hurt him!"

Hands clenched at her sides, she stopped and lifted her chin. "So you've said."

"So why can't you believe me?"

Tears sparkled in her hazel eyes, and Reid's heart broke for her obvious pain. "Because! I just…"

When she didn't finish her sentence, he filled the silence with the details she needed to know. "He passed out while we were interviewing a witness in the Holmes case. Just…fainted. I was able to revive him, and he started throwing up, said he had blurred vision. He told me to get his emergency diabetes kit that he kept in the cooler in the back of our cruiser, and I did. Then I called 911, even though he said it wasn't necessary. He kept saying he'd be fine once he had some insulin. After I tested his blood sugar, found it way high, I gave him a shot using the vial of insulin in his kit. I had no reason to think it had been tampered with. Who the hell thinks their friend's emergency insulin has been replaced with potassium chloride?"

Her shoulders drew back, and her eyes narrowed. "Maybe a better question is who the hell *replaced* his insulin with potassium?"

Reid spread his hands. "I agree! A very good question. One that has gone unanswered because of the witch hunt to blame me. But I didn't do it, which means the person who *did* is still out there. Doesn't that bother you? Because it sure as hell has kept me awake nights this past year and a half."

Pen flinched and gaped at him as if truly startled by what he was saying. "I didn't... I mean I thought..."

"You thought I'd gotten away with murder?" he huffed and shook his head. "But I'm telling you, I swear to you, it wasn't me. Which means whoever *did* switch out the insulin *did* get away with murder."

Her brow furrowed, and she plowed her hands through her hair. "Reid, I...I don't know. How can I trust what you're saying?" She cocked her head as if struck with an inspiration. "How do I know you're not saying this to protect yourself and throw me off track?"

He barked an incredulous laugh. "Pen! The police have said there wasn't enough evidence to arrest me for murder—or even manslaughter. Because of that argument, and only because we argued that morning, the cops still suspect me, but—"

"Officer Jamison said you threatened to kill Andrew. That you said, 'I will kill you for this!'"

"And Franny Hill, the receptionist, backed me up that what I really said was, 'Would it kill you to look into this?'"

This tidbit seemed to surprise her, as if she'd not heard about the receptionist's testimony. Figured. The people mounting the campaign against him wouldn't have shared that with her.

"The simple truth is, they had no way to prove I knew the insulin was tainted, that I had anything but pure motives to save Andrew when I gave him the injection and no reason to think I'd put the potassium chloride in the vial. So why the hell would I encourage you to have the case investigated further, if I were guilty?"

She curled her shoulders in now, her fingers rubbing her temples as she shook her head. "Reid, stop. I don't know what to think! I can't—"

"You think the only reason I wasn't charged is because I'm a Colton. Don't you? And because your father went to bat, defending me."

"That chafed," she admitted under her breath.

"Pen, Andrew was my friend. My partner." He placed a hand over his heart, pleading with her, and his voice cracked with an unexpected surge of emotion. "I didn't intend to kill him. I didn't tamper with his insulin, and I didn't know that anyone else had."

"Stop it, Reid!" she said, her voice taut and thin. "Just…s-stop!" She bent her head, covering her face with her hands, and her shoulders shook as she sobbed. "I c-can't do th-this…"

His heart squeezing painfully, Reid took her by the arms and pulled her into a firm embrace, tucking her under his chin and rubbing her back. He'd expected her to fight him, to pull away, but she wilted against him, the embodiment of defeat. "Pen, I'm sorry. So sorry for everything you're going through. I want to be there for you, if you'll let me. Andrew would have wanted me to look out for you. You know he would've."

Her head bobbed slightly in agreement. When her fingers curled into his shirt, fisting the loose material as if clinging for dear life, his pulse bumped higher.

"I…I wanted to b-blame you," she squeaked, her

head still bowed as she cried against his chest. "I needed s-someone to blame, somewhere to d-direct my anger and p-pain."

"I know. And if you want to vent on me, go ahead. I just wanted you to know the truth."

She was silent for a few moments, crying softly and wiping her eyes with the back of her hand.

"Use my shirt. It'll dry." A chilly breeze stirred her hair and lifted the scent of her shampoo to his nose. December wasn't the best month to be standing outside for a chat, but he'd endure arctic snow if it meant healing the rift between him and Penelope or easing her emotional suffering.

Then over the skittering sound of dead leaves blowing across the parking lot, Pen mumbled, "It doesn't matter."

"What? Of course it does."

"Why are you doing this? It won't bring him back. You weren't charged, so—"

He grunted. Did she really need it spelled out?

Because I care about you. He balked at putting it quite so bluntly. He didn't want her misconstruing his intent.

"Because I...value your friendship. Because I valued Andrew's friendship and wish like hell I could do that day over. Not just because I'd change the things that made me look guilty, but because I hate that we argued on our last day together."

She heaved a deeply weary and ragged sigh. "S-so did we."

Her admission was barely a whisper, but it jolted through him like a prod from a stun gun. "What?"

She raised wet, red eyes to meet his gaze. "I fussed at him. That morning b-before he left for work."

"Aw, Pen," he murmured, thumbing a tear from her cheek, then hugging her tighter. "He knew you loved him and he sure as hell loved you. Don't waste time kicking yourself about that morning."

"But his last—"

"Hey, married people fight. In my family, they fight a lot!" He chuckled dryly and earned a brief, lopsided grin from her.

Then her posture drooped, and she shook her head slowly. "I snapped at him about sleeping through Nicholas's crying, leaving it up to me to do all the baby duty the night before."

She spoke in a hushed, mournful tone that tugged at his heart. Yeah, he knew all about regrets. Though he'd meant this conversation to clear the air between them, if she wanted to unburden her soul, he'd be her listening ear.

"And when the dryer wouldn't start, I f-fussed about him ignoring his to-do list." She frowned and cast a side glance at him. "He said he'd been feeling bad recently, hadn't felt good that last night, but promised to look at the dryer that evening. I should have told him to go to the doctor, but I was tired and cranky and I didn't cut him a break. Before he left for the station, I yelled about something else trivial. I don't even remember what. His wet towel on the floor, maybe? A spill on the counter? But I remember feeling like a first-class witch after he left. I texted him an apology, but he never replied."

She shivered, and he knew it was as much from grief as the brisk wind. Her cheeks were pink from the cold, her nose rosy from crying, and for both reasons, he tugged her close again, offering an embrace meant both to warm her and comfort her. Although she was finally opening up to him, and he hated to do anything to mess with that, he was concerned for her comfort. He savored the feeling of her silky hair under his cheek, her arms around him, her scent teasing his senses for a few more precious moments. Who knew when he'd get the opportunity to hold her like this again?

Finally, when an especially strong shiver rolled through her, he offered, "Maybe we should continue this conversation in my truck."

Pen took a step back and met his gaze with a discerning stare. "You'll explain to me why you accused Andrew of stealing from the evidence room? Of being a closet junkie?"

He jerked a nod. "I will."

Chapter 6

"I found it as hard as anyone to explain what was going on," Reid said after recounting his story. "I worked with Andrew, trusted him, knew him to be a top-notch detective. But I couldn't deny his behavior had been off in recent weeks. He complained of not feeling well, and when I found the drugs under the seat of our cruiser...well, I knew *I* hadn't put them there. Then the report came out that drugs from a sting operation were missing from the evidence room, and—"

"You *assumed* Andrew had taken them," she interrupted, not bothering to mask her hurt and consternation. But the source of her pain was shifting. If Reid was telling the truth, then Andrew did look guilty of terrible things. The man she'd married and loved for eight years couldn't have done the things Reid was laying out. But...

His story had a ring of truth. She'd seen some of what he mentioned for herself. Andrew's poor health in his last few weeks, his acting odd and seeming distracted.

"I didn't want to believe what the evidence pointed to, but before I could look into alternate explanations,

I had to confront him with my suspicions, ask him for his side of things."

She exhaled deeply. "So your fight that day…"

"Wasn't supposed to be a fight. I tried not to be accusatory, to give him the benefit of the doubt, but when I started laying it all out…" Reid met her gaze, his dark blue eyes full of remorse.

"He got angry. Shouted at you. Escalated the discussion to a yelling match."

His sigh answered for him, before he gave a tight nod. "That's what the people at the station overheard. We were in an interrogation room. I thought we'd have more privacy there, but clearly my choice of locations only put his back up."

She made a tiny noise of dismay. "Of course it did."

He raised a hand. "I know. My bad. I admit I made mistakes. I handled it badly and have a lot of regrets about how things unraveled. But I didn't kill him or it. Later that day, when he fainted while we were in the field interviewing a witness, I did what I thought I needed to help him. He'd been nauseated and told me to get his emergency kit from the cruiser and —"

"Yeah," she said, stopping him with a hand on his arm. "I know this part."

"But do you believe me? I don't care if anyone else in the department or the justice system or all of Texas believes me, so long as you do."

Pen swallowed hard as she met his stare.

His gaze warmed. His navy eyes were intense, penetrating. Soul searing. Her tremble now had nothing to do with the chill.

"You're the only one who matters to me," he whispered.

Her heart stuttered at the wounded look he gave her.

She realized her hand was still on his arm, and she withdrew it quickly, curling her fingers into her tingling palm. "Wh-why?"

The raspy question slipped out before she could swallow it, choke it back down. *Why* was dangerous. *Why* left her vulnerable, showed she cared enough about him to need an answer.

"I think you know why," he said in a voice as soft as a caress, as tender as a kiss.

And therein lay the real dilemma. She knew exactly why, and it scared her to the core.

He shouldn't have been so honest with Pen.

An awkward silence filled his truck as he drove her back to her house. He'd given her a lot to consider, and the knit in her brow said she was deep in tangled thoughts.

His regret wasn't for telling her about the events of the day Andrew died. No, he wanted her to understand what had transpired, give her the version of those events she hadn't yet heard. But he'd all but admitted his long-held feelings for her. If pressed on the issue, he supposed he could deny any deeper meaning. *I just meant you're my friend, and I want your forgiveness, your trust. You're his widow, and your opinion is the only one that matters.*

But the gut-wrenching ache in her tone, the raw emotion in her eyes and quiver of vulnerability in the rasped *why?* had punctured his defenses, undermined his better judgment.

Add to that the disturbing information they'd uncovered at her father's house, the indications Andrew was onto something incriminating—and the bombshell that Penelope might not know she was adopted. His own emotions were in upheaval today, and her question had blindsided him.

At a red light, Reid tapped the steering wheel with the side of his fist. When he added his own father's disappearance and other recent tumult at the Colton Valley Ranch, he had quite enough to ruminate on before adding today's mysteries to the roster. He pondered the fact that Hugh Barrington had been key in stirring up false hope about Eldridge's whereabouts last month. Was there a connection to what Andrew was researching? Maybe not, but he didn't buy into the theory of coincidence, either.

He continued to mull over these thoughts as he turned onto the neighborhood street where Pen lived. The long residential lane was lined with carbon-copy houses with winter dead yards and a variety of Christmas decorations on display.

Reid had been down this street enough times to be familiar with the lay of the land, but he still took note of the details. Old habits and all…

Most of the driveways were either empty, since the owner would have been at work at this hour, or had some fashion of minivan or SUV which belonged to the stay-at-home mom or babysitter. Sure, there were exceptions. He'd met the Clarks' across-the-street neighbor, Ned Smithe, who did shift work, and his legal-assistant wife, at a Super Bowl party two years ago. The pickup truck in the driveway would be Ned's, sleeping off a graveyard shift. As they drove past, Penelope returned a wave to an older gentleman raking leaves at the end of the street. All was quiet. Normal. *Americana*… The term popped into his mind.

What would it be like to live in a middle-class neighborhood like this one instead of a sprawling ranch with quarrelsome siblings and stepparents? To have neighbors over to watch the game or call friendly greetings to someone working in their yard? The simplicity of the lifestyle and idyllic imagery appealed to him. Although, he admitted, he enjoyed some of the creature comforts of having wealth. Having household staff to cook and clean. An infinity pool and tennis court. Privacy when it was warranted to keep the family circus on the down low.

He glanced in Penelope's direction and amended his previous question. What would it be like to live with Pen in a neighborhood like this? His chest tightened. Where had that idea come from? He wasn't sure, but he knew he needed to rein it in. She was his partner's widow. Making a move on her would feel…*wrong* somehow. How could he even think of taking advantage of Andrew's death by moving in on is wife?

As they approached Pen's house, he noticed a light blue sedan that had been parked down the street pull away from the curb. He'd been briefly distracted by his wild sidetrack thought, but he'd not seen anyone get in the car. Of course, that didn't mean—

A brief flash of sunlight on metal snagged his attention. An odd intuition sent a prickle of alarm to his core. He backed off the accelerator, slowing to a crawl when he saw the driver's window lower. "Pen, do you know—"

A handgun appeared at the sedan's window.

"Gun!"

The muzzle flash and crack of his windshield were simultaneous.

Pen screamed.

"Get down!" he yelled even as he yanked her arm, pulling her down on the seat. He ducked, too, as another shot slammed into his front hood. He shifted automatically into cop mode. Crisis mode. *Protect Pen. Consider civilians—the old man raking. ID the gunman. Age, race, anything!*

The sedan rolled straight toward them. He narrowed

his eyes, lifting a hand to block the sun's glare behind the approaching car. Another bullet hit the side of the truck with an ominous thunk.

"Reid!" Pen cried, reaching for him, tugging at his jacket sleeve as if to pull him down onto the floorboard with her.

He only had a split moment to decide: flee or stand and defend. The cop in him refused to retreat. He had a better chance of protecting Pen by shielding her, and he'd rather catch or kill the bastard responsible than run from him.

"Glove box!" he returned, and she scrambled for the Smith & Wesson .40 he kept stored there.

He had only a second to study the person in the driver's seat as the sedan neared. Reid's angle was bad, seated higher in his truck than the guy in the car. The shooter's face was largely hidden by the bill of a ball cap. Dark winter coat. Caucasian male.

Pen raised her head for a look, the pistol clutched in a two-handed firing grip.

Another muzzle flash had Reid diving for cover. "I said get down!"

He watched the roof of the blue car pull alongside them, and he pushed her head down again. Reid shielded Penelope as the shooter took direct aim now through the truck's driver-side window.

"Sonofabitch!" Reid snarled, raising an arm for protection as shards of glass from his blasted-out window rained down on them.

Penelope yelped, and Reid's gut swooped. "Are you hit?"

"I don't think—"

Tires squealed as the car raced away.

Pen shoved at him and climbed onto the seat, twisting toward the shattered back window. She aimed the Smith & Wesson at the fleeing vehicle, and Reid grabbed her wrist. "No!"

"I can shoot! Andrew taught me!"

He, too, surged up to look out the back window, squinting at the suspect's back bumper. "There are by-standers!"

"But… Damn it!" she growled and lowered her hands. Hands shaking, she set the pistol on the seat beside her.

He shared her frustration and gritted his teeth in disgust. "Write this down… BHD43. That's as much of the plate as I got."

Flicking away bits of the broken window, she dug in her purse and found a pen and an old receipt. Trembling, she jotted down the partial plate number.

Reid, too, was shaking, the aftermath of his spiked adrenaline, and he carefully shook the shards of broken window from his shirt and out of his hair. "Careful of all the glass."

"Right. I—" She paused and swallowed hard. "What the hell was that about? A drive-by in this neighbor-hood?"

"I don't think it was a drive-by in the sense that you mean." He cut the engine, leaving his truck in the spot where they'd been attacked. By doing so, the police would be better able to trace the trajectory, find the bullets for a ballistics report and analyze the crime scene. He mentally replayed what had transpired and came up with a chilling conclusion.

They'd been targeted. The blue sedan had been parked down the block, waiting for them. But why?

He faced Pen and pushed her hair back from her face. Touching his finger to a small cut on her face, he wiped away the crimson bead there. "You're bleeding. Mostly nicks, but you need first aid."

She cast a side glance at him and gave a short, humorless laugh. "Have you looked in a mirror? I'm not the only one."

He didn't care about himself. He'd sustained far worse in the line of duty over the years. And a guy didn't grow up with as many rowdy siblings and half siblings and all the inherent rivalry without scrapes and bruises on a daily basis.

The older man who'd been raking appeared at the passenger-side window. "Are y'all all right? Hell's bells! I can't believe what this world's coming to!"

"We're not hit, but you might check on the neighbors. A stray bullet could have pierced a door or window." Reid turned to survey the houses, looking for obvious damage.

"I don't feel so good." Pen pressed a hand to her mouth.

She did look pale. Nausea in the wake of such a scare was common enough. Reid put a hand on the back of her head and pushed her forward. "Bend over. Head between your legs."

The older neighbor pulled a chunky old flip phone from his pocket. "I'm calling 911. You should get her an ice pack for that bump on her head."

Bump? Reid ducked his head and pulled Pen's chin toward him so he could see the other side of her face. Sure enough, a goose egg was swelling at her temple. "Damn, Pen. Did I do that when I shoved you down?"

She covered the injury with her hand and shrugged. "No sweat. Better a bump on the head than a bullet in my brain." Her eyes glistened with unshed tears. "You probably saved my life."

"I don't know about that."

"I do," her neighbor said, lifting his phone to his ear and pointing to the passenger headrest.

When he saw what the man was pointing to, ice streaked to Reid's marrow. A bullet was lodged in the ripped foam, where Pen's head had been seconds earlier.

Chapter 7

"Yeah, I need to report a shooting..." the older man said, turning his attention to his phone.

"Reid..." Penelope carefully shook the sharp bits of glass from her sweatshirt and the top of her tennis shoes. "If this wasn't a random drive-by, then...are you saying you think it was planned?" She raised wide eyes of distress to his. "That someone wanted to kill *us*?"

As a cop, he'd known the risks he faced on the job. But having someone he cared about put in the line of fire shook him hard. If they had, in fact, been targeted—and he would operate under that assumption until proven wrong—he had to take measures to protect Penelope.

He reached for her cheek, careful to dust aside the slivers of broken window clinging to her shoulder and in her hair. "Maybe. We have to consider it a possibility." He held her gaze. "But I promise I will not let anyone hurt you. I'll get to the bottom of this."

A detective made his fair share of enemies in the line of duty. Reid didn't know of anyone who wanted him dead, but that meant little. God only knew who he'd pissed off, who might have recently gotten parole and might be coming for revenge.

And just because Andrew had been gone for more than a year didn't mean his enemies knew about his death. This attack could even be tied to the odd circumstances surrounding Andrew's death. If Andrew didn't put those stolen drugs in their squad car, who did? And most important, who had replaced Andrew's insulin with potassium? Someone had been setting Andrew up, maybe even setting Reid up to take the fall for killing his partner. This attack, he knew, could very well be related to Andrew's death. Reid simply didn't believe in coincidences.

As he opened his truck door and eased out, the tinkle of glass shards littering the street scraped his nerves. Even if he replaced the windows, had the interior professionally vacuumed and repaired, he'd likely be finding bits of safety glass in odd places for the rest of the truck's life. Not that he couldn't afford a new one, even a whole fleet of trucks. It just ticked him off to need a new truck because of some punk shooter. Even angrier that the dirtwad had endangered Pen.

Come after me if you must, scumbag, but if you hurt my family or friends, I'll end you.

"So…you really think—" Pen drew a shuddering breath as she climbed from the front seat and slid to the ground on wobbly legs. He put an arm under hers to steady her, and she clung to it with a white-knuckle grip. "But who? Why on earth…?"

"I don't know." But a low, uneasy gnawing had started in Reid's belly. The itch of something dark and dangerous tickled his spine. His premonitions weren't often wrong. Could the shooter have been sent because they were found snooping in Hugh Barrington's office?

"Reid? What?" Pen stepped in front of him, one hand fisting on his shirtfront. "You look like someone just walked on your grave."

He tried to shake off the gut feeling about Barrington. "It's...nothing. I—"

Barrington's involvement in the attack seemed unlikely on the surface. First, it had been no more than two hours since they'd been at the Barrington estate. Sure, they'd detoured by the park for their talk, so there might have been time to call a hit man if the butler had reported their activity to Barrington the minute they left. Or could Stanley have called in the shooter, with or without Barrington's knowledge?

No coincidences...

Reid's jaw tightened, and his gut knotted as he tried to decipher the unlikely turn of events when Penelope gasped in terror. She grabbed both of Reid's arms and rasped, "Nicholas!"

Reid blinked once as his brain shifted gears, following her line of thought, and a bolt of fear shot to his heart.

"If this was targeted at me...or related to Andrew, they..." She seemed to have trouble catching her breath. "They could go after Nicholas! I have to get him from the church. Now!" She wrenched herself out of his grip, her steps unsteady as she spun away.

"Pen, slow down. Don't panic." He scrubbed a hand down his cheek, thinking fast. "We can't take my truck. The cops will need it for the crime scene. Where are your keys?"

"H-here." She fumbled for a moment in her pocketbook before dumping the contents, including the jewelry box, on the street. She grabbed her keys and phone, shoved the necklace and her wallet back in the purse and started at a run for her driveway.

"Tell the cops we'll be back. We have to get her kid!" he shouted to the elderly man who, at their abrupt departure, sent a startled look after them.

"I'll drive!" he shouted, and she tossed him the keys over the hood of her Ford Explorer. Gunning the engine, he pealed out of her driveway and raced back toward the neighborhood entrance.

"Buckle up and hold on," he told her as he punched the gas.

He'd lied to her neighbor. If someone was trying to kill Penelope, even just maybe, he would not be bringing her or her small son back to her house. Andrew's family was now officially in protective custody, Reid Colton–style.

Penelope wouldn't take an easy breath until Nicholas was in her arms. She squeezed the armrest of her Explorer as Reid whizzed down back streets, taking the shortest route to the church.

As Reid drove to the church, she'd shed her sweatshirt, just in case there were still bits of embedded glass clinging to it, and used the brush from the gym bag she kept in the backseat to rid her hair of any last shards before retrieving her son.

The velvet box of jewels peeked up at her from her purse, and she frowned. "Do you think… Is it possible someone knew we had the jewels with us? That it was a failed robbery attempt?"

"I think you're on the right track, but I don't think it is about the jewels."

The hard line of Reid's mouth sent a frisson of something cold and dark to her soul. "What are you saying?"

"Think about it, Pen. Your father's butler saw us in his office. He has to know by now that we were there snooping. That we were in his safe."

"My father! You think my *father* sent that man to shoot us?" She chortled a scoff of disbelief. But fingers of fear and doubt squeezed her heart. "My *father*…"

Every time she repeated the assertion, a tiny piece of her skepticism chipped away. Could Hugh Barrington, who'd never been especially warm or generous with her, who'd coldly ignored her mother in the last months of her illness—who kept a getaway stash in his safe—really be as cruel and heartless, as criminally cold-blooded, as to put a hit on her and Reid to protect his own interests?

Nausea swelled in her gut. She wanted desperately to deny it. And yet…Andrew had been keeping a file on him. Someone had replaced Andrew's insulin with potassium chloride.

"But…we were only in his office a couple hours ago. For him to have arranged a hit on us that quickly would mean—"

"Stanley was on the phone to him before we made it back to my truck. I guarantee that."

She turned a stunned look to Reid, her insides churning. Her father!

"Does it really surprise you that your father could have a gunman for hire in his little black book? With one call he could have made the arrangements, given the guy your address, knowing eventually you'd have to go back to your house."

Acid built in her stomach as the harsh truth settled like a rock. "Pull over."

"What?"

"Pull over!" she shouted, even as she unbuckled her seat belt and opened the passenger door.

He braked hard, swerving to the curb just as she stumbled out of the Explorer and indelicately lost her lunch on the side of the road.

"Pen!" His voice held a sharp note of concern.

She waved a hand behind her, as she coughed and wiped her mouth on the back of her hand. "I… I'm okay," she lied. She was trembling to her core. Heartsick. Terrified. She wasn't sure she'd ever be *okay* again.

She flopped back onto the passenger seat and motioned for him to drive on. "Go. Hurry. We have to get Nicholas, before…"

She closed her eyes, not allowing herself to finish the thought. Nicholas *had* to be all right. She simply couldn't live with any other possibility.

Finally Reid wheeled into the church lot and parked on the side nearest the children's wing.

When they hurried up to the nursery door, the volunteers at the Mother's Day Out were concerned by the cuts on her face and gave Reid suspicious looks. She assured them with a stiff smile that she was fine, just shaken by the "minor accident" that broke the car window. After signing her son out and carrying him, with Reid escorting her, back to her Explorer, she buckled Nicholas into his safety seat. She climbed in the back with him as Reid slid into the driver's seat. If the drive-by shooter found them again, she wanted to be closer to her son, be better able to protect him, shield him. And in the meantime, as needy as it sounded, she wanted to be able to see Nicholas, touch him, reassure herself that he was safe. Sometimes, especially since Andrew's death, she just needed an extra degree of connection to her son. Today was one of those days. In spades.

"Give me your cell phone." Reid extended his hand toward her, and she blinked at him.

"Why?"

He frowned his irritation with her reluctance. "I don't want anyone tracking us."

The seriousness of their situation smacked into her again, stealing her breath. Reid's cloak-and-dagger tactics brought the reality home. She was on the run, hiding from a killer. Potentially sent by her *father*.

Reid wiggled his fingers impatiently. "Come on!"

Fear balled in her gut like a cold stone as she fished in her purse for her phone. She handed it over and watched in dismay as he pried off the back and removed the battery and SIM card. He tossed the pieces onto the passenger seat, then performed the same disassembly on his own mobile phone. With their phones' GPS-tracking abilities disabled, Reid cranked the engine and sped out of the church parking lot.

Nicholas watched her with wide, curious eyes, blinking an unspoken question about what was happening. She tried to mask her fear, not wanting to upset him, but her son was perceptive for a two-year-old. Mommy didn't usually sit in the backseat. A strange man was driving their car. He'd been too young the last time Reid had been at their house to remember the sandy-haired man behind the wheel of their SUV. Nicholas's curious brown gaze was so like his father's it hurt her heart sometimes to look at him.

"Mommy?" Her son tipped his little head in inquiry, his button nose wrinkling.

Her chest contracted as her love for him swelled at the precious sound of his baby voice addressing her. When would every tiny thing he did stop being such a fascination and point of pride to her? Never, she hoped.

"It's okay, sweet pea. That's Mommy's friend." *Mommy's friend.* Or was he? She might not have thought so this morning when she woke up, but a lot had happened to change her view of Reid in the last few hours. *He saved your life.*

Reid glanced over his shoulder and smiled at Nicholas.

"Hi, buddy. How ya doin'?" He turned back to watch the road, but Pen saw his gaze flick to the rearview mirror over and again watching her, studying Nicholas. "He's looking more like his dad as he gets older, isn't he?"

She drew a breath intended to relieve the tightness constricting her lungs, but the sound of gunfire still echoed in her memory, and she couldn't relax. "Yeah. He does."

"I can't believe how big he's getting." He met her gaze in the mirror and huffed a wry laugh. "Why do people say that? Like they're surprised a kid is growing up?" He shook his head and twisted his mouth. "And yet that's really what I thought when I saw him—how much he's grown and changed." He chuckled dryly. "Some fine detective work there, huh?"

She hummed an acknowledgment but wasn't in the mood for banal conversation. Maybe he was trying to distract her, calm her down, but too much had happened today for her to maintain the illusion of idle chatter. Keeping her composure in front of Nicholas was taking all her energy. She forced a stiff grin for her son's sake and smoothed his silky hair with her fingers. "Did you have fun playing at the church, sweet pea? Did you play blocks?"

"Bwocks?" Nicholas parroted.

His vocabulary was expanding rapidly in recent days as he mimicked what she said. She could only guess whether he understood what he was saying, but her money was on her son's ability to connect the dots. Nicholas had an intelligence in his watchful gaze that spoke of precocious levels of understanding. Or maybe that was her biased view as his mother.

She tweaked his chin and whispered, "You're Mommy's smart little boy, aren't you?"

He reached for her face and poked one of the cuts. "Mommy booboo?"

Wrapping her fingers around his hand, she turned up his wrist to kiss it. "Just a little one. Mommy's okay."

He wrinkled his nose. "Kiss it?"

She had to fight a sudden onslaught of tears. "Will you?" She leaned closer to her boy, and he pressed a tender kiss to her cheek.

"Ahw bettah."

She bit the inside of her cheek and blinked back tears as she smiled at Nicholas. "Yep. All better. Thank you, sweet pea."

Nicholas gave her a sweet smile, then looked past her out the car window. "Fwench fwies?"

The little stinker had spotted the golden arches as they drove past the fast-food restaurant where she sometimes took him for a treat.

"Not today, honey. We'll get a snack at home." She ruffled his hair, then, realizing where they were, jerked her attention back to the window. "Reid, where are you going? This isn't the way to my house."

"We're not going back to your house," he said, his tone flat and uncompromising.

"What are you talking about? Of course we are!"

"No. Too risky."

She gaped at his profile, too stunned by his pronouncement to respond for a moment. "Reid..."

"Look, whoever that guy was, he was waiting outside your house. Do you really want to go back and give him a second chance to finish the job?"

"But...where can we—" She glanced at Nicholas. He might be too young to understand, but just in case she modified her language. "How do we know he wasn't aiming for you? Maybe you're the one who has the target on his back."

"We don't know. But he was waiting outside *your* house. Which is why you're not going back there until I figure out—for sure—who was behind the attack and why. And put an end to the threat."

"If there's a threat. It *could* have been a random thing. A case of mistaken identity, or a fluke..."

He sent her a look that asked, *You don't really believe that, do you?*

"Reid, I can't—"

"Pen, I know you don't want to believe it was your dad, but it comes down to this—are you willing to put your child at risk if all your doubts prove wrong?"

A shudder rolled through her. Despite her denials, her attempts to rationalize the irrational, in her gut she knew Reid was right. She couldn't do anything that would put Nicholas in harm's way. As incredible as it seemed, the evidence pointed to the frightening fact that—whether it was her father or not—*someone* had tried to kill her today. And they could try again.

Chapter 8

Reid took a circuitous route as he drove Pen and her son to his lake house. Knowing he could be followed, he made sure to watch his tail and take irregular turns, sometimes doubling back and quite often making zig-zagging turns. Only when he was certain no one was tailing them did he drive to his property outside of the Dallas metro area. He'd bought the place several years earlier through a blind corporation he'd set up so he'd have a safe house to go to if one of his police investigations ever got too hot. He'd primarily used the lake house as a getaway when things at Colton Valley Ranch got too crazed, when he needed an escape from classic Colton-style drama.

Because he'd originally intended it to be a secure retreat when he felt his life was at risk from the enemies he made through his job, he'd taken extra measures at the lake house. A state-of-the-art alarm system, dead bolts, security cameras, secure Wi-Fi and reinforced windows. He'd spared no expense because…well, he *could*. He had his share of the Colton wealth at his disposal, and if he couldn't spend it to create a safe zone for himself, a retreat where he could not only relax and rejuvenate, but do so in safety and luxury, then what was the point of having vast amounts of cash at his disposal?

His salary at the police department had been irrelevant to him. He'd worked because he'd have been bored living the life of a rich playboy. As a detective, he'd been challenged mentally and physically. The element of danger had appealed to his thirst for excitement, and the service he'd performed the community by arresting criminals and solving murders gave him a sense of purpose. That purpose was what he'd missed most in the past year. He hated feeling useless, hated knocking around the huge Colton estate and having no direction in his life.

His father's disappearance had fueled his days in recent weeks, given him a mystery to puzzle out, but the lack of progress in finding the old man was proving an aggravation in more ways than one. Now, he supposed, he'd need to set aside Eldridge's disappearance to look into who had shot up his truck. Knowing the elderly neighbor had called the police, Reid also knew there would be questions about why they'd left the scene. He'd be in touch with his contacts within the Plano PD to set things right there and find out as much as he could about the official investigation into the shooting.

But he wouldn't leave the search for the shooter entirely to the police. Not when he had his own skills, his own insights and motivation to catch the person responsible. He'd not only find the shooter, but also the person who'd hired the gunman. Maybe that person was Hugh Barrington; maybe not. Either way, he had an itchy feeling that told him something significant was behind the attempt on his and Pen's lives. The shooting wasn't random.

He turned off the rural highway, down the narrow dirt

path that was more like a cow trail leading to his lake house, and Pen sat taller on the backseat, her gaze darting about the isolated property. Fitting to his mood, a line of gunmetal clouds crept in from the north to blot out the December sun and cast the world in a dreary shadow. As they bumped down the rutted trail, branches from overgrown scrub bushes and winter-dead weeds scraped the sides of Pen's Explorer like skeletal hands grabbing at them. The fingernails-on-blackboard screeching sent a shiver to Reid's marrow.

Judging by the pained expression on Pen's face, the noise, or maybe the implied damage to her SUV, unnerved her, as well.

"Sorry. I'll spring for a new paint job when this is over," he said, meeting her eyes in the rearview mirror.

She shook her head. "That's the least of my worries right now. Where are we?"

"At a property I bought a few years ago for this very purpose."

"You anticipated having someone trying to kill us?"

"Not you, specifically. But I figured in my line of work I could earn a dangerous enemy. Or need to hide a witness. Or…" He shrugged. "More often than not, I use it when I'm hiding from my family."

She snorted a deprecating laugh. "Well, that I can understand. What I meant was *where* are we? We've been driving a long time."

"Mmm-hmm." He could tell his noncommittal hum of agreement didn't appease her curiosity. If anything, his avoidance irritated her further. "Once I get you and pipsqueak settled, I'll go into town to get you some things. Change of clothes or two, toiletries. Anything specific you want me to get you?"

"How about an answer to my question? Where are we?" Her scowl matched her tone.

"Better you don't know. That way you can't accidentally give yourself away." They emerged from the tunnel of overgrowth to a field that stretched down to the lake house and waterfront.

Pen craned her neck, leaning toward the front seat to peer through the windshield at the terrain. "A lake? Which lake?" When he stayed silent, she grunted her exasperation. "Who am I going to tell?"

"Nothing personal. Just precaution." Braking in front of the three-vehicle garage, he shifted the car into Park, then climbed out. When he'd punched the security code into the panel by the garage, the door rumbled and rolled open. He pulled the Explorer into the only open space in the garage and cut the ignition. The two spaces to the left were taken by his water ski boat, covered for the season with a giant tarp, and his Range Rover. Parked behind the garage was an older four-wheel-drive Jeep Wrangler he never drove anymore but hadn't bothered to get rid of yet. As he exited the Explorer and cast a glance around his garage, he spotted damage to the insulation around the roof vents. Probably raccoons or squirrels had gnawed their way in to make a winter nest. He huffed a sigh and made a mental note to repair the damage. He scooped the pieces of their disassembled cell phones from the passenger seat.

After helping Penelope unbuckle Nicholas from his child seat, he led them into the house through the door from the garage. He paused in the mudroom, flipping switches to turn on lights, adjusting the heat to a more comfortable setting and entering the passcode to close the garage doors and rearm the security system. With a few more buttons and a typed password on a small keypad, he turned on the secured Wi-Fi.

"This way," he said and hitched his head toward the kitchen.

Leading Nicholas by the hand, she followed him into the fully equipped kitchen, her gaze taking in all the newest gadgets and screens. "Pretty fancy technology for a lake house."

"Remote doesn't have to mean ill-equipped. I furnished the place with the expectation I might have to work a case from here. And I like keeping my electronics updated." He opened a drawer by the refrigerator and dumped in the keys to Pen's Explorer as well as the pieces of the phones and the batteries.

"Only the best for a Colton," she muttered, her tone dark with sarcasm.

"Is that going to be a problem for us?"

She turned a startled look toward him. "Your gadgets?"

"My being a Colton. In the past, I never got the sense that my last name was an issue for you, but that's at least the third time you've derided my family connection."

Chagrin darkened her face. "I'm sorry. I know I owe you better. Especially since you've done so much to help me today. I'm just…edgy." She scoffed. "To put it mildly. More like scared as hell. Confused. Angry." Her face crumpled as tears filled her eyes.

Reid moved toward her, lifting his arms to hug her, and she raised a hand to ward him off.

"No." She shook her head and swiped at her eyes. "I'll be fine."

She schooled her expression and took a deep breath. Then with a tight, tremulous smile, she lifted Nicholas into her arms and started for the next room. "So show me the place."

Reid ushered her into the living room, trying to see the house from her point of view. The decor was decidedly masculine. Since he'd been creating a space for himself and had no woman in his life to compromise with on colors or styles, he'd chosen what he liked. Dark bold shades of maroon, navy, dark green. His leather couch was extra large to accommodate his height if he chose to stretch out on it while he watched the huge flat-screen TV mounted over the river-stone fireplace. The stained concrete floor meant no carpet to vacuum, but he could see the wheels turning in Penelope's head. No doubt she was thinking of how hard the surface would be for her young son to play on.

As he surveyed his belongings, he realized how child-unfriendly the place was. His abundance of technology put buttons and knobs in easy reach of curious, sticky fingers. His coffee and end tables had glass tops and were adorned with heavy, breakable knickknacks. And then there was his gun cabinet...

He saw her bite her bottom lip and scowl as her gaze went to the glass-front cabinet where his hunting rifles and shotgun were stored.

"It's locked," he assured her. "But in the interest of full disclosure, I also have a handgun in the master bedroom. In the nightstand drawer."

"You'll have to move it. Lock it up with those." She pointed at the gun case.

"Of course." He blew out a lungful of air through pursed lips. "And a good bit of other childproofing, I'd guess."

Nicholas whined and kicked his legs. "Down!"

"You guess correctly. What am I supposed to do with Nicholas?"

"Until we can make this room safer, let's see what shape the guest bedrooms are in. Can he sleep in a real bed?"

"Do you have a guardrail for it?"

"No." Wow. He really hadn't thought this one through before he brought them here. He'd been concerned only about them being hidden, safe from whoever had shot at them.

Pen raked her hair back with her free hand. "I can move the bed against a wall. Maybe slide the dresser up next to it."

"No." He shook his head and stalked to a side table where he opened a drawer and took out pen and paper. "Here. Make a list. Everything you need for yourself and Nicholas. Safety equipment, food, clothes, diapers."

She gave a short humorless laugh. "Thank God we have a few extra diapers in his bag from Mother's Day Out. But if we stay here, I'm going to need supplies by morning at the latest."

"I'll go tonight. I can have everything back here in a few hours."

She stared at him, her expression skeptical. "Reid, I don't think this is—"

"Can you trust me on this?"

She lifted an eyebrow as if to say, *Are you kidding me?*

"Please," he added. "I thought you believed me about what happened with Andrew."

"Maybe. I..." Her shoulders slumped. "I haven't really had a chance to process it. My hesitance is not really about what happened with Andrew. Not completely. I just..." She blew out a tired breath. "So much has happened today. My head is spinning."

He closed the distance between them and stroked a hand down her arm. Grasping her elbow, he drew her even closer and held her gaze. "Can you at least believe I'm your friend? That I care about what happens to you and Nicholas, and I'm trying to do what is best for you?"

She moistened her lips, and just the glimpse of her tongue sliding along the seam of her mouth sent a shock wave of lust pounding through him.

He dropped her arm and took an awkward step back, as if Andrew had planted a hand in his chest and shoved. *That's* my *wife, man. Stay away!*

Penelope lowered her chin to stare at the floor for a moment before nodding. When she raised her head again, tears had filled her eyes. "It's just… Damn it, Reid. I'm scared. I don't know what to think, who to trust. Andrew is gone, and my father might be a crook. Someone hates me enough to have me killed, and everything I'd been told about your involvement with Andrew's death may have been lies."

He raised a finger. "Not lies exactly, but half truths. Deceptive half truths." She pulled a face, displaying her frustration with his quibble over semantics, and he pressed on to the more important point. "And I wouldn't say the shooting today was based on hatred."

Her eyebrows darted up in disbelief. "Then what—"

"Fear. Someone has something to lose if they don't get rid of you. Get rid of *us*. Remember I was there, too."

Now her expression crumpled into confusion.

"That something could be money, position, power, love—"

She frowned dubiously. "Love?"

He hesitated a beat. "I have to ask… Are you having an affair with anyone? A married man maybe?"

She scoffed an incredulous laugh. "No! How could you even think—"

"Okay!" He held up both hands in surrender. "I'm just trying to get a handle on who might be behind this." Rubbing his palms on his jeans, he sighed. "I'm still inclined to think this has to do with your father, but I don't want to miss something because of tunnel vision."

Her face paled, but she didn't argue, which said a lot about her own thought processes on the matter. She carried her squirming son to the couch and dropped heavily on the cushions. "Oh, my God," she whispered, her gaze growing distant and disturbed. Nicholas wiggled free from her slackened grasp and toddled across the floor, taking in his new environment with eyes rounded in wonder.

"I know it's hard for you to believe your own father would try to hurt you, but we can't—"

"No."

"Pen, we have to consider…"

"Not hard to believe…" she muttered, still staring into near space. "Believable. He's heartless when it serves him. He…" She swallowed hard and blinked rapidly as if clearing tears from her eyes. "He was cold and dismissive of my mother when she got sick. I've seen him treat the house staff like dirt. He can be a self-centered bastard over and again and lose no sleep over it."

Casting a glance to the toddler to check on him, Reid joined her on the couch, his thoughts spiraling in new directions. "Pen, if your father knew Andrew was building a case against him…" He scrubbed a hand down his cheek and scratched the stubble on his chin. He didn't like the direction his train of thought was going, but he couldn't ignore the nagging feeling in his gut.

"My father had something to do with Andrew's death," she said in a rasp, completing the sentence for him. She lifted bleak eyes to him. Swallowed hard. "He could have tampered with Andrew's insulin. He had the opportunity."

Reid sat back, eyeing Pen and digesting her assertion. "Opportunity? When?"

"A couple months after Nicholas was born, he showed up at our house saying he wanted to get to know his only grandson. Forget that we hadn't talked more than five minutes in three years. Suddenly he wants a relationship with his grandchild. Not me, mind you. Nicholas." Bitterness weighted her tone, and she shook her head as she turned to search the room for her wandering child. Nicholas had found a stack of magazines he was spreading out on the floor, crumpling the covers in his fist.

She made a move to get up, and he waved her back onto the couch. "Let him have 'em. They're not important. Finish what you were saying. He came to your house to see Nicholas, and…"

"He came a few times, but he never spent much time with the baby. I mean, Nicholas was only a couple months old at the time. He could hardly hold a conversation with him or throw a baseball in the yard."

"What did he do?"

"He sat in the family room with me, and we had extremely awkward conversations about the weather and how cute the baby was. I'd offer him something to drink and leave him alone in the family room for a while so I could start a pot of coffee. Once, I recall, he excused himself to use the bathroom and was gone for a long time."

Nicholas abandoned the magazines and headed for the large window with a view of the backyard and lake. Reid kept half of his attention on the boy as he plastered slobbery hands on the glass and pressed his runny nose to the window.

"Out?" Nicholas chirped.

"Andrew wasn't home with you?" he asked, facing Pen again.

"No. He never came by when Andrew was home. And he never stayed more than thirty minutes or so." She rubbed a hand on her opposite arm and glared at the coffee table as she dredged up the memories. "He'd look in on the baby or hold him for maybe five minutes before passing him back to me, have a stilted chat for a few minutes, disappear to the bathroom for ten or so minutes and then say he wasn't feeling well, or he had a meeting to rush off to or some excuse and take off. I was always relieved to see him go. The visits were so… strained. And strange."

"Did Andrew keep his insulin in the bathroom?"

She raised an odd look before her expression became crestfallen. "No. He stored it in the refrigerator."

"What about other medicines Andrew took or products he used?"

"Sure. Basic things like painkillers, antacids, mouthwash and toothpaste…"

Nicholas had grown bored with the backyard view and toddled over to the bookshelf. Reid sat forward, keeping a more attentive eye on the boy now. He had valuable items displayed on the shelves. "Did he ever go into the kitchen without you? Could he have tampered with the insulin without you knowing?"

Penelope turned her palms up. "Probably. I…" She raked both hands through her hair and scrunched her eyes closed. "God, Reid. It's been almost two years. A lot has happened since then. I don't remem—"

A crash interrupted her, and both his and Pen's gazes flew to the bookshelf. Nicholas had started to climb, knocking a candy dish to the floor. Reid bolted from his seat and snatched the toddler into his arms just as the baby lost his footing and toppled backward.

"Nicholas!" Pen gasped as she rushed forward.

"He's okay." Reid exhaled a breath made shaky by a post-adrenaline shudder. "I got him."

Pen stroked her son's head and raised her eyes, bright with emotion, to his. "You saved him, you mean. That's twice today. You saved me from the shooter, and now Nicholas from falling on his head."

The little boy twisted and craned his head to look to the floor, unfazed by his tumble or the adults fawning. He pointed a chubby finger at the spilled sweets and broken glass. "Candy?"

"I'll get a broom to clean up. Then we'll get busy baby-proofing."

After several minutes and much persuasion, Penelope was able to convince Nicholas to stay in the guest bed and take a nap. Reid had helped her make the twin bed more secure for the toddler by shoving it against a wall, moving a chest of drawers and removing the mounted trophy bass from the wall over his head.

Guilt nipped at her for having been inattentive enough to let Nicholas even start climbing the bookcase in pursuit of the candy. Reid had tried to assuage her self-reproach, blaming himself, pointing to the kid-unfriendliness of his house. She could argue that her head was swimming with all the crazy twists and turns of the day and that she suffered the lingering chill of having been shot at. She'd also been distracted by Reid's questions about her father's access to Andrew's insulin. But, in truth, she had no good excuses for her negligence. She was a mother, first and foremost, and Nicholas's safety should have trumped all the other chaos and mind-clutter of the day.

Penelope watched her son sleep peacefully for a few minutes, her heart swelling with a tender ache of affection. As much as she'd love to snuggle up next to her boy and nap herself, she and Reid had too much to do making the lake house safe for Nicholas. They needed to lay in supplies for their stay and start digging into the paperwork and computer files they'd acquired today from her father's office and Andrew's secret stash.

She rubbed her throbbing temple where a stress headache had built to a pounding pitch and joined Reid in the living room.

He glanced up from his task when she entered. "I found an empty box in my storage room. We can pack up anything and everything a two-year-old could break or get hurt from."

She barked a short laugh. "So…essentially every piece of art, technology or furniture in the room."

He shrugged. "If that's what it takes. My entertainment center has a locking door, and we can move the remotes for the flat screen and Blu-ray player to the top of the mantel. I've already put the gun from my nightstand in the cabinet with the rifles, and the display case has been secured."

"Maybe I should just go to a hotel. Or I could hire private security to guard us at our house, or…"

Reid sat back on his heels and studied her with a frown denting his forehead. "You could. But hotels and security guards cost money. I'm offering you a safe refuge and my protection for free."

She sighed. "It's not about the money."

"No, it's not. Because I can easily afford to pay for a hotel for you or a private guard, but—"

"It's not your job to pay for my hotel! I'm not a charity case!" She couldn't say why the idea of Reid covering any of her expenses galled her so much. Probably residual resentment of the Coltons and their wealth. Their the-world-belongs-to-us attitudes. "I can go stay with Andrew's parents in Georgia. They have room and would be thrilled to have the time with Nicholas."

"A logical place to go. Which is why the shooter could easily track you to your in-laws. Do you want to put them in the line of fire?"

She gritted her teeth in frustration. "Of course not."

He arched an eyebrow at her peevish tone. "The point is I want to be the one protecting you." He paused and frowned as if he realized how his declaration must have sounded to her. "What I mean is…I don't know who we can trust. I have the time, the lake house and the ability, and I want to know the job is being done right. Don't you want Nicholas in the safest possible location?"

She told him what she thought of his sly tactic with a low growl before muttering, "Of course I do."

The implications and magnitude of everything she'd learned and been through today coalesced inside her. A bitter, scalding brew of deception and pain and fear. Tears rushed to her eyes, and she covered her face with her hands as the sobs broke like waves on the shore of a storm-tossed lake, one after another.

The sofa dipped as Reid settled beside her, drawing her into his arms and pulling her against his chest. "I wasn't trying to upset you, Pen. I know this is hard for you, but the first step in protecting yourself is taking off your blinders. You have to see clearly what's happening, know who you can trust and who you can't if you're going to stay safe."

"So…how am I supposed to know who I can trust?

I'm so confused and scared right now I can't get any of this to make sense."

Reid squeezed her hand. "That's why I'm here. Trust me."

As if he'd given her permission to fall apart, she wilted against him, too emotionally spent and tied in knots to resist the comfort and reassurance he offered. After months of staying strong and keeping up appearances for her son's sake, she let herself weep from the depths of her soul. The release was cathartic, and she felt surprisingly safe crying in front of Reid. The loss of her husband, the betrayal of her father, the stress of being a single mother...she cleansed herself of all the pent-up fear and grief.

"You're going to be all right, Pen. I promise."

Reid stroked her back, and she buried her face in the soft fabric of his shirt. He smelled like laundry detergent, crisp winter air and a subtle male musk that turned her insides to jelly. The warmth of his arms around her, the solid strength of his chest and reassuring thump of his heartbeat against her ear conspired to woo her into a sense of security and well-being she'd not known since Andrew died. She might be a strong, capable woman, an independent widow by necessity and a competent single mother, but she craved companionship. She missed having someone to share the trials of life with and bolster her when her spirits flagged.

That was all this was, she told herself as she snuggled deeper into Reid's embrace. He filled a void. Being held by Reid felt good, but only because she was scared and felt alone. Any comforting arms would have sufficed. Any shoulder to dampen with her tears. Anyone...

But then Reid nudged her chin up and dried her cheeks with his thumbs. She met the fathomless blue of his concerned gaze and knew she'd been lying to herself. Reid made the difference. And just what was she supposed to do with that revelation?

Chapter 9

Shopping list in hand, Reid left a few minutes later to collect the items Penelope and Nicholas would need for their stay at his lake house. After a stop at the super-center store nearest the Colton ranch, he popped by the family home to get a few of his own things, grab a quick shower and have a word with his half brother Zane. His half brother was head of security for Colton Inc., and considering all the trouble the family had been involved in lately, he decided it would be prudent to let Zane know at least some of what he'd learned today.

As it happened, his half brother was in the kitchen digging through the refrigerator when Reid stopped through to grab a bottle of water. "Hey, I'm glad I ran into you. We need to talk."

"Look, if this is about the leftover lasagna," Zane said, raising a defensive hand, "first come first serve, man. You snooze, you lose."

"Lasagna?" Reid snorted.

"Fowler whined about it this morning. I tell ya, Mira-bella may be the pregnant one," he said of his new bride, "But I'm the one eating for two. Sympathy appetite or something maybe? Or else fatherhood nerves are making me hungry. I'm having to double up on my workouts to keep the pounds off." With that he bit into an apple with one hand and carried a pan from the refrigerator with the other.

Reid shook his head. "No, this has nothing to do with your eating for two."

"Okay...what?" Zane asked as he chewed.

"I want you to keep a sharp eye out around here and at the office for trouble."

His half brother's dark eyebrows dipped low in concern. "Trouble? What *now*?"

"I'd rather not go into all of it until I have the proof I need to press charges, but I've learned some...*interesting* things today about someone in our employ. And I suspect he's the one who sent a gunman after us—"

"What!" Zane sputtered around his mouthful of apple. "Wait. Who is *us*? Who was with you?"

"Don't worry about that. I want to protect her until we can find the evidence we need to arrest the person behind the attack."

Zane lifted a corner of his mouth in a smug grin. "Her, eh? Now, *that* is interesting..."

He sneered at Zane. "Don't be a jerk. There's nothing between us."

Nothing mutual, anyway. Nothing he could admit to or act on. Pen was Andrew's widow, and she'd made it clear for the last eighteen months just how little affection she had for her husband's killer.

"Hmm. Defensive much?" Zane's smile grew.

Reid balled his hands, struggling for patience. "Would you quit with the juvenile insinuations? Did you hear me say we were shot at? That the threat could come here to the ranch?"

Zane shrugged as he took a bite of the fruit. "You're here and seem to be in one piece—" he aimed a finger at Reid's face "—other than a nick or two. I'm assuming your girlfriend is all right, as well, or you'd have mentioned that by now."

"She's not my girlfriend."

"All right, *Sheldon*." He said with a smirk and waved him off. "She's a *girl* who's your *friend*. Got it."

Reid growled quietly and gritted his teeth. Teasing and pranks were part and parcel to the siblings—blood, half and step—in his family, with some relationships being more rancorous than others. But he was in no mood for Zane's ribbing. "My love life is not the issue. I'm asking you to keep an eye out around here. I plan to stay with Pen to be sure she's safe until we can—"

"Whoa! Pen? As in Penelope Barrington?"

Reid mentally kicked himself for the slip. "Yeah. Except she's Penelope Barrington Clark. Remember?"

Zane nodded as if he'd just made the connection. "Oh, right. She was your partner's wife." Still holding the partially eaten apple, he gestured toward Reid. "You introduced them, didn't you? Some policemen's benefit you dragged Andrew to?"

"I didn't drag him there. Our boss insisted we go. Mostly because he thought my last name would help raise more donations." He shook his head, frowning. "Look, that's irrelevant. What *is* important is—"

"My brother—the poster boy for police charity." Zane snickered as he bit into his apple again.

Reid sighed. He was happy that his half brother had found Mirabella and was enjoying married life, but Zane's good mood in recent days meant his teasing had increased as much as his appetite had. "Just keep an eye out around here for trouble. While I have my suspicions,

I don't know *for sure* who is behind the attack on us or just how desperate they are, but you can't be too safe."

To his credit, Zane sobered a bit and nodded. "Sure."

Turning, Reid headed up to his suite to clean up and pack.

"You missed dinner," a female voice chirped from the living room as he hurried through to the front hall.

His mother, Whitney, sat with her feet tucked under her and a drink in her hand. "Where were you?"

Reid wished he thought his mother actually cared about why he'd not been home for the evening meal, but Reid was certain her curiosity was simply nosiness.

"I'm an adult now, Mother. I don't have to report my whereabouts to you. And I'm perfectly capable of getting something to eat."

"Don't take that tone with me! I just asked where you were!" Whitney sniped.

"I'm in a hurry. I don't have time for interrogations. Mind someone else's business," he said, mounting the stairs.

"Reid! Reid, come back down here!" she shrilled. "Don't walk away from me like that!"

On the grand staircase to the upper levels of the house, he passed Moira Manfred on her way down, carrying a wad of bedsheets that smelled heavily of whiskey. The woman had been head housekeeper and wife of the family butler, Aaron Manfred, for as long as Reid could remember. "Evening, Mr. Reid."

He bobbed his head in greeting and added a polite smile. "Hi, Moira."

The woman, well into her seventies, could have retired a decade ago. But she, like her husband, was loyal to a fault and determined to work until she was physically unable. "Oh, Mr. Reid?"

He paused and faced her. "Yes?"

"Mr. Manfred is taking some time off tonight and has gone to bed early. If you need anything before retiring, let me know, and I'll get it for you."

"Sure." Reid nodded absently. He wouldn't be around, so he had no need for either the butler or his wife's help. He took a few more steps.

"Mr. Reid? Are you all right? Pardon my saying so, but you look terrible. Your face is cut, and you seem extraordinarily tired or worried."

He paused, feeling an odd sense of gratitude and warmth that the woman had noticed and seemed genuinely concerned. "It's been an interesting day, for sure. But I'm fine. Thank you."

She gave him a small smile of acknowledgment. "I'll be up to turn down your bed in a few minutes. I just have to get clean sheets and a fresh drink for Mr. Fowler."

"Not necessary. I'm not staying here tonight."

If the news surprised her, she masked it well. But then she'd had many years to practice hiding her reaction to the family's drama and last-minute changes in plans. He turned to continue upstairs but hesitated. "Moira?"

The older woman stopped and glanced back up at him. "Yes, sir?"

"Aaron has taken off a lot of evenings lately."

She raised her chin, her expression saying she was prepared to defend her husband if needed. "Yes, sir."

"Is everything all right? You said he went to bed already. He's not ill or anything, is he?"

She relaxed a bit and shook her head. "No, sir." He thought for a moment she was going to add an explanation as to why her husband had been so absent of late, perhaps ask that his hours be reduced permanently. Instead she squared her shoulders. "Mrs. Colton said it was all right for Aaron to take the evening off as long as I covered for him. I hope that's not a problem for you?"

He shook his head as he continued up the steps. "No, it's fine. I just…was making sure everything was okay with him. Not feeling sick or…"

"No, sir."

He gave the banister a little double pat. "Okay. Good."

As he strode past his sister Piper's room, the sound of laughter, both male and female, bubbled out like champagne overflowing a glass. Extravagant and effervescent. Farther down the hall, the noises coming from his brother T.C.'s suite were more amorous. He experienced a brief pang of envy for his siblings, moving on with their lives, enjoying the company of their new loves. Every one of his siblings had a new life, a new love, a new beginning. Except him.

Even his other half siblings, waspish Marceline and pretentious Fowler, had mellowed in recent weeks, making their illicit affairs public and embracing the future with their lovers.

So where did that leave him? Alone. Not lonely exactly, but maybe beginning to search, to question. He wanted to settle down someday. But he hadn't yet found that certain someone who knocked his socks off.

When Penelope's face materialized in his mind's eye, he quickly scuttled the image of her curled against him to the recesses of his brain. Pursuing that line of thought would just be asking for trouble. Any attraction he felt for her was not only unrequited, he was sure, but verboten.

Reid carefully stripped out of his dirty clothes, knowing shards of his windshield were probably still embedded in the folds and seams of his shirt and jeans. Leaving the clothes on the bathroom floor, he stepped into the hot shower spray, still ticking off reasons in his head why he needed to keep his feelings for Pen in check. One, she had a child. He wasn't ready to be a father. Good God, look at the sorry role model Eldridge had been. What did he know about raising a family?

Two, she was Andrew's widow. And if getting involved with his late partner's wife wasn't awkward enough, his part in Andrew's death, intentional or not, complicated the hell outta matters.

Three, just hours ago he'd promised to protect her. Somehow that pledge seemed like it should include protecting her from himself. From false expectations of a future together. From a broken heart. From—

He scoffed a laugh when his arrogance dawned on him. As if Penelope couldn't help but fall in love with him. He shook his head in disgust. He was a prime example of the conceit and sense of entitlement, the hubris of the Coltons that she'd always accused his family of suffering.

He swiped soapy water from his face. Before the attack, Pen had wanted nothing to do with him. She still harbored bitterness and distrust for the man who'd administered the fatal drug to her husband. Even since explaining his side, he'd sensed her reserve.

And then the shooter had sent everything about their dynamic into a tailspin. She was being forced to trust him. He was imposing his presence on her to keep her and the kid safe. The brush with danger had cracked the wall she'd put between them and given him a peek at a vulnerability and neediness she had fought hard to deny. And in unguarded moments, he'd sensed a crackle of something in the air. An energy. A magnetism. More than just his attraction to her.

Reid shut off the shower and stared at the drain as the last of the runoff disappeared. She'd reciprocated his lingering glances, reacted to his touch and allowed him to see a softer side of herself. She'd trusted him not just with her life and Nicholas's, but with glimpses of her heartache, her loneliness…her soul. He'd shared flickers of an intimacy with her that went beyond physical chemistry. When he held her during her meltdown, he could almost imagine she fit there, was created to be in his arms.

Heart thumping, Reid slipped his towel from the bar beside the shower and started drying off. He'd have to proceed with caution. In less than twenty-four hours, he'd moved from a secret attraction to his late partner's wife, to helping her uncover the extent of her father's deception and protecting her and her child from an assassin. Pen could get hurt in any number of ways in the coming weeks. The last thing he wanted was to add to her grief and pain. If she reached out to him for comfort and companionship during the rough days ahead, he'd have to keep his libido in check. Pen needed a friend now, a protector, not another reason to hate him.

Thirty minutes later, as he returned to his Range Rover, a dark blue Mercedes pulled up the drive and parked near the servants' entrance. Aaron Manfred. Who'd told his wife to say he'd gone to bed early and had her cover for him.

"Evening, Aaron," Reid called across the lawn. "How are you tonight?"

The old man startled and turned with a jerk to face him. "Oh, hello, Mr. Reid. I'm fine, thank you. And yourself?"

Reid scratched his chin, wondering for only a moment before deciding not to call the butler out on his wife's lie. The older man scuttled inside, shooting backward glances and a small wave to Reid as he went into the mansion.

Odd, Reid thought as he climbed into his vehicle, but gave it no more attention. He had bigger fish to fry, and he'd already been away from the lake house longer than he'd planned. He had to get back to Pen and Nicholas and make sure they were safe. A butler's mysterious evening excursion was small beans compared to the newly discovered fraud of the family lawyer and an assassin's attempt on his life.

Chapter 10

Penelope found a can of tomato soup in Reid's kitchen that hadn't expired and heated it up for Nicholas when he started getting whiny for his dinner. The few fish-shaped cheese crackers left in his diaper bag from Mother's Day Out rounded out his dinner, and when he finished eating she started preparing him for bed. She availed herself to the guest bathroom and used the shower gel and shampoo from the master bath to clean Nicholas up.

The woodsy, masculine scent of the cleansers was disconcerting, not just because she worried the harsh chemicals might dry out Nicholas's skin, but because it was far too easy to imagine Reid using the same products as he showered.

Heat rose to her face. She hadn't pictured a man other than her husband in the shower since before she met Andrew. That she could so easily conjure such an erotic image of Reid now had to speak to her fatigue, or her rattled nerves, or…something! Anything other than the most obvious—she still harbored secret fantasies about her teenage crush. She was a grown woman now. A mother. A widow.

Really, Penelope! She shook her head to clear it, scolding herself.

But another voice in her head countered, *You're a widow, yes. But you're not dead!*

Would she ever find someone she cared enough about to have sex again? That presupposed she would fall in love. Maybe even marry again? She wasn't a casual sex kind of gal.

"Mommy!" Nicholas shouted, slapping his hands in his bath so hard that water splashed her and slopped onto the floor.

The dousing was sufficient to yank her from her wandering thoughts. *Good God, Penelope!* The scolding voice tuned up again. *You learned your father may be a crook and had a madman try to kill you today, and* this *is where your mind goes tonight?*

"What?" she said aloud to Nicholas. "Better than dwelling on the horrible things that happened today, right?"

"Mommy…"

Her son held up his arms, indicating he was ready to get out of the bath. His chin trembled, and when she lifted him out she realized how cold she'd let the water get while she daydreamed and ruminated on her troubles.

"Oh, Nicholas! I'm sorry. Are you a Popsicle?"

Her son's brow shot up as she wrapped him in a plush towel. "Pop?"

Oops. She chuckled. "No, swectie. We don't have any Popsicles. You're the Popsicle."

"Pop!"

Oh, boy. Here it came. Despite her best efforts to distract him, Nicholas fixated on the idea of having one of his favorite summertime treats. When she couldn't produce one from thin air, he pitched a toddler fit and was still crying and churlish as she put him to bed thirty minutes later.

Being in a strange bed didn't help her son settle down, either, so by the time he drifted off in a fitful, snuffling sleep, Penelope was beyond exhausted.

She dropped onto the couch in the living room, wondering what was taking Reid so long, and trying to calm her whirling mind and a throbbing headache. She stared blankly at the stone horse statue on Reid's coffee table, one of the few items they'd deemed too heavy for Nicholas to bother, and she replayed the day in her head.

The silence of the lake house should have been soothing to her, but instead, the quiet tripped down her nerves and filled her with an antsy trepidation. Maybe being out of her element was the problem. Not only were she and Nicholas in a new environment, but being sequestered with Reid made her uneasy. They had so much history. And despite his explanations earlier today—jeez, had that just been this afternoon?—she still wasn't sure what to think about his part in Andrew's death.

Part of her wanted *someone* to blame for her loss, and Reid was the obvious target. A fresh set of chills washed through Pen. Reid's denials of malice left more questions about Andrew's death—questions that held horrifying implications, especially in light of today's discoveries about her father. Someone had put the lethal chemical in the insulin vial on purpose. If not Reid, then who? Had her father known Andrew was keeping tabs on him and killed her husband in order to silence him?

"Pen?"

She jolted at the sound of the voice behind her and spun to face Reid, clapping a hand to her chest where her heartbeat skittered. "Jeez, I didn't hear you come in."

"That's what I was afraid of. Where were you just then? You looked a million miles away."

She rubbed her temple. Her headache was only marginally better. "Just remembering. Reflecting."

"Well, less woolgathering in the future, okay? You need to be more aware of your surroundings. Especially now. A killer's not going to announce himself." Reid set a large bag on the couch and began unpacking the things he'd bought her. "Nicholas asleep?"

She nodded. Reid had changed clothes, she realized, and she wished fervently she could do the same. She was still finding tiny shards of his broken windshield in her clothes. And despite the cool temperatures outside, she'd perspired a thin sheen of anxiety sweat more than once this afternoon and felt grimy for it. "I had to battle a TTT, but he finally succumbed."

"Come again? A TTT?"

"Tired toddler tantrum. They're a horror to witness, trust me."

"I can imagine. Poor kid's been pulled from his home and routine today. I bet he was cranky."

She nodded, and let her expression speak for the undesirability of messing with her son's routine. "When did you become wise to the ways of small children?"

"I'm not a monk. I talk to people, read, observe. I've heard the term *terrible twos*. Not hard to extrapolate the cause of his TTT." He handed her a pack of diapers, wipes and snack crackers. "I bought a couple steaks and potatoes for our dinner. Don't know about you, but today has left me famished."

The thought of food made Penelope's stomach turn, but she said nothing. She didn't want to appear unappreciative of all Reid's thoughtfulness and generosity. Even if she did fear his motivation was guilt over his part in

Andrew's death. She had to put her son's safety over any awkwardness about the circumstances surrounding Reid's help.

They unpacked most of the items he'd bought, including toiletries and a couple new changes of clothes for her, before he tossed the rest of the bags aside. "The rest of this can wait. I'll broil those steaks while you change. Then I want to get a look at the thumb drive of files I downloaded from your father's computer before I call it a night."

Grateful for the chance to clean up, Penelope excused herself to the bathroom farthest from where Nicholas was sleeping, hoping the noise wouldn't wake him. The pounding hot water worked miracles on her tense muscles, though her headache remained. She'd have loved to stay in the steamy bath for hours, but knew Reid was waiting on her for dinner. After drying off, she selected one of the outfits he'd brought her—basic blue jeans and a dark green sweater—and joined him in the kitchen.

When she strolled up beside him, he glanced up from buttering a loaf of garlic bread and grinned. "So...did I choose well? Will those clothes do?"

"I'm hardly in a position to be picky. But yes, these are fine."

When he didn't return to his task right away, she tipped her head and eyed him suspiciously. "What? Did I leave a tag on or something?"

"No... I was just was noticing...Piper was right."

"Piper picked this?"

"Well, I pretended I was buying a Christmas gift for Zane's new wife. She's a redhead, too. Piper said that dark green was a good color for redheads." He stepped closer and gently brushed a hank of her damp hair back from her scratched and bruised cheek. "And she was right. That sweater brings out the green in your eyes."

Her heart pattered erratically, and she took a step back. "And the blue in my bruises?" she teased, hoping to gloss over her awkward reaction to his touch.

He frowned, then continued working on their dinner. "I'd love five minutes alone with that shooter and the man who hired him for hurting you and terrorizing you that way."

"Careful, Detective. That sounds a lot like vengeance rather than justice."

He grunted. "Sometimes vengeance is more satisfying than justice. Besides, I'm not a cop anymore."

She snitched a piece of crust that had fallen off the loaf when he'd sliced it and nibbled on the bit of bread. Her stomach growled as she savored the buttered bread. "Maybe I'm hungry after all. How long until we eat?"

"Just long enough for the bread to heat. Make yourself at home," he said, tipping his head toward the adjoining breakfast nook, "and I'll bring your plate to you."

She slid into the booth seat around the café table and rubbed the muscles in her neck. As wiped as she was, the day wasn't over yet. She wasn't about to let Reid delve into her father's computer files without her. She wanted to be on the front lines of his investigation, working beside him, an equal partner in bringing her father, the shooter and anyone else involved in these crimes to justice. Was Stanley involved? Surely he was complicit. He had to know something was dirty about his employer after all these years.

Reid carried two plates over and set one with a large steak, baked potato, salad and bread in front of her. The blend of aromas made her mouth water, but she paused long enough to bow her head and say a silent grace...

adding thanks that she, Reid and Nicholas had come through the day alive and relatively unscathed. *And give me strength for the days ahead.*

"Amen," she whispered and raised her gaze to find Reid watching her. He made no comment about her prayer, but hesitated a moment before he dived into his garlic bread.

Her faith was one of the few things she had learned from her mother, had shared with Andrew and was trying to teach Nicholas, and she knew it would be a source of strength to her in the uncertain days ahead.

"This looks good," she said as she cut a big bite of steak and poked it in her mouth. The first thing she noticed was the abundance of seasoning. Correction... overabundance of seasoning. She set down her fork, trying hard to swallow without gagging.

"Hope so. I could eat a horse." Reid forked a bite of steak into his mouth and grunted. Coughed. Spit his bite into his napkin. "Jeez!"

"What did you put on the meat?"

He sipped his water and shrugged. "A little of everything. I wasn't sure what to use so..."

She grinned and used her fork to scrape some of the seasoning from her steak. "With cooking, a lot of times, less is more."

"How would I know? We have a full-time cook at the ranch."

"You didn't pay attention when Andrew was grilling at our cookouts?"

He waved a hand at his plate and started laughing. "Obviously not."

Fatigue and the ridiculousness of the situation ganged up on her. She joined his chuckle but soon her laughter blossomed to peals of overtired mirth. They laughed until they were both wiping their eyes. The laughter felt good, even though she knew it was completely incongruous to her situation. Her stress eased, and she felt a tenuous renewed connection with Reid.

As her giggles subsided, she raked her damp hair back from her face and sighed. "Lordy, what a day."

"You can say that again." Shoving aside his steak, he sliced open his potato, and they ate in companionable silence for the next several minutes. When he'd cleared his plate, he scooted from the booth and carried his plate to the sink. "Leave the dishes until morning. Let's get a peek at those files."

In an instant, the tension that had fled briefly as they ate returned in spades. She followed him back to the den where he opened the cabinet doors to the vast collection of electronics including a high-end laptop computer. He carried the computer to a walnut desk in the corner of the living room.

She wanted to know what secrets her father had been keeping, what lies he'd told her and how deeply he'd sunk himself into criminal activity, but her heart gave a sore drub of dread as she dragged a chair in to sit next to Reid as he worked.

While the laptop booted up, he gave her a searching look. "You don't have to stay up. I know you're tired."

She scoffed. "As exhausted as I am, I may never sleep again. Getting shot at was...terrifying. I'm afraid to close my eyes. I keep seeing it replay."

He reached for her hand and squeezed it. "I know. I wish I could do something to help. Give it time. The images may never disappear, but they'll fade."

She gave him a weak, weary smile of gratitude. "Where did you tell your family you'd be tonight?"

"I didn't, really. I gave Zane a quick rundown of what was happening, just in case."

Just in case?

He must have misread her worried expression, because he hurried to add, "I didn't give him details, and he doesn't know where this house is. I trust him. But someone needed to have an idea what was happening."

"In case we're killed the next time the shooter comes gunning for us?" She hated the quaver in her voice.

Reid leaned toward her, pulling her against him. He stroked her back and massaged the base of her neck with strong fingers. "You're safe now, Pen. I'm going to protect you and Nicholas. I swear."

The laptop chimed, indicating it had finished start-up, and Reid backed away from their hug. She immediately missed the comfort and security of his arms around her. After a day as unsettling and topsy-turvy as she'd had, the thought of curling up on the sofa with Reid's body wrapped around her in a protective and reassuring embrace appealed more than it had any right.

Reid plugged the thumb drive into the side USB port and loaded the list of files. She canted closer to read the list on the screen.

"Two thousand twenty-three files?" Her heart dropped when she saw how much material they had to weed through.

"And that's just what I could get downloaded before the butler showed up and we had to cut and run."

"It'll take forever to go through all those files."

"Welcome to the scintillating world of a police detective. A lot of what I did on the job was tedious paperwork and combing through archived documents or computer files." He clicked on a folder and a whole new list of files appeared.

"That's what Andrew used to tell me when I worried about the dangers of his job. Didn't make me feel better, though. I knew it only took one bullet, one witness interview or suspect apprehension gone awry to negate all the desk work in the world."

He cut a silent but meaningful glance her way, then turning back to the computer and continuing to scroll he muttered, "And then it proved to be his partner that did him in. Not a suspect's bullet at all."

She huffed a sigh. "I shouldn't have brought him up."

"Andrew will always be a factor between us."

She ignored that truth, saying, "Are you now claiming responsibility for his death? I thought that whole speech you gave me earlier today was to shift blame away from you."

His eyebrows drew together, and his jaw hardened. "Oh, I take responsibility, all right." He paused a beat as he clicked through a few of her father's files, then added, "It just wasn't murder."

Penelope glanced down at her lap. She spun her wedding ring on her finger without really seeing or realizing what she was doing as she sorted through the tug-of-war of emotions stringing her as tight as a hunter's bow. A few hours ago, when Reid had made the same claim regarding Andrew's death, she hadn't wanted to hear it. She'd clung to the idea that he was to blame so she had a target for her anger and her dismay over the unfairness of her loss.

Now she felt a pluck of sympathy for Reid, for the guilt he lived with. Her anger had shifted inside her. She was angry with the shooter who'd tried to kill them today, necessitating that her life and her son's be disrupted and that they hide out like cowards. But the lion's share of her fury and confusion and hurt focused on her father.

If even a portion of their initial suspicions proved true, her father had been living a lie for years. Had he gotten wind of Andrew's investigation of him? Could her father be the one to blame for the agony she'd suffered in recent months?

She raised her attention back to Reid's laptop, where lists of files scrolled up the screen. When she groaned softly, he chuckled and cast a side glance at her. "What? You were thinking he'd have a file labeled Incriminating Evidence or Proof of My Illegal Activity?"

She snorted her derision. "Oh, no. My father would never be that cooperative. I'm just wondering how we're supposed to process all this. Where do we start?"

"After I make a backup of the whole thumb drive," he said, even as he dug another memory stick out of a desk drawer, "I usually make a first cursory pass through, scanning file names and types. I sort out what appears useless and what might prove helpful and make new folders. As I finish with a file I move it to a folder for reviewed items, but I preserve the integrity of the original material. A lot of times, all the information that incriminates a person is saved in the same place."

"Sounds time-consuming."

He arched an eyebrow and curled up a corner of his mouth. "Going somewhere?"

She opened her mouth to tell him how busy her schedule was, then snapped it closed again as it fully dawned on her what being sequestered in his lake house meant. She was essentially a captive. Until the threat to her and to Nicholas was removed, she didn't dare go anywhere near her usual haunts. Her shoulders drooped. "Oh. Right."

He selected a folder titled Family Photos and began opening files.

"Um…" Penelope frowned her curiosity at him. "Strange place to start. You're thinking our Christmas photos from years past hide some encrypted secrets?"

"If you had something you didn't want anyone else to run across accidentally would you save it in a file called Private or called Summer Vacation Photos?"

"Your theory being a file called Private or Personal screams juicy reading and invites invasion."

"Exactly."

"While Family Photos—" she watched him click through a series of humdrum stilted pictures of holiday dinners, awards presentations and ski trips taken before her mother got sick "—are every bit as boring as the cliché."

He scrolled a bit further through the pictures before closing the file. "Well, that appears to be what it claims, so we'll save the walk down memory lane for later."

She stood and stretched her back. "Surely there is something else I can be doing to help besides hovering over your shoulder."

He spun his chair to face her, the lines bracketing his deep blue eyes giving a clue to his own fatigue. "Truthfully, Pen, I think the best thing for you is to try to get some sleep. We'll have plenty of time tomorrow to search files and read documents."

"Does that mean you're going to bed soon, too? Because I don't want to be pushed aside on this. He is *my* father. *I* was shot at today, too. And Andrew was *my* husband. If my dad had anything to do with Andrew's death, if there's any connection to what happened to us today…" She squared her shoulders, firming her resolve. "I have a right to be part of bringing him to justice."

Chapter 11

Morning came early for Pen the next day. Nicholas woke before sunrise and, finding himself in an unfamiliar bed, called out for her rather than falling back asleep as he usually did. She hurried to reassure him before his cries woke Reid. After changing his diaper, she brought him into the twin bed she'd been sleeping in and cuddled him close. She tried to encourage him to fall back asleep, which he finally did about thirty minutes later. By then, she was wide-awake and her thoughts were spinning. Her body ached, especially her head, no doubt thanks to the knock it took when Reid shoved her out of the line of fire yesterday.

A quiver rolled through her, though she couldn't say for sure if it was from the winter-morning chill in the room, the reminder of the shooting or the idea of being sequestered with Reid Colton. Probably a combination of the three.

Easing out from under her son's sleepy embrace, she tiptoed to the bathroom, hoping to grab a shower before Nicholas woke again. But before she could start the spray warming, the scent of fresh brewed coffee found her and

like a heat-seeking missile, she found herself staggering into the kitchen in search of the promised caffeine.

Reid was standing in the kitchen in a pair of sleep
pants slung low on his hips. Only a pair of sleep pants.
His feet were bare, as was his chest, and Penelope
couldn't say which intrigued and tantalized her more.

"There's fresh coffee, if you want some," he said without turning. Considering she hadn't spoken, hadn't made
any significant noise in her bare feet, she wondered how
he'd known she was there.

"And I bought three different kinds of cereal yesterday, along with a bag of powdered-sugar donuts and some
fresh fruit." He glanced over his shoulder then, and his
gaze traveled the length of her in a manner that felt uncomfortably intimate.

Penelope tugged the edges of her cardigan together
at her sternum and cleared the morning frog from her
throat. "Coffee sound great. Thanks."

"What will the tyke eat? I bought eggs, too. I could
scramble one up for him."

She arched an eyebrow. "Based on your steak experi-
ment last night, I think I should do the cooking around
here." She paused when he grinned, then slugged him
in the arm. "You rat! That was your plan. Convince me
you suck at cooking so I do all of it?"

The taut muscles and warm skin she encountered with
her play-punch didn't escape her notice. She tucked her
hands under her armpits, pretending to be miffed, but
using the time to tamp down the tingle in her fist that
spread to her belly.

He choked on a sip of his coffee. "What? No!" He
laughed as he shook his head. "I swear I would not waste
good beef that way. If I wanted you to do all the cooking,

I'd just say, 'Pen, I don't know squat about the kitchen. If you want edible food, you should do all the cooking.'"

She narrowed her eyes and gave a mock growl. "Eggs are easy. I'll teach you. As for Nicholas, he'll be thrilled with some dry cereal he can snack on from a cup."

"In that case, what do you say we get busy going through files?" He carried his coffee into the next room where he'd already logged on to his laptop.

Cradling her own mug of joe between her hands, she scooted a chair up next to his desk chair to read over his shoulder. "A second computer would be nice. We could go through this stuff twice as quickly."

"I can probably arrange that later today. Borrow one from the ranch or just buy a new one."

She blinked and gave him a slack-jawed look. "Just... buy a new one." She gave a soft scoffing laugh. "You really don't have any idea how it sounds to ordinary people when you say things like that."

He gave her a what-the-heck side glance as he tapped the keyboard pulling up folders to search. "What are you talking about?"

"I bet you pay retail price without blinking."

He stopped working and gave her his attention now.

"As a Colton, you've never had to worry about where the money will come from for any purchase. That's not something you should take for granted. It is a blessing and something most people never experience."

For long seconds he only stared at her, his dark blue eyes searching hers, his brow beetled in thought. "You're right. I am blessed. I've spent most of the last eighteen months feeling bitter because I left my job, felt persecuted, had no one special in my life the way Zane and T.C. and the rest have. I've been pretty focused on the negatives, and haven't given much thought to all I do have."

"Believe me, I know how easy it is to get caught up in your losses and forget your haves. But when I focus on Nicholas, it's hard to stay negative. He's a gift. I have him, my health and a house that's paid for thanks to Andrew's life insurance."

Reid dragged a hand over his mouth and gave her a gentle smile that speared her heart. "You are something else, you know that?"

She dismissed his compliment with a shrug. "I'm no guru. I'm just muddling through life like everyone else."

He reached for her cheek and her pulse skipped a beat. A tremble raced through her as his thumb traced the curve of her chin. "You keep me on my toes, though. Even when Andrew was alive you had a way of hitting me with reality checks when I needed one."

She was too aware of his touch, too affected by the glide of his skin against hers. Catching enough breath in her lungs to speak without squeaking took effort. "Someone has to keep your head from getting too big."

Her attempt at levity did little to dispel the toe-curling familiarity of the moment. Intimacy was not supposed to be on her radar. Especially with Reid Colton. She gave her head a brisk shake, effectively ending the moment and stood to pace.

She had precious little time before Nicholas would wake again, and she wanted to use it helping Reid with the gigantic search ahead of them.

Spying the backpack he'd had with him at her father's house, she remembered seeing Reid slip a file from the desk under his shirt and then later into his backpack. She crossed the room and hoisted the pack to a chair. "What about the paper file you recovered? I could start there. Maybe there's—"

Reid's head whipped around. "Pen, stop! Leave that alone!"

Startled, she raised her hands, letting the backpack slump. "What?"

His chair scraped the floor as he shoved it back and hurried to snatch his pack away from her. "I just...don't want you going through my stuff."

She lifted one eyebrow in pique. "Says the man who searched the office of my childhood home and is currently invading my father's private files."

His mouth tightened and he tossed the backpack aside. "This is different."

Peeved by his hypocrisy, she folded her arms over her chest and cocked her head to the side. "Oh? How, exactly?"

Reid rubbed his hands on the seat of his jeans. "That file is not related to the case. It's something personal."

She furrowed her brow. Personal for Reid? In her father's office? "Uh...about your father?"

He twisted his lips, clearly deliberating, weighing his words. "No, not my father."

When she opened her mouth to question him further, he added, "Look, yesterday I asked you to trust me. I need that trust to cover all things. Not just concerning your safety, but also in my handling of this case." He stepped closer, taking each of her elbows in his hands. His voice dipped to a rumbling whisper that made her vibrate to her core, like plucked strings on a guitar. "I know what I'm doing, and I have your best interests at heart."

Oh, hell, she thought as she met his intense blue gaze. The intimacy was back, rattling her nerves, stirring a thrum in her blood and muddling her train of thought.

"If you'll just be patient, I'll explain everything... eventually. I just need time to sort out everything that's coming to light."

Trust Reid Colton? There was that imperative again. One she would have scoffed at in anger even two days ago. But yesterday she'd had no choice but to put her life in his hands. Trusting him had seemed practical, prudent.

But now he was keeping secrets from her, asking her to believe in him, even as he hid information.

Her heart hammered her ribs like a fist beating a wall in frustration. She knew she didn't *have* to trust him. She knew where he had put the keys to her Explorer. She could just put Nicholas in the car and drive home whenever she wanted. She could march across the room now, snatch up that backpack and fight him for a look at the file he was hiding.

Part of her wanted to do just that. But after everything that had happened yesterday, after learning all the secrets and lies her father had told her, something deep down inside her *wanted* to trust Reid. Needed to trust him. Needed an anchor to cling to in the midst of these turbulent and disturbing revelations about her family.

And his family. She had to remember that. Reid had a stake in all this. He'd been set up as the fall guy in Andrew's death. His father was missing, presumed dead, and her father had taken untold millions from the Coltons through deceit and malpractice.

She would offer him the benefit of the doubt. She would allow him some leeway, give him more time. She would trust him. And not because she had to.

Because she wanted to.

She gave him a small nod, and the tension in his face melted away.

"Thank you." He reached for her cheek again, as he

had moments earlier, but this time, instead of pulling away, she closed her eyes and savored the contact. "I won't let you down."

She startled when his warm lips placed a feathery kiss on her forehead. She blinked, raising her chin to meet his eyes. This seduction he seemed bent on felt dangerous to her. Because she enjoyed his caresses, his nearness more than she should. Was her fascination with him simply a factor of her teenage crush? Was it misplaced gratitude for his heroism and kindness yesterday surrounding the shooting? If that were all it was, how did she explain the warmth and desire that simmered in his expression?

The tenderness in his gaze held her in thrall, until a whimper from the back room broke the spell.

"I need to get Nicholas."

"Yeah," he rasped and stepped back. When she returned, carrying her sleepy toddler on her hip a few moments later, Reid was back at the computer with his head down, working hard.

She fixed Nicholas a cup of Cheerios and settled him in front of Reid's large-screen TV to watch a children's DVD that he'd bought the night before.

As with every time she used a screen to entertain her son, she experienced a pang of mommy guilt. But she needed something to keep Nicholas occupied while she and Reid worked.

"Holy cow!" Reid said, his tone saying he'd have used a much darker expression of amazement if not for Nicholas's impressionable ears. "Pen, come take a look at this."

She crossed the room and studied the screen over his shoulder. Reid was scrolling through a list of URLs. "What is that?"

"Your father's internet history for the last few weeks."

A rock of dread settled in her stomach, and she gripped the back of his chair to brace herself. "Tell me."

He rolled the cursor and clicked a link, bringing up a web page titled, "How to Stage Your Own Death." The next website he opened was a discussion of autopsies, primarily on burned bodies. What little breakfast she'd had curdled in her stomach at the sight of the charred human remains. With a gasp, Pen averted her gaze. "What else?"

"More of the same. It appears he was researching how to fake a murder and pass off a burned body as the victim." He angled his head to look up at her, his jaw rigid. "I think we now know who paid off the medical examiner last month to lie about the identity of that burned corpse they found."

"So m-my father killed your father? Is that what you're saying?"

"Not exactly. But he certainly wanted us to believe my father was dead. I told you, didn't I, that my father's will gives Hugh controlling interest in Colton Incorporated?"

"Seriously? Why would your father leave my dad—"

"I'm not at all sure he did. If your dad went to such lengths to fake Eldridge's death, he could certainly have faked the will, as well. He had the only copy of Eldridge's will anyone knows about."

Pen's mouth gaped open. "The only copy? That's... insane. That's—"

"One more reason I doubt the veracity of the document." Reid turned back to the screen and clicked another link.

Pen paced a short open space between the couch where Nicholas slouched watching TV and the desk where Reid continued working. Her restless pace meant her coffee sloshed onto her hand, and she lifted her fingers to suck clean the drips. "Give me something to do,

Reid. I'll go stir-crazy just sitting around here with all this hanging over our heads. I need to keep busy. For sanity if nothing else."

He eyed her for a minute, chewing the inside of his cheek as he thought. "Okay." Leaning forward, he pecked on the keyboard a bit, then tapped a final key with a flourish. Across the room a printer sprang to life, beeping and chugging as pages started spitting out.

The device's activity caught Nicholas's attention and her curious toddler slid off the sofa and trotted over to grab at the pages feeding out to the tray.

"Is it?" Nicholas asked in his toddler way of wanting to know what something was.

She hurried over to pry the pages from his sticky hands. "That's not for you, Nicholas."

"Mine!" His chubby hands reached for the sheets, opening and closing in "gimme" fashion.

"No. Mommy's." She took a blank sheet from the paper tray and handed it to him. "Here's yours."

Satisfied to have something to crumple, Nicholas carried the sheet back to the sofa and started shredding the blank page.

Pen faced Reid with a shake of her head. "Distraction. A key technique for handling toddlers."

"Good to know." He aimed a finger at the papers when she tried to hand them to him. "Those are for you. Look through those. See if anything stands out."

"Such as?"

"Duplicate billing. Numbers that don't add up in some way. Clients that don't quite seem legit somehow."

"Like this guy." She waved the top page at him. "He's billed for his services to Mr. George P. Burdell of Atlanta, Georgia."

Reid frowned. "Why is that suspicious? He could have clients out of town."

She scoffed. "Sure, he could. But George P. Burdell is the name of a fake student at Georgia Tech. Campus tradition and joke since...like the 1930s or before."

Reid arched a sandy eyebrow. "How do you know about him?"

"While I was a student at Agnes Scott College, I dated a guy who went to Georgia Tech. He told me about the student pranks and history of the gag. On one of my visits home for the holidays, I must have told my dad about it."

Reid snorted a laugh. "Gotcha. Good catch. So be on the lookout for other John and Jane Doe types. Pull the ones that seem suspicious."

Task assigned, Pen moved to the sofa, and Nicholas climbed in her lap to cuddle as he nibbled his cereal. She set the stack of pages on the seat beside her to flip through with one hand while she snuggled her son with the other.

"Hoss?" Nicholas said after a moment.

"What, honey?"

Her son wiggled down and patted the stone horse statue on the coffee table. "Hossie?"

She grinned at her toddler, marveling at his growing vocabulary. "Yes, that's a horse. Good boy."

He stroked a hand down the stone horse's flank and said, "Good hossie." Then juggled his cup of Cheerios as he crawled back onto the couch beside her. "My hoss."

Having mastered multitasking months ago—like most mothers—Pen skimmed sheet after sheet of text, stroked her boy's silky hair, and ruminated on all she'd learned in the past two days.

A gnawing started in her gut and grew as she paged through the documents Reid had printed out. A bill to a client for $500,000 to probate a simple will. Another bill to a client named Bob Smith. The name was such a common one…and yet wouldn't the most mundane and common names pass most easily under the radar?

Her uneasiness churned harder. Finally, after thirty minutes of stewing and sorting paperwork, questioning everything she thumbed through as potential proof of her father's dishonesty, she leaned her head back on the couch and heaved a sigh. "I want a meeting."

"Hmm?" Reid hummed distractedly.

"I want to go see my father. In person."

"No."

"Reid, I can't let this go!"

"No!"

She resettled Nicholas from her lap to the sofa cushions, and grabbed up her stacks of papers as she pushed to her feet. "He knows we were at his house yesterday. If I hide from that, we look guilty. I want to go see him, look him in the eyes and—"

"And what? Call him out? Confirm to him we're onto him?" Reid rose from his chair and marched toward her. "It's too dangerous."

"What, do you think he's going to shoot me in his office in cold blood? We already think he has a hired gun after us, how can it get any worse than that?"

Reid swiped a hand down his face, groaning. "Pen, I'm trying to protect you."

"And I appreciate that. I appreciate your putting us up here and helping get to the bottom of what he's done." She drew a shaky breath as emotion swamped her. "Especially if it turns out he had a hand in Andrew's death." She paused for a sustaining breath. "But…"

"My motives aren't entirely altruistic. I have a vested interest. If I can prove he planted the potassium in Andrew's insulin vial, or connect him to my father's disappearance, I'll have removed two large monkeys from my back."

She hugged herself as a chill washed through her. "I hate hiding. It feels…weak. I may have been a pushover as a kid, intimidated by him, but Andrew encouraged me to stand up for myself. It galls me to know he's likely run roughshod over the lives of so many people, including people I love, and he's getting away with it."

"He won't get away with it." The fire of determination blazed in his dark blue eyes. "Work *with* me. Together we can end his secret reign of terror and bring him to justice."

She turned up a hand as she nodded. "Of course. You know I'll do whatever I can."

"That includes following my lead, listening to my advice, not flying off half-cocked and blowing our investigation because you want to confront him." She opened her mouth to protest, and he cut her off with, "Nobody wants five minutes alone with him more than I do." He opened and closed his fist as if itching to punch something…or someone. "I'd love to look him in the eye and ask him how he sleeps at night while he lies to my family about his handling of our business. But we have to be patient. The time will come for all that."

Her shoulders drooped, and she looked away from his hard stare to the gray winter sky and still lake out the window. He was right, even if she hated to admit it.

She balled her hands at her sides as she digested the maddening truth. A man she'd loved—or tried to love, despite his distance and gruff nature—had most likely betrayed her in the worst possible ways.

"Fine," she said dropping back onto the sofa to continue through the pile of documents and receipts. "I won't go see him, but you have to promise me a chance to confront him after we nail the SOB."

Reid and Penelope spent the next week going through her father's computer files and studying the materials that Andrew had collected. The work was tedious, but Reid seemed to think they were making good progress building their case. They found more billing statements and tax records that corroborated the documents and notes Andrew had assembled, and her father's internet history continued to prove both enlightening and incriminating…which meant further disillusionment and heartache for Penelope.

Her father had searched such topics as the extradition laws of several foreign countries and missing-person laws in Texas, particularly the criteria for having a missing person declared dead.

On a Saturday, just over a week after arriving at Reid's lake house, the weather, in typical Texas fashion, had changed from the cold and windy of the previous week to sticky and unseasonably warm. Nicholas was restless with the limited selection of toys and television available to entertain himself, so Penelope excused herself from the tedium of sorting paperwork in order to let Nicholas play outside.

As Nicholas ran after a ball, Penelope raked her hair back from her face and stared out at the still, gray lake. A white heron slid slowly, gracefully through the shallow water at the shoreline. Sleek and serene, the regal-looking bird made her heart ache. Would her life ever have that kind of calm and tranquillity again? She couldn't remember the last time she'd felt at peace, secure and hopeful about the future. Certainly not since Andrew's death.

She'd been out on the lawn for about ten minutes, playing an easy game of catch and kick with a plastic ball, when Reid joined them. He stretched his arms over his head and arched his back, working the kinks out of his muscles, before trotting down from the house to intercept a toss Nicholas made. He made a show of lying out to catch the poorly thrown ball and rolling on the winter-brown grass after tucking the ball against his chest. Nicholas found the stunt highly amusing and, of course, imitated with a flop and roll.

She blinked her surprise, not having guessed Reid would be interested in lighthearted tussling with her toddler. But Reid passed the ball to Nicholas with an easy lob, and her boy chased down his missed catch, adding another roll in the grass and a hearty laugh.

Penelope's heart swelled at the sound of her son's mirth, and she couldn't suppress the grin that tugged her lips. On the heels of her joy, however, she knew a brief moment of regret, telling herself it should be Andrew playing with their son. Yet when Nicholas charged at Reid with his wobbling toddler gait and tackled him with a grin and a giggle, she shook off the negativity. If she were going to rebuild her life and be the kind of mother Nicholas deserved, she couldn't continue to dwell on the past, the could-have-beens.

Nicholas paused from the roughhousing and clambered to his feet, his attention snagged by something across the inlet. He pointed a chubby finger and said something to Reid. Though Reid glanced where the child pointed, his expression said he didn't understand Nicholas's jabber.

Penelope headed toward them, thinking she might translate for her son, but Nicholas saw her and shouted, "Mommy, too!"

"What?"

Her boy jumped up and tumbled to the ground with a laugh and repeated, "Mommy, too! Mommy faw down!"

She considered her clothes, a simple pair of jeans and a sweatshirt from the discount store Reid had been to. Expendable, especially if it would give her boy a moment of joy. "Fall down?" she said, then dropped to the ground and barrel rolled toward them.

Her antics sent Nicholas into peals of laughter and more childish tumbles and rolls. When she crawled across the last few feet of earth to join them, Reid reached to pluck a piece of grass from her hair. "Any idea who Miss Tee is?"

"Who?" she asked, chuckling her own amusement with Nicholas's silliness.

"That's what he said when he pointed across the water—Miss Tee."

"Miss Tee..." She searched her brain for what, or whom, her toddler could be talking about.

Hearing their discussion, Nicholas ran up to her and flung himself against her chest with a devilish grin and enough momentum to knock her backward. "Miss Tee!"

She gave him a tickle and a kiss, and when she had struggled back to a seated position, he pointed across the inlet again exclaiming, "Miss-miss Tee!"

And it clicked as she spotted a small pine tree among the hardwoods on the shore. "Christmas tree! You see that Christmas tree, don't you?"

Nicholas clapped and bounced happily. "Miss-miss tee!"

She turned to Reid with a lopsided smile, explaining, "He saw the decorated Christmas trees at the mall the last time we were there, and I promised him we'd put one up at our house soon. He's been quite excited at the prospect. Kids have memories like steel traps."

He bobbed a nod of understanding, then a thoughtful look crossed his face. "I think I have an ax in the shed." He climbed to his feet and offered her a hand up. "Let's get the boy his Christmas tree."

They walked together around the inlet to the small pine tree Nicholas had spotted, and Reid had Pen's son "help" drag the tree home after they'd cut it. He could see the pride and sentiment in Pen's expression as she watched Nicholas enjoy the outing. Though the Coltons had relied on staff to decorate the house every year, he'd heard of other families making it an annual event, heading out in the woods or to a Christmas tree farm to select and cut their tree. He knew without asking that Pen wanted family traditions like that for Nicholas. She'd always made a big deal at holidays for Andrew, and even included Reid in special meals and traditions. Corned beef and green beer at St. Patrick's Day, grilling and fireworks on the Fourth of July, king cake and jambalaya at Mardi Gras. This past eighteen months since Andrew's death, he'd missed sharing special days with his partner and his wife, so having this opportunity to kick off the Christmas season with her and Nicholas filled him with an indescribable satisfaction. A completeness that brought him a deep internal joy.

Once back at his lake house, he realized he didn't have a Christmas tree stand. Or decorations. Or lights. He should have thought about the lack of holiday cheer at his safe house and offered to bring in some decor days ago. Pen and her son deserved as much holiday cheer as he could give them. His only excuse was that he simply didn't think in terms of holiday preparations. At the ranch, the garlands and wreaths and lights just appeared around the house in the days after Thanksgiving.

But that oversight was something he could do something about. Pen tried to dissuade him from leaving to buy a houseful of decorations, but his mind was made up.

"We can improvise a stand from a bucket and make a few homemade ornaments and string some popcorn."

"You're welcome to do any of that with him that you want, of course. But...let me get some Christmas things to spruce the place up. I want to do this for you."

He could see her reluctance in her eyes, and when she opened her mouth to refuse his offer, he stepped close to her and touched a finger to her lips. A crackle like an electric shock tingled on his skin, and caught off guard by the sensation, he held his breath. Her eyes widened, though he couldn't be sure if she was simply surprised by his touch...or as affected by it as he was. Or both.

For a moment neither of them moved. He searched her gaze, lost in the changing shades of green and gold and brown in the hazel depths of her eyes. More than anything he wanted to kiss her. The pull was as strong as any urge he'd ever felt. The irritating voice that had sounded caution, had warned him away from his partner's widow, whispered again. *Don't do it... Too risky... A mistake...*

But Reid had lived most of his life on the edge, and he defaulted to reckless, selfish desire. With a hand on each of her shoulders, he drew her close and settled his mouth onto hers.

Chapter 12

Reid muffled the half gasp, half sigh that escaped her lips as he angled his lips over hers. She was still for a moment, her body rigid. He shifted closer, moving his hand to her cheek, and he felt a tremble race through her.

The warning voice spoke louder, firmer. *Leave her alone! Off-limits!*

He should back away. He knew he should, damn it!

But then her lips parted and she canted toward him. Her body brushed his, and her hand lifted to his back. Pen's fingers curled into his shirt as if clinging for support, and the tip of her tongue darted out in a tentative invitation, lightly teasing the seam of his mouth. He deepened the kiss, drawing more fully on her lips, accepting her shy foray with a testing sweep of his tongue.

She tasted sweet and tempting, like a new adventure waiting to be revealed. His alpha drive to conquer, to explore, to rise to any challenge roared to life. His fingers delved into the thick waves of her hair and he captured the back of her head as he slaked his curiosity, his need.

Only the small sound that filtered through his lust-muddled focus held him back. He didn't recognize what he'd heard right away. Only as his subconscious replayed the squeak-like noise did he realize it held notes of fear. Of regret. Of grief.

He stiffened, tightening his grip on her nape and lifting his mouth only a fraction. In the tiny crack of his composure, his conscience screamed, *You can only disappoint her. You're not what she needs. You will hurt her.*

He jerked back from her, and his heart clenched seeing the confusion and pain that filled her face. She wouldn't meet his gaze. She kept her chin down, and her brow furrowed with a deep crease.

He muttered an earthy curse word under his breath and dragged a hand down his face. "I'm sorry. I shouldn't have…"

When she continued to stare at the floor, looking rather shell-shocked and torn, he gritted his teeth and swung toward the door. "Right. So…I'll get those decorations and a few groceries and, um…" He dug his keys from his pocket and glanced at her once more. "Pen? Will you be all right if I…?" He hitched his thumb over his shoulder to finish the thought.

She blinked and dabbed at the outer corner of her eyes as she forced a smile. "Of course. I'm fine. Go."

She didn't look fine, but he didn't argue. With a rock of regret and confusion sitting on his lungs, he beat a retreat to the Range Rover. And a little distance to get his own head around what he'd done. Had he opened the door to a deeper, satisfying sexual relationship with Pen…or had he ruined their fragile friendship?

Penelope was stringing popcorn with Nicholas, Christmas tunes streaming through the television, when Reid returned from the store. Just the sound of the back door opening and his deep, dulcet voice calling, "I'm back!"

had her nerves jumping and her heart racing. She'd thought she'd pulled herself together after their toe-curling kiss—and the onslaught of guilt and second-guessing. Andrew was gone. He would want her to move on, find happiness again with someone who could be a good father to Nicholas and a loving husband to her. But was Reid Colton that man?

She couldn't deny the joy she'd felt seeing him play with Nicholas earlier. He'd been infinitely patient with her toddler's tantrums, high-maintenance needs and curiosity about every cranny of the lake house in the past several days. And she owed him so much for keeping them safe. But how could she forget the fact that he was a Colton? He'd had a hand in Andrew's death, intentionally or not. And he had a reputation for commitment phobia, happily playing the bachelor or the womanizer when it suited him.

Kissing him back had been a mistake. She couldn't lie to herself about that truth—she'd willingly returned his kiss. And although it had been an undeniably blood-heating, world-tilting, breath-stealing kiss, a kiss she hadn't stopped thinking about since it happened, she couldn't let it happen again. At least not until she figured out what she wanted from Reid. What he wanted from her. What possible sense could they make of a future together? Because with Nicholas in the picture, she couldn't tangle herself up with a man who didn't have every intention of sticking around, of being the whole package—husband, father, protector.

The rustle of packages brought her attention to the door of the kitchen where Reid appeared with several large bags. "Ho, ho, ho!"

Was his tone just a tad overbright? Tinged with stress and doubt?

"Nicholas, go see what Mr. Reid brought us." She helped her son clamber to his feet and scurry over to peek in the bags.

"I have shiny ball ornaments, tinsel, lights, angels, garlands, holly…" He pulled box after box from the sacks and set them out for Nicholas to look at. "I see you got a head start." He stuck his hand in the bag of microwave popcorn and shoved a handful in his mouth. When he licked the salt from his lips and fingertips, a fluttering stirred in her chest like a garden flag in the breeze.

Harry Connick, Jr. crooned "Sleigh Ride" from the TV, and her heart swooped and stumbled a syncopated rhythm right along with the beat set by the jazz singer. Pulling her gaze away, she continued poking popcorn on the needle and thread she'd rummaged up from his laundry room. "Patience is not a toddler trait. And this project doubles as a snack, so…win-win for me." She flashed him a smile that felt strained. How were they supposed to move past the awkwardness after that kiss?

He popped another few kernels in his mouth. "Good plan."

"Except that movie-theater flavor was all you had, and it's…well, quite buttery." She held up her hand to show him her greasy fingers.

"Mommy!" Nicholas had found a stuffed Santa and waved it at her, his eyes shining. "Tanta?"

"That's right. That's Santa Claus."

Reid lifted Nicholas onto his lap and asked, "What does Santa say?"

"Say?"

Reid took the stuffed figure and made it shake. In a low voice he demonstrated, "Ho, ho, ho!"

Nicholas grinned and blinked at him.

Reid repeated the deep laugh. "Now you try."

Nicholas reached to grab his toy back. "Tanta."

"He may be too young to understand," she started when Nicholas shook the stuffed toy and cried, "Oh, oh, oh!"

Together, Reid and Penelope laughed and congratulated the boy.

"Close enough," Reid said, setting Nicholas back on the floor. "Well, have fun." He waved a hand at the decorations. "I'm going to get back to work. I was onto something when we took this side trip down Candy Cane Lane."

"Hang on, pal." Pen climbed to her feet, looking for something to wipe her greasy hands on. "It takes two to put a tree that size in a stand. Don't cut and run yet."

Reid glanced to his idle laptop, then back to her and the pine leaning against the wall, waiting for decorations. On the TV, "Deck the Halls" started joyfully streaming as Burl Ives's "Frosty the Snowman" ended. He sighed and slid his hands into his jeans pockets. When it was clear he was about to put her off, Pen leaned down and whispered to Nicholas. Her son listened to her directions and looked up at Reid with his wide eyes blinking innocently. "Pweez, Weed?"

And who could have said no to her son's cherubic face and sweet request? Not even the Grinch himself.

In the end, Reid helped her put the tree in the stand, string up the lights, hang ornaments on the highest branches, and when the tree was ready for the angel on top, he lifted Nicholas and showed her boy where to place the finishing touch. Her heart gave a bittersweet throb. She'd have loved to have snapped a few pictures with her phone as they decked the boughs. Andrew's parents lived out of state and were always tickled to get updates and pictures of their grandson. But her phone had been disabled in order to prevent them being tracked.

As Reid turned back toward her, Nicholas still in his arms, he tipped his head and crumpled his brow. "What's wrong? Is she crooked?" He glanced back at the angel.

Pen waved off his comment. "Of course she's crooked. She's adorably crooked. Don't change a thing."

"Then what was the sad face about?"

"Just…wishing I could take a picture of the tree, of Nicholas…" *Of you holding Nicholas.* She cleared her throat. "Family times like this are meant to be recorded."

"Hmm." He ruffled Nicholas's hair as he set him on the floor. "I wouldn't know. Coltons aren't big on warm, cozy family memories." He flashed a wry grin that held a bit of regret before brightening his smile as he stepped closer to her. "But this was fun. Thanks for making me help."

He stroked a hand from her shoulder down her arm, capturing her hand to tug her close.

The shift in mood from lighthearted to sensual was palpable, and her pulse rum-pa-pum-pummed along with "The Little Drummer Boy." She swallowed hard, his searing kiss all too fresh in her memory, and worked to keep her tone airy. "Thank Nicholas. He spotted the tree."

Reid angled his head toward the toddler who was examining every bauble and shiny light on their tree with rapt fascination. "Thanks, Nick!"

"Ooo, look, Mommy! Pwesent!" He pointed to an ornament shaped like a wrapped package with a large red bow.

Reid snapped his fingers and turned to cross back to the pile of discarded bags. "That reminds me. I got you something."

"Me? Like a Christmas gift?"

"Uh, no. Like a safety gift." He pulled two burner phones out of the bag. "I don't like being out of touch when I go to the ranch or to run errands. I'll set these up so my number," he wiggled one phone, "will be on your speed dial."

She nodded. "Good idea." She watched him tear into the packages, and tucked her hair behind her ear. "Have you been back by the ranch this week?"

"Not in a few days." He glanced up. "But I'm thinking it's about time I filled them in on what's going on. That lead I was onto earlier?"

"Before we started down Candy Cane Lane?" she said, mimicking him.

He nodded. "Exactly. It concerned my father. His disappearance. It seems Hugh made a substantial payment to the ME who pronounced the burned body to be Eldridge, just before the man mysteriously disappeared."

"You can prove that?"

"I'm close to proving it. I found the bank record of the money transfer. I plan to call—" he flipped his wrist to check his watch "—tomorrow morning when the bank opens and confirm the transfer. But evidence seems to support that Hugh paid the guy to lie about the body's identity, then saw to it the guy disappeared."

A shiver rippled through her. "Disappeared as in... killed?"

His lips thinned in a frown of disgust. "At this point, that wouldn't surprise me."

Nicholas was unsurprisingly keyed up that evening, and even after a warm bath and several stories, fought his bedtime ritual. When Penelope finally got him settled and asleep, she tiptoed back out to the front room to join Reid.

"Success?"

"At last," she said, keeping her voice quiet as she entered the den.

Reid stood from the crouch in front of the stone fireplace where he had a cozy blaze crackling. He dusted off his hands and gave a lopsided grin of acknowledgment. "I'd have thought after today he'd have been exhausted and would have dropped right off."

She threaded her fingers through her hair, her own fatigue dragging at her. "In the toddler world, there's such a thing as overtired, and it actually makes it harder for the little ones to get to sleep." She sent Reid a grin. "He loves the tree and all the decorations. Thank you."

He nodded, holding her gaze, then a beat later, he waved a hand toward the couch where he'd uncorked a bottle of red wine. The room lights were turned low, so the Christmas tree glowed and twinkled with particular warmth and holiday beauty. "Come. Your turn to unwind."

She paused, a nervous flutter tickling her belly. The setup was too intimate. Too ideal. Too…tempting. Memories of the kiss they'd shared earlier in the day roared to life like tossing gasoline on flames. And now he'd created this cozy setup…

Penelope shook off her hesitation.

If she handled it right, she saw no reason not to enjoy a glass of merlot and warm herself by the fire. She chose a spot at the end of the couch, and after toeing off her shoes, she angled her body toward the fireplace and tucked her feet under her.

Reid poured them each a generous serving of the wine and took the other end of the couch. Lifting his glass toward her, he said, "Sláinte!"

"Sláinte?" She gave him a dismissive grin. "You're not Irish."

"No. Neither was my father. He was born as Texas redneck as they come, but it didn't stop him from using that toast at every dinner party he ever hosted. He thought it gave him class."

She gave a disgruntled, "Hmph. Class isn't created by saying a few magic words or having the right car and clothes. It's about how you live your life, how you treat people."

He leaned back against the cushions and took a slow sip of his wine. "Agreed. That didn't stop ole Eldridge from trying to impress folks with his cash, though. He was all about the image."

She sipped her own wine, letting the mellow flavors linger on her tongue. "Past tense?"

Reid blinked. "Hmm?"

"You referred to Eldridge in the past tense. Does that mean you think he's dead?"

He cocked his head slightly. "You sound like a cop."

Penelope turned up a palm. "Well, I did marry one. I picked up a few things over the years." She sipped again and narrowed her gaze on him. "So? Do you think of your father in the past tense now?"

"Not really. But if he is alive, where the hell is he? Why hasn't he contacted anyone? Why no ransom note?"

"So you don't believe my father really saw him last month, I take it?"

"Would you? When we have so much evidence showing he arranged for the burned body, paid off the ME to say it was Eldridge when it wasn't. The whole story, sighting included, was pretty obviously a ruse to get my father's will read." Reid angled a surly look toward her. "Did I mention Eldridge's will conveniently left controlling interest in Colton Inc. to you father? Fowler was quick to contest that, let me tell you."

"You did." She wrinkled her nose, still stunned by the news. "Why did your family believe your father left the majority of his company to his lawyer? Why didn't you question the will from the start?"

Reid took a large swig of merlot. "Because it would be just the sort of attention-seeking stunt Eldridge has pulled in the past. I gave up trying to figure him out years ago. We were shocked, of course. But it sounded like just the sort of final 'screw you' from the grave Eldridge would give to his family."

"I didn't realize things were that dicey at the Colton ranch."

He sent her a dubious look.

"Well, other than Fowler being a first-class jerk most of the time. And Marceline being rather catty," she amended.

"Catty." He flashed a wry smile and rubbed the muscles at the back of his neck with his free hand. "That's a diplomatic way to put it."

"But the rest of your family…" She tried to remember the few occasions that Reid talked about his siblings or the rare occasion when she'd been invited to Colton Valley Ranch for special events. What had the family dynamic been like?

"Let's just say, Eldridge's disappearance and presumed death brought out the dark side of the Colton clan."

"Oh?" Her tone invited him to continue.

He raised his eyebrows and twisted his mouth in disgust. "Like I mentioned before—all the finger-pointing and backstabbing in the past few months related to Eldridge's disappearance and other trouble we've encountered. I'd rather not rehash it."

"I'm sure that was stressful."

He patted his chest. "Ah, warms the cockles of my heart to know how my family comes together in a crisis," he grumbled.

She thought of how her father had pushed her mother away, shut her out when she was sick, as if he could pretend the disease wasn't ravaging his wife. "I can relate. My father was a real ass to my mom while she fought her cancer. Treated her as if she were already dead or just too much trouble to bother with."

He sent her a commiserative glance. "I remember you telling me that, years ago. How hard it was on you."

"More so for my mom. I already had a strained relationship with Hugh. But seeing the way he dismissed my mother, rarely stopped by her room to visit her when she was bed-bound…"

"Sounds like our fathers were cut from the same cloth. No wonder they got along so well. I guess you remember I've always had a pretty contentious relationship with my father."

She winced. "Sorry."

He waved her off. "Not your fault. Eldridge didn't go from redneck thief to billionaire oilman and rancher because of his parenting skills. He was always a cunning, ruthless businessman and opportunist. He married his first wife for her money and surrounded himself with people who would protect his interests and weren't afraid to be just as ruthless as their employer."

"Like my father," she finished for him. He fumbled a bit, and she shook her head. "No, no. Don't try to backtrack or be polite. It's true. I think we have ample proof of that in recent days."

He raised his glass toward her again. "To the children of sorry, distant fathers."

She grinned and clinked her wineglass to his. "We turned out okay, though. Right?"

He flashed a coy smile. "Well, you did. I'm still working on some rough edges."

She chuckled and raised her wine again, teasing, "I'll drink to that!"

He playfully clutched his heart as if she'd wounded him. After contemplating the fire for a moment he said, "For what it's worth—speaking of rough edges—I think the worst of the undercutting is behind the family. I've sensed a shift toward cooperation and mutual goals."

"Because everyone is falling in love, happier with their lives and moving forward." She finished for him, remembering his earlier comments about the family changes. Her calf began cramping, and she stretched out her legs and rubbed the stiff muscle. "And you?"

He paused with his wineglass almost to his lips. "What about me?"

"Are you...happy with your life?"

He sipped, set the glass aside, and unexpectedly took hold of her foot which was only inches from his thigh.

His touch sent shock waves through her. The first blast of adrenaline was rooted in surprise, kicking her heart rate into high gear. But as his fingers dug into the tired tendons of her feet and worked the cramping muscle in her calf, heady sensations rippled through her, as sweet and intoxicating as the wine. A moan of pleasure slipped from her throat before she could squelch it.

His hand stilled momentarily, and her breath stuck in her lungs as their eyes met. Neither of them moved, but the earth seemed to shift under her. Neither said anything, but a clear message passed between them. The air vibrated. The mood changed. They hurtled past an invisible guardrail into an abyss from which she wasn't sure she could ever return.

Reid slid his hand up to grasp her ankle, tugging her leg closer and dragging her feet onto his lap. Her wine sloshed as his actions toppled her onto her back. He took her glass from her and set it aside, his feral gaze never leaving her. She blinked at him, stunned, but didn't pull her feet from his hands as he cupped first one, then the other, rubbing them with deep, relaxing strokes.

She tipped back her head, allowing the tension in her body to flow out, surrendering to his magic touch.

Reid. That's Reid Colton you're melting for. The sobering acknowledgment was quickly silenced by a competing voice that reminded her he'd saved her life, exonerated himself regarding Andrew's death and proven himself trustworthy.

And no matter how much time has passed or how much your life has changed, he still makes your heart race as much today as when you were a teenager and fell for his devastating good looks and rakish charms. That was the issue she faced in a nutshell. She'd always been hopelessly attracted to Reid, and the signals he sent her now, his returned interest, made her head spin and her suppressed longings fire to life.

"You never answered me," she said drowsily, savoring the sweet lassitude that sank to her bones. "Are you happy with your life?"

Chapter 13

Reid twisted his mouth as he thought, then cast a sultry side glance to her. "I'm happy right now…here with you."

Her pulse staggered, and she realized that, despite the turmoil and danger they'd encountered in the past few days, she was happy right now, too. *With Reid*.

But what if she was wrong about him? What if his story about how Andrew died was a lie? What about the way her father had bowed and scraped for all the Coltons while ignoring her for her whole life? Were her feelings of hostility toward his family just a manifestation of little-girl jealousy and hurt?

She'd seen a different side to Reid when he'd become Andrew's partner and friend. He still had moments of acting the entitled rich boy, the arrogant jock she'd known in high school, but she knew more facets of Reid now. He was deeper than his shallow mother, kinder than his snobbish half siblings and had an innate sense of justice and protectiveness that had drawn him into a career he'd not needed for the income, but undertook to fulfill a sense of purpose and duty.

She sighed heavily and pinched the bridge of her nose.

"Something wrong?" he asked, his hands stilling on her feet.

"Only that you quit rubbing my feet," she replied with a lopsided grin, then grew more serious. "And I over-think things. I rationalize and nitpick things to death."

"Having an analytical mind isn't a bad thing."

"I said overthinking. I have trouble letting things go sometimes and accepting things at face value."

He focused his deep blue gaze on her and frowned. "What are you overthinking at the moment?"

She swallowed hard and curled her fingers around the hem of her sweater. "You."

His eyebrows shot up for a moment, then formed an inquisitive V. Shifting on the couch, he let her feet fall to the floor as he stretched toward her. "Is there anything I can do to help you decide your feelings about me?" His hand settled at her waist as he lay across her body, press-ing her into the cool leather cushions. "Maybe this?" He brushed his lips across the pulse point on her neck.

Her breath snagged, and her fingers curled around his shoulders.

"Or this?" Reid nipped the tip of her chin, and her head swam muzzily.

"Reid..." she rasped.

He raised his head to look deeply into her eyes. "I want you, Pen. I won't pretend otherwise any longer. But if this isn't what you want, you can tell me to go to hell, and I'll respect your feelings."

She opened her mouth to reply, but so many thoughts and emotions battled inside her, she could only stare at him mutely.

When she didn't reply, his expression darkened. He levered farther away from her as if to leave, and she tight-ened her grip on his shirt.

"Pen?" He angled his head, clearly trying to read her.

"I...need more time." Her heart thrashed in her chest like a wild animal tangled in a snare. She felt trapped, caught between loyalty to Andrew and a years-old lust for Reid. Factoring in the mind-numbing twists her life had taken, her father's deceit and the foggy road that was her future, how could she know what was right? For both her and Nicholas, because she had to put her son's needs at the top of her considerations.

Reid bowed his head briefly, his disappointment plain. "More time. Right. Because we've only known each other for fifteen some odd years. Been friends for seven."

"Andrew—"

"Has been gone for over a year," he finished for her, his voice noticeably tighter. Pain flashed in his eyes, and he shoved away from her. "All right. I promised to respect your choice, and I will."

Freed of his weight and warmth, a stark chill sliced through her. Confusion or not, she didn't want to be without him. She did desire him, value the protection he offered, appreciate his friendship.

"Wait!" she cried before he could rise from the couch. She sat up, shifting her legs under her to kneel on the cushion beside him. "Reid, I'm still sorting out my feelings, but I want..." Her throat tightened. "I need..."

He arched an eyebrow to indicate he was listening, waiting.

She drew a slow breath, her body quivering from the inside out. She threaded her fingers through the hair near his ear before cupping the back of his head and drawing him close. "This..." she whispered as she slanted her mouth over his.

Her kiss was tentative at first, testing the reality of a dream she'd had since she was a teenager. Her body hummed its approval, her blood rushing to her head and to her most intimate places.

Leaning closer, she deepened the kiss, forsaking hesitation for the need that pulsed to life inside her. For a brief time, he let her set the pace, but when she sighed her pleasure and teased the seam of his lips with her tongue, he swept an arm around her and laid her back down on the couch. He took command of the kiss, alternately caressing and plundering. With his lips, teeth and tongue, he elicited sensations from her body that rocketed straight to her marrow. His hands stroked gently, and his fingertips tantalized sensitive spots she'd never known could be so responsive.

Flesh-and-bone Reid surpassed her imagination in every way. Here was heat and skin, raw passion and sensual touch. The embodiment of excitement and temptation. Penelope savored the heat that pulsed through her, the connection and comfort of his embrace, the stir of tender emotions at her core.

But beneath it all, she knew a low drumbeat of fear. Reid was a Colton. He came from a world of power and privilege she couldn't imagine. Despite all his explanations and justifications, he still wore the stain of having administered the fatal injection that killed Andrew. He had a reputation for going through a string of casual relationships, discarding one woman for another the way one might discard dirty socks.

Would he toss her aside when the danger from the shooter, the investigation into her father was over? Possibly. Probably.

She told herself she could handle whatever happened. She wasn't naive to Reid's nature, so she could fortify and protect herself from heartache. She could savor this moment for the sheer pleasure of it and not let it draw her down a false primrose path.

She arched her back, angled her chin up, giving Reid fuller access to the sensitive pulse point at her throat. She silenced the whispers of doubt as she surrendered to sensation, to need and sensual impulses.

Eager to feel Reid's warm skin against her palms, Penelope wedged her hands between them and began tugging at the buttons of his shirt.

He shifted to the side, giving her room to work, and continued feathering kisses along her chin and cheek. "I have to tell you, Pen," Reid said in a husky whisper, "I've wanted this for a very long time. You're beautiful. I've always thought so."

She'd only fumbled through about half of his buttons before he grabbed the back of his shirt and pull it over his head. She helped untangle his hands from his sleeves, and he flung the shirt aside.

And knocked over her glass of wine.

Penelope gasped and wiggled free of him so she could sit up. She gaped in horror at the red liquid spread across the coffee table headed for the edge, ready to drip onto his carpet. "Oh, no!"

She lunged off the couch to get paper towels, and he grabbed her wrist. "Pen, it's okay. Don't freak."

"It's red wine, Reid. It'll ruin your carpet." She tugged free of his grasp.

"I don't care. If the carpet gets stained, I'll replace it."

She paused only briefly to send him a look of disbelief. "Don't be ridiculous." She snatched the roll of paper towels from the kitchen counter and hurried back, wadding several in her hand. She started mopping wine and gave him a scowl. "Just because you have money to throw away, doesn't mean you have to."

His blasé attitude toward a perfectly avoidable expense brought their differences front and center in bold unmistakable strokes.

"What's with you? I just don't think you have to panic about a spill."

"Because you can afford to replace stained carpet." An uneasy gnawing grew in her belly.

"Yes. That's part of it."

"But I can't. Maybe when I was living with my parents I could have, but even then I wouldn't have."

He covered her hands with his, stopping her as she sopped up the merlot. "What's going on with you? What is this really about?"

She bowed her head, feeling all the doubts she'd just so neatly cast aside for a few moments of bliss come crashing back down on her. "Every now and then, you say or do something that reminds me of all the differences between us. The reasons I always saw your family as arrogantly entitled and maddeningly extravagant. Wasteful, even. 'Don't bother cleaning up the wine—I'll just buy a new carpet.'"

"I was kidding...mostly. I just didn't want to see you get upset over it."

"Or the new laptop...or the way I used to see you go through cars when you were Andrew's partner. You didn't fix that engine problem with the SUV you had, you just ditched the car and got a new one." She hated the emotional wobble to her voice.

"The thing was a lemon! It had trouble from day one. Of course I replaced it."

"And you talked about new TVs, new fancy sports equipment and—"

"You resent that I have money? Is that it?" he said gently.

"—you replaced every *girl* you ever dated as soon as you decided she wasn't shiny and new anymore, too!" As soon as she said the words, she wished she could reel them back in.

She closed her eyes, bit her bottom lip and fought back the swell of tears in her throat. *Damn!*

He didn't say anything for long, heavy seconds, but eventually, she heard him rip off more paper towels, finish wiping up the spill and take the soiled towels to the kitchen.

Like a coward, she hurried to the guest bedroom before he got back. She'd shown her hand, all but told him she was scared he'd leave her, that he'd use her up then cast her aside. Reid Colton could have any woman he wanted. He had looks, wealth and personality. Why would he want to burden himself with a middle-class single mother, whose father may have been responsible for heinous crimes against Reid and his family?

No reason she could see.

Even after years on the police force, Reid was surprised—or maybe dismayed—how easily information that should be private could be breached. Outside parties with just the right amount of inside knowledge, deception and ingenuity could gather a frightening amount of personal data. Bad news for the public. Good news for him as he called Hugh Barrington's bank the next morning.

By providing Hugh's bank-account number, date of birth and home phone number, he was able to convince the local bank employee that he was Hugh. He obtained a confirmation of the money transfer to the ME's account, as well as a more recent transfer that boded ill. A large lump sum was sent last week, the same day as the shooting, to an account in a New Orleans bank.

Reid thought on his feet. What was that transfer about? He cleared his throat and improvised. "That's odd. My associate claims he never received the transfer. Maybe his name was misspelled? How do you have his name?"

"It's not a name, sir. It's a business. Mareau Towing."

"Oh, that's right! I'll remind him to check his business account. Thank you. You've been most helpful." Reid was typing *Mareau Towing in New Orleans* into the Google search box before he even disconnected from the bank.

No such business existed that he could find. So…a dummy account?

"Well?" Pen asked, looking up from playing blocks with Nicholas.

He reported what he'd learned and chewed the end of a pen as he leaned back in his desk chair to process the information. "I think it is time I filled my family in on at least some of what's going on."

Pen looked dubious. "Are you sure you can trust them?"

He considered the question, turning his chair to gaze through the plate-glass window to the rippling waves on the lake. An egret stood in the shallow water of the inlet waiting for breakfast to swim or hop by. Puffy white clouds scuttled in from the west as the breeze kicked up.

"A year ago, even six months ago, I'd have been leery. Seriously leery." He puckered his brow as he reflected on the last couple months, the changes he'd seen in the family dynamic. "But ya know what? Eldridge's disappearance has done interesting things to the family. Plenty of accusations and blame have been thrown around, most of it disproved, and yet I feel more like I can trust my siblings now than ever before. We've been through the fire together, and it's strengthened family relationships."

"The proverbial silver lining?"

He lifted a shoulder. "I suppose. I'd say a lot of the change has also come from the significant others in the family." A strange ache filled his chest at that thought, and he spun his chair back to face Penelope.

"What do you mean?" she asked as she carefully placed a block on the top of a tower. Nicholas immediately knocked the tower over with a gleeful chuckle.

The ache eased to a warmth as he watched his two guests—guests who felt less like company every day and more like people he wanted as a fixture in his life, guests who made him want to be his best self, guests who made him hopeful about the future for the first time in many years. Recognizing that truth, he could easily see why his siblings had grown more likable, become easier to trust and developed a more genuine loyalty to the family.

"Everybody's getting engaged and married, becoming parents," he explained. "Funny how being in love, sharing life with your soul mate can change a person. I guess falling in love, being truly happy brings out the best in the Coltons."

"Love brings out the best in everyone." She gave him a smile that burrowed to his soul.

"Yeah, I suppose." He scoffed a laugh and shook his head. "Even Fowler and Marceline have been nicer lately."

She made a choking sound and coughed. "What? Fowler? Even my mother said she thought he was a putz. And that was when he was just a teenager."

"Good ole rotten Fowler. He's always been as mean as a riled Texas rattlesnake toward me and the other kids in the family. But he's mellowed in the past month or so after proposing to his longtime love."

"Wonders never cease. And Marceline…" She bit her bottom lip as she narrowed her eyes in deep reflection. "My main memory of her is when your family came to our house once for a dinner party and she kept referring to us as 'new money.' Her tone made it clear that in her mind that was synonymous with pond scum."

Reid snorted. "Our family fortune is 'new money.' Eldridge and his brother had nothing as kids. Eldridge was a two-bit criminal who married money, got lucky in oil and capitalized on key investments."

"Oh, I do believe she was including your father in her denigration. She bragged about her real father having come from old money. From the 'establishment.' She made me feel so…unworthy of our wealth."

"No wonder you hated our family."

"I had a long talk with my mother that night. She told me a person's worth and value is in how they treat other people, how they use their resources and work at making the world a better place. How well they love others." Her expression reflected a mellow tenderness, a longing.

Reid tried to remember what he could about Pen's mother. She'd largely been overshadowed by her vocal and obsequious husband whenever he'd met her. "I think I'd have liked your mother if I'd known her better. Your father, and my inattentiveness, made it easy to overlook her."

"Dad loved to keep her in the shadows. I think her more charitable views on topics and her love of rescuing animals embarrassed him." She pulled her mouth into an ugly moue. "He was a jerk toward her when I was young but he was *really* unkind to her after she got sick. There were plenty of times I wished he'd been the one who'd gotten cancer, if only so he'd see how sick mom felt."

"You miss her."

She lifted her gaze to his and gave him an odd grin. "Of course. She was my rock as a child."

Reid cocked his head to the side, his thoughts swirling. Clearly Pen had her mother to thank for the gentle soul she'd turned out to be. "Why did she stay with Hugh if he was that awful to her?"

"She wasn't perfect. She freely admitted she liked the lifestyle Dad's money afforded her. The nice clothes and spa treatments. And having his money allowed her to spend more on her animal charities. The rescues. My parents managed to lead relatively separate lives, pretending to be the happy couple when social obligations required."

He nodded. "I get it. In fact, before Eldridge disappeared, I'd have said that was how my parents' marriage worked."

"And now? You don't think so anymore?"

"It's weird, but…no. At least…my mother seems to actually be grieving for Eldridge." He twisted his lips in a frown. "To an annoying degree. She's quite the drama queen and prima donna, but I'm beginning to believe her feelings are genuine. I wouldn't have said that before all this insanity started six months ago."

Pen dodged a block that Nicholas threw her direction and redirected her attention to her son. "*No*, Nicholas. Don't throw your blocks."

Reid slapped both hands down on his thighs as he pushed out of the chair. "And on that note, I'll go talk to the clan. I think we may need their help to corner your father. I've no doubt he's suspicious of us, so any contact from us will be stonewalled. But if he still values having my family on his client roster, I'm betting he'll be more ingratiating to one of my siblings."

She rose from the floor, as well, and followed him to the back door. "Anything I can do in the meantime?"

He pocketed the Range Rover keys from the kitchen drawer. "Just wish me luck."

She moved close, surprising him with a quick kiss at the corner of his mouth. "Good luck."

His pulse did a happy dance as he made his way to his vehicle. If Pen was kissing him goodbye, opening up to him about her relationship with her mother and father, his luck was already changing.

A smile tugged his lips. Talk about silver linings. If he won Pen's heart in the coming weeks, all the chaos of recent months would have been worth the trouble.

Reid planned what he wanted to say to his family as he drove toward the ranch. How much did he reveal? Who had the best chance of winning Hugh's trust and the skill to worm information from their cagey lawyer?

In the interest of time, he pulled into a parking lot and let his car idle while he took out his phone and fired off a group text to his family.

Family meeting in the main house living room ASAP. Urgent.

If he didn't have to wait for his siblings to gather from all over the ranch and town, all the better. He tossed his phone on the passenger seat and pulled back into traffic, headed to the ranch. Despite hitting every red light on the way home, he still reached the long driveway to Colton Valley Ranch within twenty minutes of sending the text. Plenty of time for most of his siblings to have assembled.

As Reid strode into the main house, he encountered Marceline coming down the grand staircase from the area of the upstairs suites where she lived. She wore a little smile as she strolled down the steps, and if Reid hadn't known about a certain ranch hand named Dylan, he'd have sworn that smile meant his half sister was up to her scheming ways. But he'd recently had a surprisingly candid talk with Marceline about her secret love for the "forbidden" cowboy, and her personality had improved greatly in recent weeks.

"We need to have a family meeting," Reid said, loud enough to draw Marceline out of her daydreams. "Now. In the living room."

"I know," she returned, with a snooty lift of her nose. "I got your text. But don't think that just because you fire off a clipped group message that I'll always be willing to respond on command. I have my own life, my own things to do and people to see."

Reid arched an eyebrow and smiled despite his half sister's curt tone. "And how is Dylan?"

Just the mention of his name brought the grin back to her face. "Good." She descended the last few steps, then cocked her head as she eyed Reid suspiciously. "You're not teasing me about him, are you? Because I have a right to be with anyone I—"

He raised both hands. "Whoa! Chill. If you'll recall, I was the one who encouraged you to do what made you happy and not let him get away."

His answer seemed to satisfy her, and with a toss of her hair, she headed into the living room. "Can we get this meeting of yours over with quickly? I have things to do."

He followed her into the living room and took a head count. Piper sat next to her new man, Cord Maxwell, alternately whispering to Cord and looking at her cell phone. T.C., his eyes closed and his head leaned back on the couch catnapping, was there, as was his mother, Whitney. Fowler, notably, was missing.

Reid dialed his oldest half brother, who answered his phone on the fifth ring with a gruff, "What is it, Reid? I'm busy."

"Tough. We all are, but this is more important. Get your ass out here for a family meeting."

"What if I'm at the office?" Fowler grumbled. "I could have business meetings with overseas investors."

"Do you?"

Fowler balked, fumbling, "Well… I—"

"That's what I thought. Family meeting. I have important news concerning the search for our father. You need to be here."

Fowler scoffed. "For the record, I resent being summoned like an underling. As the president of Colton Inc., I cannot just drop everything when you crook your finger, expecting—"

"Just hurry. We're all waiting on you." Reid hung up before his older brother had finished pontificating and grousing about being called to the meeting.

Alanna hadn't shown up, either, and Reid's next call was to the stable, where Jake McCord, Alanna's new love, answered. "We're on our way. Just cooling down the horses and putting our tack away. Five minutes."

We. Reid considered telling Jake the meeting was for family only but it seemed his family was growing. Since his siblings were pairing off and getting married, spouses had as much at stake as the rest of his siblings, he supposed.

Reid paced the room impatiently. "Where's everyone else?"

"Right here. Keep your pants on." Zane sauntered in from the back of the house near the kitchen with his fiancée, Mirabella, beside him. His half brother carried a large sandwich and seemed irked to have his meal interrupted. "So what's this urgent meeting about?"

"I'll tell you when everyone is here."

"Zane, you're getting that all over the imported rug!" Whitney squawked, flapping a hand toward the bits of lettuce and mayo dripping out the back of Zane's Dagwood-worthy meal. "At least get a plate."

Zane sent his mother a flat look, turned to an accent table where an antique pitcher and wash bowl were displayed, and held the wash bowl under his sandwich. "Happy?"

Whitney gasped her indignation. "Zane! You can't—"

"Mother, please," Reid said in a loud, firm tone. "Forget the sandwich."

Fowler arrived through the door from the foyer about the same time Alanna and Jake shuffled in from the back of the house. Reid gave Fowler a disgusted look. "You weren't even at the office?"

His oldest brother, dressed in his signature tailored suit and Stetson, straightened his tie and dismissed Reid with a haughty sneer. "I'm headed there as soon as this little chitchat of yours is over, so—" he waved his fingers "—get on with it."

With a glance around to make sure everyone was assembled and paying attention, and giving T.C.'s boots a kick to rouse him, Reid began. "I have evidence that Hugh Barrington may be involved with Eldridge's disappearance."

Piper gasped, lowering her phone for the first time to gape at him. "But he's the one who saw—"

"I know what he *said* he saw," Reid interrupted. "But, remember, the burned body proved not to be Eldridge, and nothing about his previous supposed sighting has been confirmed."

Confused looks were exchanged among his siblings. His mother blinked and shook her head. "Reid, what are you implying?"

"I'm not implying anything. I'm saying it outright. A few days ago, Hugh's daughter contacted me about some files she found, hidden in the wall of her late husband's office."

"Penelope?" T.C. asked.

"Of course, Penelope, moron. He only has one daughter," Fowler groused.

Undeterred by Fowler's sniping, Zane turned to Mirabella and explained who Penelope and Andrew were and gave her the abridged version of Andrew's death and the unproven accusations against Reid.

"So Penelope found some files..." Fowler prompted, impatiently waving his hand.

Reid recounted what Andrew's files revealed, how he and Pen had searched her father's office and computer, and how they'd been shot at soon after.

"Dear God, Reid!" Whitney cried, sitting forward and clapping her hand to her mouth in dismay. "Was anyone hurt?"

"Could you ID the shooter?" T.C. asked.

"No and no." He went on to explain how the evidence they'd found in Hugh's computer and safe showed Barrington had been swindling the Coltons and other clients for years.

"That rat bastard!" Alanna fumed.

Fowler cursed under his breath. "So it's not enough he finagled his way into Eldridge's will. That he stole our inheritance and control of the family business. He's been stealing from us for years?"

T.C. frowned and rubbed his chin. "Hang on, Fowler. Hear him out." Then to Reid, he asked, "What are you doing about it? Have you reported him to the police?"

"Not yet."

"Why not?" Whitney gasped, her hands balled tightly at her sides.

"I'm still gathering the right kind of evidence to take to the police. I don't want them to have any reason to boggle this or allow him to wiggle off the hook."

T.C. nodded. "Exactly."

"In my investigation of his internet history," he continued, "I also found proof that his computer was used to research faking a person's death. He'd searched for old news stories about bodies being stolen from funeral homes and how burned bodies would be identified."

"*Hugh* set up the burned body we thought was Dridgey-pooh?" Whitney asked, pressing a hand to her throat and looking ill.

"We already knew the medical examiner was paid off to lie and say the body was Father," Alanna said.

Reid nodded his agreement. "Right, but we didn't know who paid him off. Until now. I found proof in his bank records he sent the ME money before the guy disappeared."

"He wanted us to think Eldridge had died?" Piper asked. "Why? I thought he was father's friend?"

"To get the will read," Zane supplied darkly. "I'm beginning to think he wasn't as surprised by his inheritance as he wanted us to think."

"I knew it," Fowler grumbled, slamming a hand on the

back of the settee where Whitney sat. "I'll bury him!" He pulled his phone out and began jabbing the screen, his jaw tight.

"Hold on!" Reid put his hand over Fowler's cell phone. "Don't be rash and tip him off that we're onto him. There's more at stake here than just Eldridge's will and control of Colton Inc."

"You think he killed Dridgey-pooh?" Whitney squeaked, her eyes damp with tears.

Reid hesitated, startled anew by Whitney's reaction. For years she'd endured the stigma of being a gold digger, but her distress seemed real.

"That's what it's beginning to sound like to me." Zane finished his sandwich in one big bite and dusted crumbs from his hands.

"But if Father *is* dead, why not just produce his real body?" Piper asked. "Why fake his death and go to the lengths of stealing a burned body to pass off as Eldridge?"

T.C. grunted. "Good point."

"There's more," Reid said, taking the reins of the meeting again. "Hugh also researched fatal doses of potassium chloride."

"Potassium chloride? What the hell does that have to do with anything?" Fowler asked.

"For one thing, the internet search was made about a month before I gave Andrew what I thought was an injection of insulin." When his siblings exchanged dubious looks, Reid added. "Potassium chloride is what they found in the vial I used."

"Whoa." T.C. plowed fingers through his hair and flopped back on the formal couch. "So you think Hugh could've been involved with his son-in-law's death, too?"

"I do."

"Involved? Hell, if he planted a fatal chemical in Andrew's insulin vial, that's intent. That's premeditated murder," Zane said, his voice taut with anger.

"He had opportunity. Pen says he had access to Andrew's insulin vials to tamper with them. He could have withdrawn the insulin and filled the vial with potassium chloride concentrate when he visited their house. Or planted a bottle he'd tampered with before visiting. All he had to do then was sit back and wait for Andrew to inject himself with the fatal dose. Unfortunately for me, I administered the shot that killed him."

"Wait," Cord interrupted, raising a hand, "Pardon my asking, but if they found potassium chloride in the vial you used and you admitted to administering the shot…" He divided an awkward look between Piper and Reid, his unspoken question obvious.

"Why wasn't I arrested?" Reid finished for him. "Because I passed a polygraph saying I didn't know the real contents of the vial, that I had been trying to save Andrew, not hurt him. Because, ironically, Hugh Barrington went to bat for me, shooting down most of the department's supposed evidence against me."

"Because he's a Colton," Fowler said with his characteristic arrogance, "and the DA office knew better than try to ramrod a flimsy case against a Colton. He'd have been humiliated in court by our lawyers, and Eldridge would have seen the man's career was ruined."

Cord glanced to Piper and arched a dark eyebrow.

Reid pinched his nose, ashamed to admit there was probably a great deal of truth to Fowler's claim.

Piper lifted her chin and patted Cord on the chest. "Because he didn't do it."

Reid twitched a half smile to Piper in appreciation of her support, then turned back to the rest of the family.

"My point is, I'm working several different angles at this point. Hugh seems to have hidden a lot of dirty dealings and unsavory connections. He had a fake passport and a large sum of money in his home safe—"

"A getaway stash," Cord, a bounty hunter familiar with such activity, confirmed.

"Right." Reid rubbed his chin, trying to gather his thoughts for their next move.

"So Father's scum-sucking attorney has not only cheated us for years," Fowler began, his face growing florid as he ticked the items off on his fingers, "tried to convince us someone killed Eldridge—"

Whitney mewled a soft squeak of distress.

"—forged a fake will to give himself control of our company, and set up the murder of his son-in-law, which you got caught up in—but you want us to do nothing about it?" Fowler scoffed loudly and bitterly. "I guess I can see now why you were booted from the force."

"I wasn't booted. I left by choice," Reid defended, feeling like a cantankerous child even as he corrected his half brother. He was sick to death of defending his departure from the police department.

At least Pen seemed to believe him. Now. No one else's opinion really mattered to him. "And I didn't say we were going to do nothing. I just have to gather more evidence against Barrington, get my facts straight and all the pieces and directions of this case worked out before we go to the police. I want to turn over an airtight case to the DA, have all our proof lined out, so the jerk can't weasel his way out when confronted with what we've learned." He paused, sending a sweeping glance around the room.

"Um…" Cord said, scratching his chin, his brow furrowed deeply. "I hate to rain on your parade, but as an ex-cop, you do understand Barrington can claim the evidence you've collected was obtained illegally. It won't hold up in court."

A round of grumbles rose among his siblings, and he waved them down. "Of course I've considered that. But when I do talk to the DA, he'll be able to get search warrants for Barrington's home, office and computer. We'll subpoena people who can testify to everything we've found.

"There are ways to bring him to justice without the stuff I attained. It was a calculated risk, yes. But I have a plan."

Zane straightened, his eyes brightening with the fire of a challenge. "What do you have in mind? How can I help?"

"Thanks for the offer, but you and I are out, except in the background. He knows our law-enforcement connections and instincts." Reid turned to his oldest brother. "Fowler, you up for a little espionage work?"

Fowler's eyes narrowed viciously. "Let me at him. What do I do?"

"Fowler?" Marceline squawked. "You trust *him* to get evidence against Hugh?"

"I have to echo her skepticism, man," T.C. said, giving Fowler a dubious glance. "He's hardly subtle. Maybe I could—"

"Thanks," Reid interrupted, "but it's because of his reputation as a blowhard that I want to use him. He's the person Hugh will least suspect as cooperating with the family or police on a sting."

Fowler gave his family a sour, petty frown. "Are you kidding? Not subtle? Man, I've schmoozed and sweet-talked more men in business deals than I can count. Fortune 500 business leaders come into my office thinking they're going to strong-arm me, and I negotiate terms that have them all but eating out of my hand. How do you think our company grew as big as it has?"

Alanna snorted wryly. "Down, boy. You've got the job."

T.C. shook his head. "Yeah, okay, just don't screw it up, all right?"

Fowler's hand gesture sent T.C. an unspoken, and crude, reply.

"I need you to cozy up to Barrington. Make him think that, in light of Eldridge's supposed will, you want to partner with him in running the company. That you want to help him transition into a position of more authority and—"

"What?" Whitney shot to her feet, shaking her head. "You just said this beast is responsible for all kinds of terrible things and you want Fowler to *help* him steal the company from us?"

"Pay attention, Mother," Piper said. "It'll be an act. He's gonna try to trick Barrington. Am I right?"

Reid jerked a nod and, her indignation appeased, Whitney took her seat again, pouting.

"So butter him up, and…" Fowler waved a hand.

"Finagle any information you can. See if you can get him to trap himself with contradictory statements. Back him into corners and see how he extricates himself. And record everything. Your phone has that capacity, doesn't it?"

"Um…" Cord sat forward again and raised a finger.

Reid acknowledged him with a nod. "If you meet in his office or yours, Fowler, legally, you have to let him know you're recording."

"But a conversation in public, say at a restaurant or

park, doesn't meet the same standard for expected privacy." Cord lifted a shoulder in a shrug. "Just sayin'."

"So what do you think?" Reid faced Fowler, giving him a level stare. "Think you can weasel information out of Hugh without tipping him off?"

Fowler gave him a smug grin and adjusted his tie. "Oh, you can count on it."

Chapter 14

That evening after Nicholas was asleep, Penelope joined Reid in the living room where he sat with his head leaned back on the couch, staring blankly up at the ceiling.

"Are you okay?" she asked, settling next to him. She sat close enough for her thigh to touch his, well aware of what had happened—or almost happened—on this same couch just a couple days earlier. Was she tempting fate, cozying up to him tonight? Of course. Was a sexual tryst with Reid Colton what she wanted? On that matter, her mind vacillated. Oh, she wanted Reid. She knew sleeping with him would be pure pleasure. But in her heart of hearts, she wanted to make love to him, not just have mind-blowing sex. She wanted meaning and commitment and…all the things she feared Reid could never offer her.

She wanted…to be wanted. To be valued. To be needed. And how could a man who wanted for nothing, who had the world at his feet, who could snare any blonde bombshell at whom he crooked his finger, possibly need anything she had to give?

And yet the instinct in her to help, to heal, to care

drew her to him tonight, wanting to ease whatever distress had his mouth drawn tight, his gaze distant and his brow creased.

When he didn't answer her query, she put a hand on his knee and jostled him. "Earth to Reid. What's going on? Wanna talk about it?"

He angled his head and slanted a look at her. "Just thinking about…everything."

His vague response needled her. His generic answer was just another form of evasion, of keeping her at arm's length.

She gave a wry snort. "Oh, good. Only everything. I was afraid it was something specific."

He arched a sandy-brown eyebrow that told her he heard the bitterness in her tone. After another moment of quiet, he said, "So I talked to the family today."

"And?"

He rose from the sofa and stalked over to the wet bar to uncork a bottle of wine they'd started at dinner. He refilled both of their glasses and carried them back to the sofa. "They were predictably upset with Hugh's betrayal."

She exhaled heavily as she took her glass from him. "Why does that make me feel…guilty? Like I should share some of the blame?"

He shook his head as he scowled. "Don't even go there. Nothing your father has done is your fault."

"I know that. It's just a guilt-by-association thing. He's my father, so I hate how that paints me thanks to my relation to him." She clutched her wineglass tighter, an acid fury and frustration with her father seething in her gut. "Even though I saw how he treated my mother when she was sick, it just shocks me, galls me to think my father could be so…greedy. So—" she waved her free hand, trying to find the right word "—so cold toward his own flesh and blood. And then I pray in my next breath such selfishness and heartlessness aren't hereditary. I'd hate to think Nicholas, despite my best efforts to the contrary, could turn out so morally bankrupt by some cruel trick of nature over nurture."

She sipped her wine, her gaze meeting Reid's over the rim of her glass. He opened his mouth as if he wanted to reply, but then pressed his lips in a taut line, his sandy brown eyebrows drawing into a frown over a keen blue stare.

"Reid? What is it? What were you going to say?"

He flashed a fake smile. "Nothing."

She huffed her irritation with his continued distancing tactics. "Reid, talk to me. I hate it when you shut me out like that!"

He gave her a negligent shrug. "Just…agreeing your dad is a piece of work. And to say I seriously doubt Nicholas will be anything like Hugh Barrington." He gave her knee a reassuring squeeze. "Not with you for his mother."

"So you don't think heredity can trump environment?" She tilted her head, pondering the awful possibilities. "What if my father is the way he is because of some genetically controlled mental illness? What if Nicholas got some gene for—"

"Pen, no." Reid shook his head and gave her an odd, guilty-looking grin.

"I'm just saying…he could have."

He shook his head harder. "No, he couldn't. Just… trust me on this?"

She cocked her head farther to the side, studying his peculiar expression. He seemed unable to meet her gaze now, and that alone spoke of some deception or compunction on his part. A tickle of uneasiness quivered in her gut.

"Reid? Tell me."

His expression grew pained, but he still refused to look at her.

Her hand trembling, she set her wineglass aside and slid down the couch toward him. She gripped his forearm, digging her fingers into his muscles. "I'm sick of hidden agendas and deception and feeling like there's a storm about to break that I have no control over." She tightened her grip, shaking his arm. "How can I move forward without fear if I'm worried there's a reason to be looking over my shoulder or questioning everything I've put my faith in?"

He lowered his chin, his eyes closed. "Hugh Barrington isn't your father."

She froze, replaying his words in her head as if to reassure herself she'd heard him correctly. "What are you saying? Of course he—"

"No. He's not." Finally he raised his head and looked at her. His eyes were soft and full of concern…along with a brutal honesty. "Not biologically, anyway."

Her spine stiffened as she processed his assertion. "If you're implying that my mother cheated on—"

"No!" he said quickly, wrapping his hand around hers where it still clutched his arm. "You were adopted, Pen. I found the legal papers when we searched Hugh's office."

She blinked, stunned. *Adopted?*

"I thought maybe you knew, but—"

"No…" she whispered, still digesting the revelation, trying to refocus the camera of her memory through this new lens. Her heart drubbed a slow, strong beat as if staggering under this new weight.

He scrunched his face into a wince of regret. "I'm sorry if I—"

"No." She repeated the sentiment with a vigorous

shake of her head. "If it's true, then I have the right to know. My parents should have told me. I..." She paused to inhale and release a ragged breath, still mentally stumbling. "Adopted? It explains a lot about my father's distance and lack of connection to me, but...my mother—"

"I shouldn't have said anything." Reid raked his free hand through his hair as he leaned his head against the back of the couch.

"Yes, you should have. I'm glad you told me. It's just..." She blew out a puff of breath, overwhelmed. "A lot to process."

"Which is my point."

He pulled his arm from her grip and speared his fingers under the curtain of auburn hair at her nape. His long fingers began massaging the knotted muscles of her neck, and she instantly felt a heady rush of warmth loosen the tension inside her. Reid Colton's magic caress was more relaxing than any hot bath, more intoxicating than the finest wine.

"You didn't need anything else worrying you right now. It could have kept until this mess with your father was settled and you were able to go home."

"Except that he isn't really my father..." She was still testing the concept and examining it from all sides. "And that makes me feel...strangely relieved."

And a bit grief stricken. Her real mother hadn't wanted her. She'd been given away...

He canted his head to one side, lifting an eyebrow as he studied her. "I can see feeling relief concerning Hugh. But I'm sure it raises a lot of questions. Maybe opens old wounds? I hate to think I was the cause of any new pain for you."

She leaned against the sofa, rolling her head to the side, then forward, giving him better access to her achy neck and coiled muscles. "I asked. And you're not to blame for the secrets my parents kept from me. Or my awful relationship with my father." She closed her eyes as a pang shot to her heart. "But I'm disappointed my mother never said anything."

"Maybe she'd planned to, before she got sick. Telling your kid they're adopted when, 'oh, by the way, I'm also sick and dying,' would have been a lot for a kid of… what? Twelve?"

"Thirteen. Possibly the most awkward age for a girl." She sighed and put her head on his shoulder, lifting her feet to the sofa and snuggling against him. "I see your point."

"Besides, I'm betting your mother was the one behind the adoption. She *chose* you. She wanted you."

The air snagged in her lungs, and she struggled to draw a new breath. His reassurance arrowed to her core, cracked the vise of grief and loosened the stranglehold of hurt on her soul.

"She loved you, even if your father proved—"

"An ass?"

He chuckled and wrapped an arm around her, drawing her closer. "I was going to say a disappointment, but… I like your word better." He placed a kiss on the top of her head.

She relaxed against him, savoring the connection. His presence took the edge off of what could have been devastating news, had she learned it under other circumstances. Knowing she'd been adopted cast so much of her childhood in a new light, whether it should or not. She reflected on some key moments, searching for clues she may have missed. The feeling that returned over and again as she thought of her younger years was isolation.

And not just from her father. Maybe she'd had a second sense that she didn't belong all along…

"You know, until I met Andrew, I always felt so alone in the world. I know my mother tried to help me make friends, but I never really fit in at all those cotillions and social clubs and society teas." She furrowed her brow in deeper thought. "Maybe that's why I've always had a soft spot for animals. They made me feel wanted, needed. I had something in common with those homeless animals and never knew it. I'd been a stray, adopted by my family…"

"Pen, keep in mind that your mother wanted you. You don't know why your birth mother gave you up, but you were given a home with the Barringtons because your mother *wanted* you."

The rumble of his baritone voice and the vibration of his chest beneath her ear as he spoke his affirmation were comforting. The assurance he offered touched a raw, aching part of her heart.

She nodded, still analyzing her past. "I hope you're right. But the truth is, I think I sensed something. I know I felt alone more often than not. And when Andrew died, I was right back at square one, all by myself."

"No," he argued, his tone full of passion, "you're not alone. For one thing, you have Nicholas."

"That's not the same. I'm his mother, and while it helps to have somebody to share my life with and take care of, he can't replace the companionship, the bond I had with Andrew. The friendship."

Reid grunted as if he couldn't stand to hear the truth. "You have friends. I know you do. Neighbors that we cooked out with and church members…and—" He exhaled a puff of breath, his hand tightening on her shoulder. "You have me."

She could hear the increased thumping of his heart beneath her ear, could feel the heavy beat against her cheek.

Though his offer touched her, it niggled, as well. "Why?"

He scoffed. "What do you mean, *why*?"

"What does it sound like? I want to know why you're here, why you're taking care of me and offering to help me."

"Because...we're friends."

"Are we?" She didn't want blanket statements of support or friendship made out of pity. She hadn't talked about her lonely childhood to gain his sympathy. If she were to accept Reid as a constant in her life, as a rock of strength she could depend on, she needed to know his offer was genuine and not born of guilt.

"I... Yeah. I think so. Don't you?"

"Then this isn't some kind of a guilt trip over Andrew? I mean, we were never close before I married Andrew, so why now? What's changed?" She pushed away from him, angling her body so she could face him and see his expression. "I appreciate that you're here now, that you've done so much to help me these past few weeks, but...what about later? A year from now? Ten years?"

She looked deep into the blue stare that met hers, knowing if she looked into his eyes she would see the truth.

And what she saw was his hesitation, his own conflict and uncertainty.

"I don't have a crystal ball, Pen. I can't say what will happen ten years from now."

Her heart sank, and she pushed to her feet, blinking back the sting of tears. "Thank you," she said, "for being honest."

She left him sitting on the couch as she'd found him—

alone and staring into near space with a frown clouding his countenance.

Although she was disappointed, perhaps even a little heartbroken, at least she knew where she stood with Reid. His answer was the reality check she needed to help her rein in her feelings, which had taken a dangerous detour she could now correct. Reid Colton was still Reid Colton—an ultra-rich, well-meaning playboy who could never give her the kind of lifelong love and commitment she needed. No matter how much she wanted him.

Chapter 15

"Excuse me, Mr. Barrington," Hugh's secretary said via his desk intercom a few days later, "Fowler Colton to see you."

Fowler Colton?

Hugh grimaced, a gut reflex, conditioned over the past several years of his dealing with Eldridge's oldest son. He drummed his fingers on his desk, trying to come up with an excuse not to see the president of Colton Inc.

If a smarmier, more contemptible bastard ever existed... Hugh stopped himself midthought. He actually could name a few people in league with Fowler. Eldridge was up there. And if he were honest, his business associates and clients might say he himself was a pretty wretched bastard—if they knew the truth about him. Which he'd gone to great lengths to prevent.

A sharp, painful tightness gripped his chest when he thought of the contract he'd put out on Penelope and Reid Colton. He didn't want to get rid of his daughter. But he had to protect his self-interests at all costs. His schemes and behind-the-scenes machinations couldn't be discovered. If he were sent to prison, he'd—

"Mr. Barrington? Shall I send in Mr. Colton?" Ethyl repeated, interrupting his thoughts.

With a mental groan, he replied, "Tell him I—"

His office door burst open, and Fowler Colton boldly strode in. "Tell me yourself, Hugh. My family has been your best client for years. I won't be put off like some two-bit car accident injury complainant."

Hugh shot to his feet, straightening his tie and plastering on his most ingratiating smile. "Of course, Fowler. I was going to say, 'Tell him to come right in.'"

Acid churned in his gut, not only from the prospect of dealing with Fowler, but also from the wearisome act of kowtowing to the high-and-mighty Coltons after all his efforts of recent months to put them in their place. He waved a hand toward one of two wingback chairs that faced his desk at angles. After offering his unwanted guest both coffee and whiskey, and having both declined, Hugh asked, "What can I do for you?"

Fowler doffed his trademark Stetson and set it on one chair before unbuttoning his suit coat and taking a seat in the second. "Well, it's pretty simple, Hugh."

Hugh gritted his teeth, irritated by being addressed so casually by someone young enough to be his son. What ever happened to good old-fashioned Texas manners? Even as a precocious, uppity child, Fowler had lacked respect for his elders and called most adults by their first name. Because he'd always been taller than his age group and had cold, pale, calculating eyes, Fowler had gotten away with more than most children, even those of the Colton brood.

"In light of the terms of Eldridge's will, which left you a controlling share in Colton Inc., we need to make sure we are on the same page. And while that burned body proved not to be Eldridge, one day we will have to bury

Eldridge, and knowing his last wishes in his will leaves me with a choice. Comply with Father's wishes or make waves." Fowler pressed his mouth into a frown. "I'm here to express my willingness to work with you for the best interests of the company."

Hugh worked to mask his surprise. *Controlling share of Colton Inc.* The family had bought his lie? Hugh's heart rate accelerated, and he gripped the arms of his chair to keep from fidgeting and giving himself away. He cleared the nervous thickness from his throat and said, "Thank you. I appreciate your cooperation and support. I know how difficult the past few months have been for the family."

"Do you?" Fowler asked, arching one thick brown eyebrow. His pale blue eyes seemed especially cunning. Or was that just a trick of light? Or Hugh's guilty conscience?

He chose to ignore Fowler's challenge. "I look forward to putting the troublesome days behind us and moving forward together. There is no reason Colton Inc., under our joint leadership, cannot continue to thrive and be a profitable company for many years to come."

Fowler's expression said he wasn't happy about losing control of his family business, but Hugh hadn't expected anything else. "You do understand, though, that until we can confirm Eldridge's death or have the court declare him to be presumed dead, the will is not yet in effect."

Hugh fell silent, wary, and waited for Fowler's next move. For several tense beats, neither man spoke or moved. They eyed each other like dogs jockeying over one bone.

"Hugh," Fowler said at last, "I won't lie. The prospect of losing control over the company my father spent the better part of his life building from the ground up was a major blow to me. I considered fighting you over it." He curled up a corner of his mouth in a sly grin. "Literally. I imagined more than once dragging you into a back alley and beating you until you signed a release returning the company to our family."

Hugh forced a chuckle, but it sounded stiff even to his ears. His palms grew damp, but he didn't want to show Fowler his effect on him by wiping them dry.

"But…" the repugnant Colton upstart continued, "in the end, if Eldridge wanted you to have controlling interest in the company, he had to have a good reason. He didn't build Colton Inc. into the empire it is today without having a keen business sense and always doing what was best for the company."

Hugh nodded heartily. "True. Very true. Your father was a great businessman."

"And because you've been right beside him through the years, guiding him and protecting his assets, I know the company means something to you, as well. I know he respected you and your opinions."

Hugh would have relished the flattery, if Fowler didn't look constipated as he spoke. The SOB was clearly about to choke on the words. Hugh had to bite the inside of his cheek to keep the gloating grin that twitched his lips from blossoming to full flower. The old coot *had* trusted him, and Hugh had known just how to use that to his advantage.

"So…" Fowler drew a deep breath and turned up one palm. "In order to smooth the eventual transition, I will accept his wishes, and I suggest we begin bringing you up to speed on the projects and deals in the pipeline. The longer Eldridge is missing, the more I tend to believe he must be dead. The will may be on hold now, but knowing what will come, we should proceed accordingly. In the best interest of the company." He sat forward and offered his hand. "Partners?"

Now Hugh had no choice but to quickly swipe his hand on his pants leg before gripping Fowler's for a firm shake. "You got it. I look forward to our alliance." His turn to almost choke on his words. Though he was still skeptical he had Fowler's full confidence and support, the eldest Colton progeny had skillfully hidden any secret agenda.

Or was he just paranoid that his deception would still be discovered? If that ever happened, Fowler would unleash his famous temper…and put Hugh *under* the jail.

Jail. Hugh suppressed a shudder. He'd die before he let that happen.

One night at the beginning of Pen's third week of living at the lake house under Reid's protection, Nicholas was acting especially cranky and resisting bedtime. Reid could hear the whining toddler at the other end of the house, and he pitied Pen for her trying task of getting the boy to sleep.

Reid was almost finished cleaning up the kitchen when Penelope stalked in, raking her hair back from her face. Sounds of Nicholas's discontent were still echoing down the hall from the bedroom.

"Where are the keys to my car?" Pen asked, fatigue and frustration heavy in her tone.

"Why?"

Her expression darkened. "Didn't your mother teach you not to answer a question with a question?"

"Like you just did?" he replied with a smirk.

"Reid, I'm in no mood."

Knowing better than to tease her any further when

she was feeling frazzled, he opened the drawer where he'd stashed the keys and dangled them on his finger.

She reached for the key ring, and he closed his fingers around the fob and drew his hand back. "If you need something out of the Explorer, I'll get it. Just tell me what I'm looking for."

She extended her hand farther toward him. "I need the car. I'm going for a drive."

He gave a humorless chortle. "No, you're not."

"Reid!" Her face tensed. "You can't keep me here like a prisoner!"

"You're running away? Leaving Nicholas because he won't stop crying?"

"Don't be obtuse." She tilted her head slightly and paused a beat as if struggling for patience. "I'm taking Nicholas for a drive. Driving him around is the only way to get him to fall asleep when he gets wound up like this." She thrust her hand at him again, "Keys. Please."

He rubbed his thumb over the ridge of bumpy metal and considered her request. "The only way? What about…warm milk or a back rub or…"

"Over the years, I've tried all of it. Driving him around works the best." When he gave her a skeptical look, she added, "Lots of parents do it. Don't judge me! Where's the harm?"

He grunted. "Fine. But you're not taking the Explorer. It's too recognizable. And you're not going alone. I'll drive."

"Reid, you don't have to—"

"I do. I promised to protect you, and I can hardly do that if you're out on the road alone while I sit around here like a bump on a log."

"I'm not running away. I promise. I'll come back when he's asleep."

"You really think you could find this place again? You were paying that much attention when we drove out here?"

"Well, I…"

"Just accept my offer to drive and get your coat." He hitched his head to the door of the kitchen where Nicholas, red faced and sniffling, had just appeared. "When you're ready to go, I'll meet you at the Range Rover."

Her shoulders dropped in defeat. "Will you move his car seat, then?"

"I'm on it."

Pen had her son bundled in a blanket and her own coat on in short order, and once Nicholas was buckled in his car seat, she rewrapped him in the blanket.

"No coat for him?"

"New studies say it's not safe." She tucked the ends of the blanket under his feet. "The car seat straps won't be snug enough with a coat on him."

Why hadn't he known that? As a police officer, he'd been required to stay on top of safety regulations and warnings in order to enforce not only the law but to advise the public of the safest practices. He'd allowed his attention to such matters to lapse in recent months. He didn't have a kid, so why bother following safety seat recommendations? Except that he had new nephews and/or nieces on the way. A new generation of Coltons to look out for and protect.

As well as Nicholas.

They got on the road, and Reid angled the rearview mirror so he could better see Pen's son. Even before they made it all the way down the long bumpy driveway to the highway, the toddler had quieted to a snuffle and was trying to see the night-darkened view out his window.

A sensation like the warmth and satisfaction of that

first sip of hot coffee on a cold morning filled his chest. Affection, he realized. Because whether he wanted to admit it or not, he was growing attached to the little boy. Nicholas's endearing grin, wide and insightful eyes and infectious laugh had burrowed into Reid's heart and taken root. Even his crying spells and tantrums didn't irritate him the way they had in the first few days. He'd begun to understand how the toddler ticked and what precipitated a meltdown.

But along with the mellow tenderness that filled him, a stark edginess crept in at the periphery, as well. Reid had a new appreciation for the demands of parenting. The job of raising a child was huge, never-ending and quite possibly, even more pressure-packed than being a policeman. As a detective, Reid could go days or weeks without facing an emergency situation where he literally had a person's life in his hands. But a parent was responsible for their child's life every minute of every day. Feeding them, keeping them from getting hurt, keeping them clean and warm and happy...

Not to mention how a parent's example, interactions and instruction shaped their child's personality, outlook on life and preparedness for the future. Just considering all the ramifications made Reid's hands sweat, even in the cold car. He rubbed his palms, one at a time, on his chest. He wasn't ready to be a father. He cared deeply for Pen and appreciated her son in a new light, but how could he tie himself down to that mountain of responsibility and pressure?

"Are you mad at me?" Pen asked softly as she gave him a long, scrutinizing look.

"Huh? No. Why?"

"You just looked so...upset. You were scowling and

so quiet. I thought maybe you were angry at me for de-fying you and insisting we drive out."

"No. It's not that. I'm…" he flipped up one palm on the steering wheel "…just thinking."

"For what it's worth," she whispered, peering into the backseat, "it's working. His eyes are getting droopy."

Reid checked the mirror and smiled at Nicholas's ef-forts to fight sleep.

By unspoken agreement, he and Pen remained silent, allowing the whir of the tires and light sway of the vehi-cle to lull Nicholas. When he did ask Pen a question about how soon was too soon to return to the lake house to en-sure the boy stayed asleep, he got no response. Glancing her way, he found her head lolled to the side and her lips parted slightly in sleep.

He smiled and resisted the urge to stroke her cheek for fear of waking her. She needed her sleep as badly as Nicholas did. He knew she'd been restless and had had trouble sleeping over the past several days. The whole situation with her father, the attempt on their lives and the stress of caring for Nicholas in a new environment were weighing on her. He'd seen the circles under her eyes grow darker each day.

So he kept driving. He'd drive all night if it meant she got some much needed rest. He used the time to rumi-nate on his own concerns and plans. Repairs he needed to make at the lake house, the unsolved case of his miss-ing father, the next steps in proving Hugh Barrington's deceit and corruption. He needed to get a copy of Hugh's phone records. He still needed to see if he could link a known hit man to the fictitious Mareau Towing, where the sizable bank draft had been sent on the day of the gunman's attack. He needed—

"Reid?"

He whipped his head toward Pen, who blinked sleepily at the scenery out the window. "Why are we here?"

He brought his attention to where he'd driven and groaned. The fences of the farthest pastures of his family's ranch whizzed by and the turnoff to the mansion loomed in the distance. He snorted his wry amusement. "Autopilot, I guess. I wasn't really thinking about where I was."

She gave him a reluctant glance. "Do you want to stop in as long as we're here?"

"Naw. I've got nothing particular to report to them. Nothing to pick up." He craned his neck to check on Nicholas. "Besides, little guy is asleep. Let's just head back to the lake."

She nodded her agreement, and while Reid was deciding whether to turn around on the driveway or make a loop by following the highway to the next street, he spotted a pair of headlights coming down the drive from the house. He squinted to see who was leaving the house at this late hour. Evenings out drinking or partying weren't uncommon for any of his siblings in the past, but the Colton clan as a whole had become much more the homebodies in recent months, now that his brothers and sisters had someone to stay home with.

So who…? A prickle of suspicion nipped at his spine. Thinking quickly, he pulled onto a rutted lane that the ranch hands used as access to the farthest pastures and turned off his headlights and engine. "Get down."

"What?" Pen's tone held a note of panic, as she clearly remembered the last time he'd instructed her to duck in a front seat.

"I don't know yet who that is." He nodded toward the vehicle that was turning from the drive onto the highway, aiming in their direction. "And I don't want the wrong person to see you with me."

She unfastened her seat belt quickly and slid low on the seat, just before the dark Mercedes rolled past. Though Reid recognized Aaron Manfred's car, he squinted to verify that the driver, his angular face illuminated by his dashboard lights, was, in fact, his father's longtime butler. The older man didn't so much as glance at Reid's darkened vehicle sitting just outside the range of his headlights.

"I'll be damned," he muttered.

"What? Can I get up now?"

"Yeah." He waited until Aaron was well down the highway before starting the Range Rover again and turning on his headlights. "Where does he keep going at this hour?" he mumbled to himself.

"Who was it?" Pen rebuckled her seat belt and cast a curious gaze down the dark highway.

"Aaron Manfred." Reid pulled onto the road and set out after Aaron.

"Your father's butler? Why is it a big deal that he's going out somewhere?"

"It's not, in and of itself. But this isn't the first mysterious nighttime trip he's made. He's actually making it something of a habit lately." He shot her a lopsided grin. "You up for a little spy work?"

"Spy work?" she wrinkled her nose. "What, are you going to follow him?"

"Damn right. I don't have a problem with him leaving in the evenings, but the sneaky way he's done it raises questions for me. He's been having his wife tell us he can't fill his duties in the evening because he doesn't feel well. That he's tiring easily these days. That little lie, his leaving without telling the family where he's going, has me curious."

Pen pivoted on the seat and checked on Nicholas. "He's still asleep, so... I guess there's no harm."

She barely had the words out before she was lost to a jaw-cracking yawn.

Reid gave her a small grin. "Put the seat back and catch some z's yourself. You don't have to stay awake on my account."

"You sure? I can help you spy if you want?"

Aaron turned at a crossroad, and keeping a manageable distance between them, Reid followed. "I'm good. If I need you, I'll give you a nudge."

She nodded, reaching below the seat to push the button that angled her seat back. She turned toward him, tucking a foot under her, and her eyes closed before she'd even settled her head. Reid couldn't resist stroking a hand along her cheek, which looked especially pale and smooth in the bluish glow of his dash lights.

"G'night." She gave a soft, sleepy hum as he tucked her hair behind her ear and gave her chin a final caress. The murmur of tired satisfaction rippled through him, a more potent intoxicant than a shot of the best whiskey he had at his lake house.

Giving his head a small shake, he gripped the steering wheel harder. *Focus.* He needed to keep Aaron in his sights without letting their butler know he was being followed. He doubted Aaron would recognize the Range Rover, especially at night, but he didn't need to take the chance that the older man would realize someone was tailing him.

Pen drew a deep breath in her sleep that was just shy of a snore, and Reid smiled. She'd be horrified to think she'd snored in front of him. She may have rejected her father and his upper-class lifestyle, but she was still, at heart, the lady her mother had raised her to be.

Aaron entered the on-ramp of the interstate headed into Dallas, and Reid twisted his mouth. "Where are you going, old man?"

If Aaron were just out on a quick errand, he'd already passed any number of grocery stores, bank ATMs, all-night drug stores, fast-food restaurants and liquor stores.

He tailed the butler into downtown Dallas and off the interstate, onto the streets of a low-income part of town. He hung back a bit as Aaron took one turn after another until finally slowing to a stop in front of a multi-story older brick building in a low-rent neighborhood. He stopped a block back, but near enough to watch what transpired. "What the hell?"

Reid knew his family paid Aaron well. If he was renting a place in this neighborhood, it was not for lack of funds. A woman bundled up against the cold in a long coat and hat stepped out of the high-rise building where Aaron had stopped, and Reid goggled. Was the family's trusted butler having an affair?

Reid squinted as the woman turned and tossed a bundle of what looked like laundry into the backseat of the Mercedes before climbing in the front seat. He caught a good view of her face and grunted his surprise. "Moira?"

Both Aaron and his wife were up to nighttime shenanigans? Both of them were sneaking off and making mystery trips away from the ranch? Clearly they were in cahoots, and covering for each other when either of them needed an alibi with the family. "At least he's not cheating on her," he groused, then gave a wry chuckle.

"What?" Pen whispered, her voice heavy with sleep. She sat up, adjusting her seat so she could look around. "Where are we? Who's cheating?"

Moira closed the car door, and Aaron drove away from the curb. Checking for cross traffic from the side street, Reid continued his pursuit.

"No one is cheating. At least not on their spouse, but…" He aimed his finger toward the Mercedes. "I followed Aaron into downtown Dallas. He picked up his wife at this place," Reid motioned toward the building as he slowly drove past. "You recognize it?"

She blinked tiredly at the front door and cocked her head to the side to look up at the facade. "Don't know it. I don't see any signs saying what the building is or any businesses inside. What street are we on?" He told her their location, and she rubbed the sleep from her eyes with the pads of her fingers. "Can't say I've ever even been in this part of town before. What do you think she was doing?"

"Your guess is as good as mine." Reid angled his head to study the front entrances of the stores and edifices as they cruised down the nearly empty city street. Many of the buildings were shuttered, signs declaring them for lease or condemned. He spotted a barbershop, a liquor store and a greasy-spoon diner. "Something seriously fishy is going on. Aaron and Moira would never—"

Penelope gasped and cried, "Reid, stop!"

Startled by her shout, he slammed on the brakes, and before he could stop her, she'd unfastened her seat belt and was shouldering open the passenger door. "There was a kitten in the road. I don't think you hit it, but…"

"What? Wait, Pen…" He grabbed for her arm to stop her, but she was out of the car in a flash. He called to her, "Are you sure it wasn't a rat?"

As he shifted into Park, he checked his rearview mirror and saw nothing in the street. His sudden stop had wakened Nicholas, and the little boy rubbed his eyes and whimpered.

Could he leave Nicholas in the car alone long enough to fetch Pen? He didn't dare. Not at night in this questionable part of town. But he didn't want Pen out on the street unguarded, either. He opened his door and leaned out. "Pen, come on! What are you doing? Get back in the car."

He peered through the darkness down the street in time to see Aaron's Mercedes make the turn onto a side road a few blocks ahead. If Penelope didn't get back in the car pronto, he would lose the butler and his wife. "Pen, now!".

Penelope crept around the Range Rover, peering under the vehicle and calling quietly, "Kitty? Here, kitty."

She could hear Reid yelling for her to return to the car, but until she knew the kitten was safe, she couldn't in good conscience walk away. Her love of animals and soft spot for homeless animals was one of the things she'd shared with her mother. One of the things she always knocked heads with her father over. Before her mother died, Pen and her mom had kept a continuous stream of rescued dogs, cats and even a rabbit and ferret over the years.

"Jeez, Pen. At least answer me!" Reid shouted, his voice rife with frustration and...worry?

"I hear you, but it's going to be below freezing tonight." Not finding the kitten under the car, she moved across the street toward the opposite sidewalk. "The poor thing could die. Not to mention the fact it's running into traffic and could get hit."

"What traffic? Besides Aaron, we're the only car out here!" Reid had climbed from his Range Rover and stood in the V of the open front door.

A dilapidated truck rolled past at that moment as if to prove Reid wrong, chugging clouds of exhaust behind it. Reid waved away the fumes with his hand and coughed. "Pen!"

"Stay with Nicholas. I'll just be a minute." She lifted a crushed cardboard box that leaned against a brick wall and heard a scurrying sound. "Kitty?"

"And what do you plan to do with a kitten?" Reid called.

She waved him off and crouched to look deeper into the pile of trash, praying she didn't encounter one of the sewer rats Reid had mentioned. What would she do with the kitten? She didn't know, beyond taking it back to the lake house tonight and giving it the TLC it deserved.

"Kitty, where are you?"

A tiny mewl answered her, and she zeroed in on the kitten's location. When she moved another crumpled box, a white and orange kitten scrambled out. "I won't hurt you, honey. Calm down."

As she neared the frightened kitten, it tried to bolt away again, and she made a grab for it, just catching its tail. Not ideal. She didn't want to hurt the poor thing, but it stopped the cat from getting away. With her free hand she scooped the kitten under the belly and lifted the squirming, terrified feline to her chest. She held its back feet together to keep it from clawing her as she nestled it against her. She hurried back to the Range Rover crooning, "Easy, baby. I won't hurt you. You're okay."

She hurried back to the Range Rover, and when Reid saw her coming, he climbed out of the car and ran around to open the passenger door for her.

"What in the hell do you plan to do with *that*?" he said with a meaningful glance to the kitten clutched to her chest.

"I'm taking it back to the house with us."

He opened his mouth as if to argue, but he could apparently see in her expression her mind would not be changed, and he said nothing. Releasing a small sigh, he helped her buckle her seat belt, since her hands were full with the wiggling cat.

"Pull my scarf off me," she said when he'd returned to the driver's seat.

He did, then helped her wind the wrap around the kitten, effectively trapping his scrabbling paws wielding needlelike claws. Once she had a secure hold on the kitten, he pulled away from the curb with a disgusted look on his face.

"You're wearing the same sour expression my father used to wear when my mother and I rescued animals."

Her statement clearly rattled him, and he shot her a stunned glance. "I don't like that comparison in the least."

"I know you're mad at me, but—"

"Not mad...exactly. Just..." He blew out a lip-buzzing breath of exasperation. "I know you have a soft spot for animals. And I know your soft spot includes underdogs of all sorts. It's one of the reasons I love—" He cut himself off and blinked rapidly, his expression growing briefly stunned...or panicked?

Love. Had he been about to say he loved her? The notion made her heart swoop and her pulse twitter.

"One of the things I admire most about you," he said in a measured, careful cadence and tone.

"Reid," she murmured while stroking the kitten's nose with her thumb, hoping to soothe the frightened feline. And maybe seeking a little calming comfort herself. Why did Reid's almost-confession have her so jumpy, so... prickling with expectant energy? Maybe it was just a post-adrenaline reaction to her chase after the cat, but suddenly she was hyperaware of everything about Reid. The sounds of his exaggerated breathing, his wide hands gripping the steering wheel, his subtle musk scent. His brooding countenance as he navigated the streets of downtown Dallas, and the tension in his square jaw.

"You know that I don't have any food or litter or anything for a cat at my house."

She nodded. "So would you make a quick stop so I can buy all those things?"

He rolled his eyes and twisted his mouth into an I-should-have-seen-that-coming frown. "You also realize that your cat rescue expedition means we lost track of Aaron."

She sent him a remorseful moue. "I'm sorry about that. What do you suppose Moira was doing here?"

"I haven't the foggiest idea, but I guaran-damn-tee you I'm going to find out."

She rubbed the bedraggled kitten's ears, and said quietly, "Your butler and his wife aren't entitled to a private life? They have to approve every move with you or your siblings?"

"I'm not saying that. It's the *way* they've handled these night trips away from the house that have my spider-senses tingling. They're being evasive and secretive, and in my experience that spells trouble."

She thought about the Colton butler and his wife, trying to come up with a logical explanation to counter Reid's suspicions. "You know, I can't help thinking of how much my father depends on his butler and vice versa. You have to wonder how Eldridge's disappearance has affected the Manfreds. They're probably grieving for him in their own way. Maybe...I don't know...

maybe they're seeing a counselor and are embarrassed to tell you?"

He sent her a wry, skeptical glance. "I think that's kinda reaching. They—" He stopped abruptly, his expression washing with dismay, then intensity. He slowed to a stop in the middle of the block and squeezed the steering wheel. "I'll be damned."

"What?"

"Pen, you're a genius."

She chuckled. "I am?"

He shifted into Park and turned to face her. "The Manfreds are loyal to Eldridge. And they've been surprisingly stoic throughout this whole ordeal. What if they know something we don't?"

She sat taller, and her heart thrashed the way the kitten had when she'd captured it. "You think they killed him?"

He shook his head, and thumped the steering wheel with his fist. "No. They aren't killers."

"Then…" And then she caught his meaning. "You think they have your father stashed in that building." She turned in the seat to look back down the city street in the direction they'd just come.

His face lit. "Worth checking out."

Reid made a U-turn and drove back down the street to the building where he'd seen Moira climb into Aaron's car. "Stay here and keep the doors locked."

Pen held her breath as he approached the door to the building and tested it. The door didn't open. Reid paced around the entrance, walked to the back and stared up at the windows to the upper floors before returning to the Range Rover.

"I'd bet my inheritance he's here. But I don't see a way in." He cranked the engine again and gave the facade of the building one last look before pulling away from the curb.

"So...do you confront them? Or...what?"

He gave her a mysterious grin. "I think I'm going with *'or what.'*"

Chapter 16

The next morning, after going to the drive-through window of his favorite coffee shop for a cup of dark roast, Reid drove back to the area in downtown Dallas where he'd spotted Moira and Aaron the night before. He parked his car in the pay lot just down the street, but with a clear line of sight, from the building in question. He leaned his seat back, getting comfortable, prepared to wait. He'd been on many stakeouts in his days with the police department, but none as important to him as this one. Was Eldridge holed up in this run-down part of Dallas? If so, had he come willingly or—

A loud rapping on his window yanked Reid from his musings. A heavyset balding man, huddling against the brisk December gloom in a heavy, hooded coat, stared in the driver's-side window.

Reid cracked open the window. "There a problem?"

"You gotta pay if you're stayin'. Five dollars for the first 30 minutes and three for each additional hour." Even from his distance, Reid could smell the cigarettes on the guy's breath.

"Right." He dug in his wallet and extracted three

twenties. He lowered the window some more and handed them to the attendant. "That should cover me for a while."

The attendant looked at the bills and grunted. "That it will." He started to walk away, then turned back toward Reid. "You all right? When I walked up, you looked..." He hesitated as if looking for the right word.

Reid gave him a halfhearted grin. "I'm fine." Before the attendant could walk more than a step, Reid called to him, "Can I ask ya something?" He earned a shrug in response. "What do you know about an older guy who lives in the building over there with the green awning? He'd have moved in about June? Skinny guy, short for a man. Midseventies."

The attendant twisted his mouth as he thought and gave another shrug. "I don't know. Maybe..."

Sighing, Reid pulled a couple more bills from his wallet. "Think harder. He might have been with another older gentleman or a petite woman with straight gray hair. Or getting in or out of a dark blue Mercedes?"

The attendant's face brightened. "Now you're speakin' my language. Cars I notice." He rubbed his face with a gloved hand. "Let's see...I remember a blue Mercedes coming around here a couple times maybe..." He gave Reid a speculative glance. "Maybe even on a regular schedule, but...that info will cost ya another couple Jacksons."

Reid scowled darkly at the extortionist but peeled two more twenties from his wallet. "How regular? What schedule?"

With a smug grin, the parking attendant shoved the bills in his pants pocket. "If they stick to routine, the Mercedes should be around to drop off the old guy in about an hour."

"Drop him off? When did they leave? Where do they go?"

"How the hell should I know where they go? I'm here working the lot. But they leave about nine a.m. every Wednesday and come back around eleven thirty. The old lady sometimes helps the shorter man you mentioned to walk inside. The Mercedes will circle the block and come back to pick her up." The attendant reached in his coat pocket and pulled out a crumpled pack of cigarettes and tapped one out. "Why are you asking about the guy? You a cop?"

Reid gave the attendant a noncommittal shrug like he'd received. "Something like that. Thanks for the info."

He rolled up his window, signaling an end to the conversation, and the guy shuffled back to his tiny booth.

Reid checked his watch. Returning in about an hour, huh? So the butler and his wife had been making daytime runs each week, as well. Interesting.

He lifted his cup of coffee and took a sip. He had nothing but time. Before he left downtown today, he'd find Eldridge and get some answers.

After feeding the new kitten and Nicholas their respective breakfasts, Penelope took her son down to the boat dock for a change of scenery. The kitten, which Penelope had dubbed Lucky, had warmed up to his rescuers the night before after recovering from his trip to the lake house and gobbling a large bowl of canned food. And Reid, for all his fussing about the cat, seemed a little smitten with Lucky that morning. Until Lucky had used Reid's leg as a ladder to climb up to the counter where Reid was making scrambled eggs.

Pen chuckled to herself remembering the look of amusement on Reid's face as the orange fuzz ball, tiny claws extended, clambered up his jeans. And his grunt of pain as those tiny claws dug into his skin when Lucky reached the thinner material of Reid's T-shirt.

Once at the floating pier, Nicholas spent his time gathering rocks on the shore and bringing them out to the dock to fling into the water with glee. The kid had a room full of toys Reid had bought him, but he was happiest throwing rocks. *Boys!*

Penelope cast a gaze around at the peaceful setting. Reid had such a lovely setup here at the lake house: The quiet inlet, the surrounding woods, the tranquil water. Although the hardwood trees had dropped their leaves, the barren branches still had a serene sort of beauty. But even the calm of the water couldn't take the edge off her nerves as she waited to hear back from Reid's excursion today. Would he find his father? Was *her* father somehow involved with Eldridge's disappearance? It wouldn't surprise her. And, damn it, what did that say about how wide the gulf between them had grown?

Spotting the white egret that frequented the water's edge, perched on a fallen log across the cove, she squatted next to Nicholas and pointed to the bird. "Look, sweetie. See the bird?"

"Buhd?" Nicholas scanned the shoreline, clutching at her jacket sleeve, and his face brightened when he spotted the water fowl. "Big buhd!"

She stayed in a crouch beside him, trying to see the lake setting from his perspective. A world of new sights, sounds, scents and discoveries. She allowed her thoughts to drift to Andrew, and all the firsts he'd never see with their son. A heaviness settled in her, and determined not to go down that track, not to get waylaid in regret, she shook her head and resolutely pulled her thoughts back to the here and now. Enjoying that moment with her son for the gift it was.

"H'llo? Mommy, h'llo?"

Called from her perusal of the lightly rippling water, she glanced at Nicholas. "Hmm?"

He'd managed to slide the emergency cell phone from her pocket without her noticing. He held the phone to his ear with a look of deep concentration. He babbled a few words, then fell silent before saying, "H'llo? H'llo?"

She chuckled. "Little mimic monkey." She held out her hand to him. "But that's not a toy. Give it to Mommy, please."

When he didn't obey, she repeated her request more firmly.

He turned from her and trotted a few steps away, moving close to the edge of the dock.

"Nicholas, be careful!" Pushing to her feet she moved quickly toward him to catch the back of his coat.

"No!" In a fit of two-year-old temper, Nicholas threw the secure cell into the lake.

Penelope gasped. "Nicholas! No! Bad behavior!"

Her toddler dropped on his behind and loosed a wail. "No, Mommy! Bad, Mommy!"

She growled under her breath. So much for savoring precious moments with her son. "Derailed by a terrible-twos tantrum."

Pen hurried to the edge of the wood planks and lay on her stomach to reach into the cold water. She fished out the phone and tried to turn it on. The screen flashed on for a moment before flickering off.

"Oh, Nicholas!" She sighed as she scooped her unhappy boy into her arms and headed back to the house, praying Reid kept an ample supply of rice in his cabinet for a cell phone salvage effort.

The kitten greeted them with tiny mews as they came in the porch door and with a squeal of delight, Nicholas stopped to pat Lucky.

"Be gentle!" she warned and headed into the kitchen to explore Reid's cabinets.

She knew Reid's solution to the waterlogged phone would be to buy another one. But she wanted to prove to him that replacing things wasn't always the answer. With time and a little care, the phone could be resurrected. She hoped. Saving a phone didn't matter to her nearly as much as the principle she wanted to demonstrate. Some things were worth saving, even if it took a special effort. Phones, kittens…and relationships.

Approximately seventy-five minutes later, Reid yanked himself from deliberations on his relationship with Pen—*even if we settle the questions surrounding her father, Eldridge, and Andrew's death, am I ready to settle down? Be a father to Nicholas?*—when Aaron's dark blue Mercedes rolled to a stop in front of the apartment building. The back door of the sedan opened and a man wearing a trench coat, fedora, an obviously fake mustache and dark glasses—Reid snorted at the trite, useless disguise— eased carefully out to the sidewalk. He used a cane to hobble slowly toward the building's door.

Reid was out of his car and jogging across the street in a matter of seconds. "Hey!" he called, then louder, "Eldridge?"

The stooped, trench coat–clad figure froze, then turned slowly toward Reid. When he spied his son, Eldridge's expression appeared startled at first, then surprisingly relieved. His fake mustache looked all the more cheesy up close. "So…you found me."

"A trench coat and fake mustache? Could you possibly be more cliché?" Reid shook his head at his father, who lifted his chin haughtily.

"It worked for Bogart. That's good enough for me."

Reid poked his hands in his pockets and rocked back on his heels. "Really? When did it work for Bogart? Which movie?"

Eldridge glared at him. "I don't remember which one, I just... What do you want, Reid?"

Reid's chest felt light with relief while at the same time his gut twisted with anger. "Answers. What are you up to? Why did you disappear on us without a word? We thought you were dead!"

"Sir?" Aaron called through a lowered window of the Mercedes. "Should I—"

Eldridge waved off his butler. "It's all right. Go on home. I'll talk to him."

Aaron didn't look convinced, but neither did the butler argue. Giving Reid one last concerned glance, he pulled away from the curb.

Eldridge ripped off the limp mustache and rubbed his upper lip. "There's a greasy spoon on the next block. Buy me lunch and I'll explain everything."

Reid glanced down the street to the crooked sign that read Ken's Eats and frowned.

"I know," his father said before he could comment. "Horrendous ambiance, but the food is good and the waitress likes me."

Cocking his head, he gave his father a skeptical look. "Define *like*."

"I tip her well. Money can be very influential. Haven't you learned that by now?"

"I prefer to win over women the old-fashioned way— with my charm and good looks."

His father started tottering down the sidewalk. "Funny,

I don't see a ring on your finger. Your method must not be working too well."

He started to mention his budding relationship with Penelope but swallowed the words. Did he have a relationship with his ex-partner's wife? He had feelings for her, but if he wasn't willing or able to commit to her, to be the father to Nicholas the boy deserved…

Instead, he just quirked an eyebrow and fell in step beside Eldridge. "Point taken, old man."

Once inside the greasy-spoon diner, Reid scanned the interior, looking for an open booth. If the number of patrons was any indication, Eldridge just might be right about the quality of the food. He was just about to suggest they take a pair of empty spots at the end of the lunch counter when the waitress, a fiftysomething redhead who reminded him of Lucille Ball with a pixie cut, sashayed up to Eldridge with a toothy grin.

"Well, if it ain't my favorite customer. How ya doing today, Burt?"

Reid shot his father a puzzled look. "Burt?"

Eldridge waved a hand to shush him. "My regular table available, sugar?"

"It will be in two shakes of a lamb's tail!" She hustled off to an end booth where she began clearing empty dishes from the table where a customer sat idly reading his newspaper.

Eldridge canted toward Reid and muttered, "Hardly serves me to hide out from my family, have the world think something's happened to me and then tell a loud-mouth like her my real name, now, does it?"

Reid shook his head in wry amusement. "Whatever you say, *Burt*."

The customer who'd been booted from his table gave them a glare as he passed.

Having cleared and wiped down the table where the newspaper reader had been sitting, their waitress gave a shrill whistle. "All ready, Burt."

Eldridge led the way to the vacated booth and took the far seat.

"Black coffee, right?" she asked Eldridge and he nodded.

"Same," Reid told her, and she hurried away to get their drinks. He glanced at the bench seat Eldridge had taken and rubbed his chin. "Um, that's where I was going to sit."

Eldridge gave him a blank look and aimed a finger at the bench across from him. "What difference does it make? Sit there."

Reid tucked his hands in his jeans pockets and shifted his weight. "I always sit facing the entrance. It's a cop thing."

Eldridge looked at him as if his son had rocks for brains. "Why?" Then, "You're not a cop anymore, so..." He waved his hand toward the other seat again.

A sharp pain sliced through him, and he tightened his jaw, trying to school his face, not let Eldridge see how his remark had stung him. Clearing his throat, he said, "Once a cop always a cop. I'm talking about a mind-set, not the job."

His father sighed, but slowly slid from his seat. "For what it's worth, I knew it would be you that found me. Hoped it would be you."

Reid stiffened, raising his chin a notch. "What? Why?"

"'Cause you're a good detective. No matter how things went down about your partner's death, I knew you had the right stuff to figure out I was alive and come find me." His father slid into the opposite booth bench with a groan. "Damn these old bones. Some days, I don't feel worth shootin'."

As Reid settled in his seat at the table, he gave Eldridge a nod of thanks, both for moving and for his words of support. If the old man had given him even a shred of that kind of backing and faith in previous years, maybe they'd have had a chance at a functional father/son relationship.

Eldridge wiggled a finger at him. "This police thing with the seat facing the entrance...you think you're gonna see trouble coming? Is that it?"

He shrugged. "Better than if my back's to the door."

Eldridge harrumphed. "And what if there are two doors? What if trouble comes in through the kitchen?"

Reid pinched the bridge of his nose and exhaled, striving for patience. "What if you tell me now why you disappeared? You've had us all in a panic for months!"

"A panic, eh? Is that why it took you more than five months to find me?"

"You staged a scene at the ranch that made us think you'd been kidnapped, possibly killed. The cops have been looking for— "

"And you? What have you been doing? My son, the former detective... I thought a missing-person case would help get your mojo back."

Reid scowled. "Are you saying this was all a test for me?"

Eldridge flicked a hand. "Hell no. This was a test for everyone."

Reid shook his head as if he'd not heard his father correctly. "Come again?"

The waitress—Celia, her name tag read—brought their coffee at that moment and they both fell silent.

"Anything to eat, Burt, darlin'? The lunch special is

beef stew, corn bread and coleslaw. Or I can have Mac make up one of those bacon cheeseburgers you like."

"Bacon cheeseburger?" Reid repeated. "Your cardiologist know you're eating that kind of crap?"

Eldridge sneered at him. "I'll eat whatever I damn well please. At my age, I should be able to enjoy my food without judgment from you or doctors or anyone else."

"You tell 'em, Burt!" Celia said, nodding. "So a cheeseburger all the way?"

Reid frowned at his father while Eldridge considered his choice for moment. "Actually the stew sounds good. Reid?"

He held up two fingers, indicating she should make it two of the lunch specials.

As Celia walked away, Eldridge mumbled, "I'm dying anyway. Might as well speed up the process with a bacon cheeseburger or two."

Reid propped his arms on the table and leaned toward his father, pitching his voice low. "Something you want to tell me about your health, old man? Is that what this whole fiasco has been about?"

Eldridge looked away, his fingers drumming restlessly on the Formica tabletop. "Tell me something, Reid. What's been happening at the house since I disappeared? How did my *loving family*—" his tone belied the words "—respond to my absence? My presumed death?"

Fowler watched the gray December clouds scuttle across the sky, a reflection of his mood. He should be happy. Tiffany was having his baby, and she had agreed to marry him. He could settle down with her and raise their baby together and live happily ever after. *Whatever the hell that meant.* Tiffany seemed to think their future was going to be all roses and candlelight. And she did make him happy. The sex was certainly good, especially now that they were engaged. Tiff was more adventurous in bed now. And being pregnant had upped her libido. Good news all around. But…

But.

Fowler ground his back teeth together and squeezed the armrest of his leather desk chair as he stared out his office window at the horizon. There was always a *but*, wasn't there? He should be completely happy, *but* he wasn't. Too many things were still unresolved. Too many people still needed their comeuppance before he'd be satisfied. Too many questions needed answers. Fowler hated unfinished business, especially if he came out on the short end.

Eldridge was still missing. Hugh Barrington still hadn't been arrested. And the control and running of Colton Inc. was still going to fall into the wrong hands if Eldridge's will was enforced.

He couldn't do anything about his missing father, and his personal lawyers were looking into challenging his father's will. But Hugh Barrington was a pebble in his Stefano Bemer wingtips. He was tired of pussyfooting around with the man. The family had trusted him to coax information from Hugh, but Fowler was out of patience.

Resolved to force Hugh into a corner, Fowler slapped his hands on the arms of his chair as he lunged out of the seat and strode to his office door. He snagged his suit coat from the coat tree as he marched out, barking at his secretary, "I'm going out."

"How long will you be gone?" she called after him.

"As long as it takes to nail Barrington's ass to the wall!"

Chapter 17

After his meltdown over the cell phone, Penelope had put Nicholas down for a nap and set about trying to salvage the burner cell phone. Once she'd done all she could with the mobile phone, she tried to kill time reading. But her thoughts kept straying to Reid, his mission to find his father, and her future. Would Reid be part of her life in the months and years to come?

Hearing Nicholas's plaintive-sounding cry, Penelope hurried in to check on her napping son. The minute she saw him sitting up on the bed, his eyes bleary and his cheeks flushed, she knew something was desperately wrong.

"I'm here, sweetie. What is it?" she cooed as she sat on the edge of the bed.

Rather than reach for her, as he usually did when she retrieved him from his naps, Nicholas tugged at his ear and stared blankly ahead as he sobbed pitifully. A light touch to his forehead confirmed her fear. Her baby was burning up with fever.

Worry swept through her, knocking her breath from her like a giant wave in the ocean. Crisis moments like this were the times she missed Andrew the most, when she felt the most overwhelmed by the job of single-parenting. Andrew had always been so good in an emergency. His first-responder training and laid-back personality had helped calm her when her first instinct was to panic.

Easing Nicholas into her arms, she stroked her son's fiery head and fought down the swell of emotion crowding her thoughts. She needed to think clearly. The first thing Andrew always told her was not to panic. Drawing a deep breath, she focused her thoughts.

Nicholas needed a doctor. Possibly an antibiotic if his ears had an infection, which based on his history was quite likely. Calling for an ambulance seemed an extreme measure, especially when she didn't know exactly where she was to give them an address.

She checked her watch. The pediatric clinic she typically used only worked half days on Fridays and would be open only another thirty minutes. Could she get there in time?

Nicholas had had badly infected ears in the past, and her doctor had warned her that failure to get him help quickly could mean his eardrum could burst. She had already been talking with her pediatrician about surgery to implant tubes in her baby's ears when the holidays were over. Now she wished she'd done the procedure earlier.

Acid anxiety swirled in her gut. She squeezed her eyes shut and forced herself to take a calming breath. *Pull it together, Penelope. Think. Do. Nicholas needs you now.*

Exhaling through her mouth, she gathered her thoughts as she paced the floor with Nicholas limp on her shoulder, whining pitifully. She went to yoga class with one of the nurses who worked at the pediatric clinic. Maybe

Linda would convince the doctor to stay late if she told them she was on her way?

Shifting Nicholas onto her hip, she hurried into the kitchen. She'd seen Reid stash the keys to her Explorer in the drawer by the refrigerator. The same drawer where he'd put her cell phone when they'd arrived. Taking both from the drawer, she fumbled to put the phone back together. Like most mothers, she'd become adept at performing tasks while also holding a squirming child, but her nerves made her hands clumsy and it took several tries to get the battery to snap in place and the back cover securely snapped on. She hesitated the briefest moment before turning on the cell phone. Reid had purposely removed the batteries to prevent anyone tracking the phones through GPS. But she *had* to reach the doctor. And she needed to call Reid to tell him what was going on.

Her first call was to the doctor's office, a number she kept stored in her phone. She explained to the receptionist who she was and that she had an emergency. "I'm sure I can be there in forty minutes or so if you could please wait on me."

After extracting a promise from the office to see Nicholas after hours, she hurried to the Explorer. She'd call Reid from the road. She wasn't at all sure she could reach the clinic as quickly as she'd promised. Her recollection of the time it took Reid to drive them into downtown a few days earlier was foggy since she'd slept in the car. The lake house was probably more like fifty minutes or an hour from town. And while she knew she could take Nicholas to the emergency room, she foresaw an interminable wait at the ER. Overworked doctors and nurses who weren't familiar with Nicholas's medical history.

As she buckled her son into his car seat, his cries grew

to a frenzied pitch. She knew the tenor and volume well from past illnesses. He was in real pain.

"I'm sorry, sweetie. Hang in there." She quickly rifled through his diaper bag until she found a bottle of children's acetaminophen drops. Hands shaking, she administered a dose, recapped the bottle and bolted to the driver's seat.

Before cranking the engine, she plugged the address for the pediatric clinic into her map application and searched for driving directions. Next, she dug the scrap of paper out of her pocket that had the phone number for Reid's burner cell. She put the phone on speaker; while it rang from her lap, she backed out of the garage and headed down the bumpy lane toward the country road.

"Turn left in a quarter mile," her phone app said, while Reid's burner cell rang without an answer.

"Mommy…" Nicholas cried pitifully.

"Hang on, darling. We're going to get you help." She turned onto the rural road, left a terse voice mail for Reid, then tapped the disconnect icon. Where was he? Why wasn't he answering?

She gripped the steering wheel as she accelerated down the highway, then glanced in her rearview mirror in time to see Nicholas throw up the medicine she'd just given him. Her heart kicked hard seeing the droopy look of his eyes and the flush of his cheeks.

Speed limits be damned. Her baby needed help… *quickly*.

Reid flattened his hand on the diner's table. "The family reacted to your disappearance about the way you'd expect. Backbiting, accusations, finger-pointing."

Eldridge's shoulders slumped, and he met Reid's gaze. "Even Whitney?"

Reid scratched his head, trying to remember everything he'd heard Whitney say or do. "She's done her share of finger-pointing, largely to shift the spotlight off herself. She was one of the first people suspected. She stood to inherit a lot of power and wealth, depending on the terms of your will. But after the will was read, it was obvious to everyone she really loves you. She didn't care about what you did—or rather didn't—leave her. She just wanted her, quote, 'Dridgey-pooh back.' From the looks of it, she truly mourned for you during the short time we believed the burned body was you."

Eldridge heaved a relieved sigh and smiled. "Ah, Whitney..." Then he frowned darkly. "What burned body?"

Reid explained how, the month before, Hugh Barrington had claimed to have seen Eldridge shoved in a car at gunpoint and how the same car was seen later, crashed and burned with a charred body inside. "We all thought it was you for a few days, until a second medical examiner looked at the case and called us. When we tried to find the first ME and question him, the guy had disappeared."

Reid's burner cell buzzed at his hip, and he flipped it up to check the number. At a glance, he knew it wasn't the secure cell he'd left for Pen, although the number on the caller ID did look familiar. But Penelope was the only person for whom he'd interrupt his discussion with Eldridge. He re-clipped the phone at his waist and regarded his father.

Eldridge's hands twitched and fidgeted on the tabletop, and his dour expression echoed his agitation. "So who do you think Hugh saw getting kidnapped? Do they know who the burned body *did* belong to?"

Reid glanced out the large picture window beside their

booth to the slow-moving traffic on the street. "We have reason to believe Hugh arranged for a body to be stolen from a funeral home or morgue. Probably thanks to more greased palms."

"Hugh?" The surprise in Eldridge's tone drew Reid's attention back to his father. "Why do you suspect Hugh?"

"Well, the terms of your will certainly gave him reason to want people to think you were dead." At Eldridge's befuddled look, Reid added, "Controlling interest in Colton Inc.?" He barked a humorless laugh. "Let me tell you, Fowler was not pleased by that surprise."

His father's eyes were as large and round as their coffee mugs, his complexion as white as their napkins. "Controlling interest—" he sputtered. Now his cheeks grew florid, his jaw tightening. "I did *not* leave any part of my company to Hugh Barrington. What kind of stunt are you trying to pull?"

"Me?" He flopped back on the booth seat and blinked at his father, stunned. The heat of anger rushed through him. "I'm not pulling anything! You're the one who—" He cut himself off and, teeth clenched, he drew a slow, calming breath. "You didn't leave controlling interest of the company to Hugh?"

"Hell no!" Eldridge shouted, slamming his fist on the table so hard their coffee sloshed.

Reid folded his arms over his chest and stared at his father while his mind took off in new directions, factoring this in with everything else he'd learned about Hugh Barrington.

"Did Barrington…did that *bastard lawyer* tell you he got majority stake in *my company*?"

Reid arched an eyebrow. "You know, having more than one copy of your will would have allowed us to verify his claim. You should know better business practice than—"

"*One copy*? That's insane! Of course I have more than one copy." Eldridge looked apoplectic. He blinked rapidly, the veins in his neck pulsing, and his voice was so tight he could barely speak. "Did Barrington say...? But Aaron knew... After all the years I've trusted that smarmy ambulance chaser!"

Reid wanted to agree on that point. His father should have known his lawyer better, shouldn't have trusted him so implicitly. But then Eldridge wasn't the only one Hugh had deceived. And pointing out Eldridge's lack of discernment wasn't going to help the current conversation, so he bit his tongue.

"So..." His father seemed to be having trouble breathing. "All these months, my Whittie-pooh has thought I didn't leave her anything?"

Reid groaned. "Can we not use the nauseating pet names for the rest of this conversation?"

Celia returned with their plates, and Reid surveyed what she put in front of him. If his food tasted half as good as it smelled, he might have to make this dive a regular lunch spot.

He picked up his fork and regarded Eldridge warily. "Like I said, the will was only read last month when we thought the burned body was you. All the months prior, no one knew what it said."

Eldridge was stroking his chest and breathing heavily, his face dark with fury. He ignored his food, and after a moment, Reid grew worried. When his father appeared to be having trouble breathing, his face turning beet red, Reid slid toward the end of the booth bench and lunged toward his father, shouting to their waitress, "Call an ambulance!"

* * *

Before he stepped off the elevator, Fowler opened the voice-recorder app on his phone and slid the cell into the inside breast pocket of his suit coat. As the doors slid open, he tugged on the cuffs of his shirt and strode into the reception area of Barrington's office.

Hugh's secretary looked up from her computer, and Fowler barked, "Is he in?"

"Well, yes, but—"

"Tell him I'm here." Fowler shoved down the twinge of impatience jumping inside him as he waited for Barrington's secretary to announce him. He was tempted to barge into the old coot's office unannounced but doing so would get Barrington's back up, start the meeting with a note of discord, and Fowler wanted Hugh lulled into a false sense that everything was copacetic.

When he was allowed in to see the lawyer, Fowler feigned one of his charming, ain't-business-great smiles that had helped him wrangle more than one deal for Colton Inc. and coaxed a few pretty blondes into his bed, too.

After the usual tooth-grinding pleasantries, Fowler took a seat across from Hugh and launched his attack. "I'd like to discuss my father's will."

He saw the none-too-subtle tensing of Barrington's shoulders. Not for the first time, Fowler looked at Barrington and thought of Fred Flintstone, the short but muscular cartoon character with the thick swath of dark hair. "What about it?"

"I'm just wondering your thoughts on the drafting of his will. As Eldridge's lawyer, didn't it concern you that there was only one copy? That he went to someone else to have it written?"

Barrington leaned back in his swivel chair, steepling

his fingers in a relaxed manner incongruous with the nervous tic of his right eye behind his silver framed glasses. "I knew I could keep it safe, so I didn't question his wish to have only one—"

"And you didn't question why he used another lawyer?"

Hugh blinked. Swallowed hard. "I...trusted Eldridge had good reason—"

"So why didn't that lawyer keep a copy?"

Hugh's jaw tightened. "You'd have to ask the lawyer."

"I'd like to. So who would this other lawyer be?"

Barrington's eye was twitching harder, and he hesitated before saying carefully, "Fowler, let's be honest..."

"Please." Fowler turned up a palm of invitation, although he was certain the "honesty" Barrington proffered in his next breath would be anything but.

"We both know your father was a bit...eccentric."

Fowler arched an eyebrow. Eccentric wasn't the half of it.

"There were many times in our association that your father asked me to conduct our business in unorthodox ways." Hugh paused and gave Fowler a you-know-what-I-mean smirk. "Because of who he was and the power he had in the business community, because of our history together and friendship—" here he pressed a hand over his heart as if to seem more sincere "—I often made exceptions for Eldridge that weren't typical business or legal protocol. Not illegal, mind you," he added quickly with a stilted chuckle, "but definitely not my standard practice."

Fowler calmly folded his hands in his lap. "Hugh, let *me* be honest. I think you are full of shit."

Barrington's face fell, and he blinked rapidly as if trying to decide if he'd heard correctly.

Fowler might have laughed if he weren't seething inside at the lying sycophant's betrayal. "You see, I believe you altered Eldridge's will so that you were the main beneficiary."

Barrington sat taller in his chair, sputtering, "I... I did not!"

"Furthermore, I know my father would not have trusted you, or any one person to keep the *only* copy of his will safe. He was far too savvy of a businessman and far too suspicious by nature to trust something as important as the dispersion of all his worldly goods to one copy of one document."

"But he did!"

Fowler continued, his tone flat but deadly. "I will find the other copies of his will, his *real* will, and I will use them to not just contest the one you have, but to have you disbarred and prosecuted for fraud, malpractice, theft, malfeasance—whatever the hell my attorney can make stick."

Penelope wished she had emergency lights on her Explorer so traffic would yield her the right-of-way. Frustration and impatience gnawed at her as she waited for a short string of cars in front of her to each wait for an opening in traffic at the most recent stop sign. She couldn't remember having to stop so often when she'd ridden with Reid into town a few nights ago. Perhaps the GPS app was sending her the shortest route rather than the fastest. Or maybe in her haste she'd typed in the wrong address. Or maybe—

As she approached the intersection, she noticed a gold SUV headed toward the crossroad. The SUV was traveling fast. Too fast for her to safely pull out. Damn it!

The gold SUV whizzed into the intersection and skidded to a stop, blocking traffic in both directions.

"Oh, for crying out loud!" Pen groused, plowing her hands into her hair, tempted to pull out handfuls from the root. "Move!"

The SUV's passenger door and both backseat doors opened, and two men climbed out. They were both large, with football-player builds and scowling expressions. And guns.

When she saw the weapons, her breath whooshed from her lungs. *No! Not again!*

"Nicholas!" she rasped as panic swelled in her chest. The two thugs marched toward her, weapons raised. She hit the button on her armrest that locked the doors, but locks were no defense against bullets. If they shot up her car, Nicholas would be unprotected.

Get out of here! Hands shaking, she jammed the Explorer into Reverse and punched the accelerator. Only to come to a crunching halt as another car slammed her from behind. Trapping her.

Get help! The impact had slung her phone from the seat onto the floor. Quickly, she fished it up and tried to dial 911. One of the men appeared at her window. The other had circled the fender to Nicholas's side door.

The thug outside her window held his gun trained on her head. "Get out!"

She continued dialing, waiting for an emergency operator. *Pleasepleaseplease!*

The thug rapped the gun on her window. "Drop the phone and get out! Now!"

At the back door, thug two yanked on the handle, trying to get to her son.

"911, what's your emergency?"

Before she could answer, a loud bang made her yelp. Her driver's-side window shattered. Nicholas shrieked in terror. Shock and fear paralyzed her voice and brain for precious seconds. *No, no, no!*

The gunman reached through the broken window, manually unlocked her door and flung it open. Seizing her elbow in a painful grip, he jerked at her arm. "I said, get the hell outta the car!"

He pushed her to the back door, while another man climbed behind the steering wheel.

"No!" she screamed, fighting the hold the other man had on her. Her only thought was of helping her baby, saving him. "Nicholas! Don't hurt him!"

The warm muzzle of her captor's handgun touched her temple.

"Shut up and move or I'll waste ya right here." The dark grating tone of his voice told her he'd harbor no regret over doing just that.

He shoved her into her backseat next to Nicholas, then followed her in, while a third man piled in the front passenger seat. Her only chance of saving her son was to do as the man said and pray she stayed alive long enough to rescue Nicholas. Her kidnapper wrenched her phone from her grip and disconnected her link to 911. Dropping her phone on the floor, he crushed the screen with his heel.

She was slung against the man to her left as the driver took a turn at top speed. The man in the front seat pulled out his own cell phone and pushed one button before putting the phone to his ear.

"Yeah," he grunted, "we got her and the kid. No. He wasn't with 'em."

He, no doubt, meant Reid. Her heart twisted, both glad he wasn't going to die like she figured she would, and also wishing fervently he were with her now. She'd feel a hell of a lot more optimistic about her predicament if Reid were here.

Her thoughts were scattered snippets, jumping one direction then another. Her captors' faces. Escape. Nicholas's crying. Regrets. Planning. Panic.

As the reality of her situation sharpened and shock loosened its grip on her brain, a rock of truth settled in the pit of her stomach. She was to blame for these men finding her and Nicholas. She'd turned on her phone, made calls, used her GPS. Reid had been right about her cell signal being monitored. The minute she'd put the battery back in her phone, these men had begun tracing her location, pinpointing where to intercept her.

She pressed her lips to Nicholas's hot forehead, a pulse of tension throbbing under her skull. She'd had to do *something* for her son. He still needed a doctor. That these terrible men had interfered with getting Nicholas medical help only fueled her fury and frustration.

"My son is sick," she said to the man beside her, her tone pleading. "He needs a doctor. Please let me take him to—"

With a glare, the man growled, "Shut it."

The guy on the phone listened for a moment, then said, "We could use them as bait. Right. Yeah, he'll want proof of life, but then we can pop 'em."

A chill shimmied through her, and her tears poured faster. Not for her own life, but for Nicholas's. Her ears buzzed with adrenaline, but she sucked in a stuttering breath and tried to clear her head. She needed to listen to the one-sided conversation for any clue as to who these men were, where they were going. And she needed to send a signal to Reid, warning him of the danger he was in. She might die today because of her actions, but she'd do whatever she could to protect her son. And to save Reid's life.

Eldridge glared at Reid and flapped a dismissive hand toward the waitress. "No. No ambulance. I'm not all right, but I don't need an ambulance. Just a new lawyer, so I can sue that two-faced Hugh Barrington for all he's worth!" The old man flattened both hands on the table and drew a wheezing breath. "When I'm done with that rat bastard…"

Reid returned to his seat but kept a close eye on his father. Eldridge's color began to improve, though his jaw remained clenched tight, and his eyes flickered with animosity.

Remembering the earlier comment about Eldridge's health, Reid pressed, "Why did you say you're dying? Are you ill?" He had to admit his father didn't look so good, even before they'd broached the topic of his will or Hugh's deception.

Eldridge gave a low, gruff cough. "Hell, boy. We're all dying. Some of us will just get there sooner than others. I'm seventy-five, have a former smoker's lungs and the liver of a man who enjoyed quite a few whiskey sours back in the day."

Reid shook his head. "So then…"

"I have cancer."

Heart jolting, he studied his father's face looking for some sign the old man was pulling his leg. But Eldridge wouldn't look at him, a sure indication he was serious. Slowly, reluctantly he asked, "What…kind? What's your prognosis?"

Eldridge was quiet for a long time, ignoring his food and squeezing the handle of his spoon until his knuckles blanched. Finally he mumbled, "Prostate." He aimed a finger at Reid and warned him sharply. "Don't you dare say anything about this to Whitney. She doesn't need to know."

"She's your wife! Of course she should kn—"

"I said *no*. I don't want her worrying about something she can't do anything about. When I go home—if I go home—I'll tell her myself, if and when I decide to."

Now Reid leaned forward and pointed a finger at his father. "*When* you go home. Not if. You've hidden out and left us worrying and questioning each other long enough, old man."

"Soon. I want to finish this round of radiation treatments first. That's where I was this morning. Every Wednesday morning for the last three months. If I get a good report next week, I plan to come home by Christmas. I want a chance to say goodbye."

Reid grunted. "Don't be defeatist. Prostate cancer is beatable. It has a high recovery rate if detected early enough."

Eldridge averted his gaze toward the window again. "Yeah, that's the hearts and roses my doctors keep prattling on about. They keep telling me I'll be fine, but…it's cancer, damn it. I've known too many people who died from the big C to believe the doctors are doing anything but blowing sunshine up my ass, so I'll pay for expensive treatments and more office visits."

"Listen here, old man," Reid drilled a finger to the sticky tabletop and nailed his father with a no-nonsense glare. "You *will* do what the doctors tell you, and you *will* recover. You will adopt a better attitude and quit being a miserable old cuss about your diagnosis, because there are millions—no, billions—of people who are sicker, poorer, have harder lives than you and don't bellyache half as much as you. And you *will* bring your sorry ass home ASAP. Got it?"

Eldridge sat back and crossed his arms over his chest, giving Reid a stubborn frown. "Says who? You don't get to tell me what I will and won't do."

"Oh, really? After all the hell you've put your family through these past months, disappearing with no word and leading us to believe you were kidnapped or killed, I have every right." He aimed a finger at Eldridge. "You owe us this much. You owe Whitney better than grieving for a man who's not dead." He paused a beat, gritting his teeth before adding, "And you owe your conniving lawyer a come-to-Jesus confrontation for the years of lies and theft and manipulation."

Eldridge inhaled slowly and, his gaze distant, took a bite of his stew. Reid would wager his father didn't taste the stew, that he tasted nothing but the bitterness of his lawyer's betrayal. Turbulent shadows chased across his face like the skittering black clouds of a fast-approaching storm. "That I do, son. That I do."

Chapter 18

"Now, see here!" Hugh shot out of his seat and puffed out his barrel chest.

"I don't have all the proof I need now," Fowler said, "but Reid assures me he's building a case against you that—"

"Reid? That washed-up cop can't prove anything! I'm the one who will be filing charges against him for libel, and theft of property and—"

"Reid says you tried to have him and Penelope killed. We are onto you, Barrington. All of your misdeeds and deception and crimes—"

Hugh aimed a finger at Fowler. "You listen to me, Colton…"

"No!" Fowler sat forward in his chair impatiently, tired of Barrington's games. "You listen to me, *Hugh*—"

Barrington's phone interrupted with a jarring old-fashioned ring, but Fowler continued, "If you think our family is going to sit back and—"

The older man had the gall to ignore Fowler and lift the receiver. "Barrington."

"We're not finished!" Fowler fumed. "How dare you take—"

Hugh turned his back to Fowler as he listened to the caller.

Fowler leaned forward, prepared to knock the phone from the lawyer's hand.

"You've taken them both? Alive?"

Fowler stilled, the lawyer's words chilling him.

"No. Leave them alive. He'll take the bait and try to rescue them. When he does, finish them all. Yes, the kid, too. I have no time or interest in raising another brat."

Fowler straightened his spine. What the hell?

"That's what I'm paying you for. Handle it. And don't call this line again. Ever." Hugh slammed down the receiver and drew a fortifying breath. His back still to Fowler, he flexed and balled his hands in a jittery fashion before squaring his shoulders and facing his visitor with a smug look. "So what were you saying about your brother having evidence against me?"

Fowler tightened his jaw, wary of Barrington's mood change and suspicious phone call. He had an oily feeling in his gut that the lawyer wasn't talking about leaving wild game alive or baiting traps for pests in his house. But the alternative meant...

A new, quieter wave of rage and disgust rolled through Fowler, but he shoved it down as he slowly sank back in his chair. "Just what I said. Reid's been investigating you. He's building a case against you, and he'll soon have enough evidence to put your ass in jail."

Hugh lifted his chin, the older man's expression suddenly far too confident and gloating for Fowler's liking.

"I'd be very careful what I threatened," Barrington said. "That call was a report from one of my men saying they'd captured Penelope and Nicholas."

Captured? Fowler's pulse shot up at the term.

"It's only a matter time before they have Reid in their custody, as well." He hiked up a corner of his mouth in a one-sided grin. "Because you know for damn sure he's going to come after her. The sap. He probably believes he's in love with her. I saw the way he's looked at her through the years. His feelings were pretty obvious."

Fowler stilled and narrowed a wary glare on Hugh. "What do you mean...captured?"

"I mean exactly that. They are in my men's custody, and I will make sure they're unable to use any of the information they *stole* against me."

Fowler scooted to the front edge of his chair and leaned toward the vile man. Even knowing the fraud and deception Hugh had been practicing against his family for years, Fowler was shocked at what he was hearing. This had to be a stunt. A ploy to throw Fowler off guard or—

He blinked hard. "You'd kill them? You... You're talking about your own daughter, your grandson. You can't mean that you intend to let these men kill your own flesh and blood!"

Hugh's face grew dark, angry. "I mean exactly that," he grated as he began restlessly pacing, "I've bowed and scraped to your father and his ilk for too long to let anyone take it from me. I cannot, *will not* go to jail, and I will do whatever it takes to make sure of it." He drew a ragged breath and added, "And for the record, she's not my daughter. She's just a concession I made years ago, because my bleeding-heart wife couldn't have her own children. She wanted somebody to coddle, so we adopted Penelope when she was a baby."

Fowler couldn't believe his ears. The man was heartless. *Insane.* "But she's still family—"

Hugh dismissed the connection with a haughty snort. "Like you, a high-and-mighty Colton, care anything about family. The name Colton is synonymous with backstabbing and looking out for number one."

Fowler took umbrage and stiffened his spine. "Maybe once. But things are changing. Even for me."

Hugh waved away Fowler's claim like so much rubbish, and continued, "I don't have any particular attachments to Penelope. We've never been close. In fact, our relationship has always been adversarial." His breathing was fast, shallow, and he flicked a hand as he continued, "She and Reid started this when your snooping brother broke into my office with Penelope and stole valuable information from me." He nodded, as if agreeing with his sick justifications. "They made themselves my enemy, and I have to protect my own interests." Another smug grin curved his thin mouth. "I learned that watching your family."

A frisson of ice slithered down Fowler's spine. This merciless, rattled version of the family lawyer was deeply disturbing. "Are you responsible for my father's disappearance? Did you kill Eldridge, too?"

Hugh sneered. "I wish I could take credit for that. But I have no idea where your father is."

As his disbelief morphed into righteous indignation and revulsion, Fowler was pricked with a sense of urgency. He needed to alert the police, to de-escalate the situation with Penelope and Reid. He slid his phone from his breast pocket and began thumbing the screen to enter his passcode. "You don't really think you'll get away with this? Contracting three murders on top of all the fraud and malpractice?"

Hugh paced to his credenza and poured himself a

large whiskey. "I've been getting away with it for years. I learned from the best how to cover my tracks."

Fowler almost laughed. How was his current gloating covering his tracks? The voice recorder was taking down everything Hugh had said, but he needed more. Where were his men taking Penelope? Could he warn Reid before his half brother walked into a trap? He'd never much liked Reid or any of Whitney's children, but that didn't mean he wanted him murdered.

"Too bad Reid caught on. Now too many people know what you've done."

"Which is why your brother has to die. I refuse to spend my remaining years in some stinking jail cell." He took a long swallow of whiskey. "I only need a couple hours, and I'll be gone. Maybe to Mexico. Definitely somewhere warm with no extradition to the US." Hugh slammed down his drink and stalked back to open his desk drawer. "But I can't allow anyone to talk about what they know. I'll do whatever it takes to keep my secrets hidden."

A prickle of alarm shot through Fowler a split second before Hugh pulled a revolver from his desk. And aimed it at Fowler.

Pure gut instinct took over. Fight or flight. Fowler chose fight.

He launched himself across Hugh's desk, hands outstretched. He heard the click as Hugh tried to shoot, but the gun didn't fire. An empty chamber or an unloaded weapon?

No time to find out. He grabbed at Hugh's wrists, trying to shove his hands up.

"Mr. Barrington!" the secretary screeched from the office door.

"Call the cops!" Fowler barked. He blocked Hugh's arm when he tried to angle the gun in his direction.

An earsplitting blast jarred Fowler. He froze for a split second. The chemical tang of gunpowder filled his nose. A numb ringing muted his hearing. And then he felt the pain.

Penelope sat with her back rigid, fear tensing all her muscles. She listened with her heart in her throat as the men discussed their next move.

"I say just take her into the woods and finish 'em both. Leave 'em for the animals to eat." The man to her left, who had bad teeth and a tattoo of a fist on his neck, gave her an evil grin. "Crows gotta eat same as worms."

Her stomach rolled at the morbid line she recognized from a Clint Eastwood movie she'd watched with Andrew. No doubt Tattoo Neck thought he was clever, quoting the line.

"Not yet. We still need Colton," the man in the front seat countered. "Barrington said to use her as bait for Colton, then get rid of them both."

A shiver chased up her spine hearing her father's name, having this confirmation that her own father was behind the kidnapping and her impending murder. Rage and hurt seethed in her belly, a toxic brew that left her nauseated and heartsick.

"So then we're going back to Lenny's to wait?" the driver asked.

"Hell no! We can't risk my neighbors hearing anything or seeing her," Tattoo growled.

"So where do we go with her until we have Colton?" the driver asked.

"Back to Colton's hideout." The man with the buzz cut in the front passenger seat tapped the screen of his phone. To the driver, he said, "We picked up the first signal about two miles from here. At the lake."

Penelope's heart scampered, but she fought the panic. She had only a few minutes to make a plan. Her only advantage was knowledge of the house layout. How long would it be before Reid showed up? Could she signal him in some way, warn him?

Tattoo jabbed his gun toward Nicholas, who continued crying pitifully. "Shut that kid up, or I'll pop him now!"

She recoiled, ice sluicing through her as she angled her body to shield her son. "He's scared! And sick! We were headed to the doctor when you stopped us."

Tattoo scowled, then jerked his head toward Nicholas. "What's that on his neck?"

When Penelope cast a glance down at her baby, she spotted a blood-stained fluid dripping from his ear.

White-hot pain stole Fowler's breath. The sonofabitch had shot him! Disbelief and horror rode shotgun to the burning ache that paralyzed him momentarily. When he was finally able to suck in a gurgling breath, he clutch at the hole in his side and lifted his palm to stare numbly at the red staining his hand.

Barrington took advantage of Fowler's incapacitation, shoving at him to free his legs. And roll away.

Fowler fumbled to grab at Barrington's pant leg as the lawyer untangled himself and staggered to his feet.

"Stop…him!" he rasped to the secretary, gaping at them from the door.

To which Hugh, waving his weapon, countered, "Out of my way, woman!"

Yelping, the secretary stumbled backward as Barrington plowed through the door.

Fowler struggled to his knees. The burning sensation

arcing through his midsection was enough to make his head spin and nausea swirl in his gut.

Was this what it felt like to die? He thought of Tiffany and the life they might not get a chance to build together. But most, he thought of his failure today. He'd handled the situation with Barrington all wrong. He'd flown off the handle, letting his damn impatience and need for vengeance push a dangerous man into a corner. Who did he think he was? He wasn't a cop like Reid or a trained secret agent like Jake McCord.

He could hear the frantic sobbing voice of Hugh's secretary on the phone calling an ambulance and asking for police assistance.

Fowler closed his eyes and gritted his teeth. He needed to get off the floor. With a groan of agony, he struggled to his knees. He might have blown this encounter, but he could warn Reid about Barrington's hit men. With a hand slippery from blood, he fumbled his cell phone from the floor where it had fallen in the tussle and tapped the screen, leaving red fingerprints as he dialed.

Reid didn't answer. Instead, the call went straight to voice mail. "Damn it, Reid!" he groused, then with a labored breath he blurted, "Barrington shot me…and… men have Penelope. Orders to…kill her! Hugh's…running."

Then his peripheral vision blurred, and his head felt thick and heavy. He saw a fuzzy image of Hugh's secretary running toward him…and then the world went black.

Pen's heart seized. She was too late. Nicholas's eardrum had burst and was seeping the built-up effusion. She gave a whimper of dismay. "Please," she begged, tears filling her eyes, "his eardrum ruptured. We have to get him to the doctor! He could have hearing loss or a worse infection if a doctor doesn't—"

"Shut. Up!" Tattoo waved the gun in her face again. "His ear ain't gonna be a problem once he's dead!"

Bitter tears pooled in her eyes. "You're foul. A monster!"

"So what are you going to do, now that you know the truth?" Eldridge asked, leveling a defeated stare at Reid.

"I won't stay quiet, if that's what you're asking. Whitney deserves to know you are alive. I won't be party to your deception. Hell, the whole family has suffered unnecessarily because of this stunt of yours."

"But you can't deny it worked to root out the traitor in my life. Barrington will pay for what he's done!" Eldridge hammered the tabletop with a stiff fist. Then, his expression softening, he added, "And it's proven to me the strength of the family bonds that I'd doubted."

"So the ends justify the means to you?" Reid shook his head. "Our pain and stress and worry over the last six months mean nothing to you?"

Eldridge frowned. "I won't keep apologizing for that."

"You've apologized to me but you still have to ask your wife and the rest of the family for forgiveness."

"Well, but...all's well that ends—"

"Don't!" Reid dug in his pocket for enough money to cover the food and a generous tip and slapped it on the table. "If all you've got left for me are trite expressions, then we're done here. Come home or don't. I don't care. But Whitney will know you're alive and where you're living. She deserves that. I'll give you until Christmas Eve to call her or show up at the ranch for yourself. Then I'm telling her what I know." He slid out of the booth and strode toward the exit.

"Reid!" his father called after him, but he didn't stop. He'd heard enough. When he reached the sidewalk outside the greasy spoon, he paused long enough to check his messages on his cell phone. He had three. He frowned at the number. Having three messages wasn't uncommon under ordinary circumstances, but only a couple of people had the number for this burner cell.

A tingle of alarm pinched the nape of his neck as he quickly went through all the prompts to replay his messages. The first was from Pen.

"Reid, it's me. Nicholas has spiked a high fever and likely has an ear infection." The panic in her voice heightened his concern. "He needs a doctor, and I couldn't wait for you to return. I'm sorry, but my baby needs help. I've taken my Explorer and am headed to his pediatrician. Call my old cell when you get this message."

"Damn it!" he groused, not just because Nicholas was sick, but because Pen had taken it upon herself to leave the safety of his lake house to get him medical attention. Then the rest of her message sank in, and he cursed again, louder and more profanely. Call her old cell? That was the number he didn't recognize and had ignored while he was meeting with Eldridge. A number that Hugh Barrington knew. A number that was almost certainly being watched so Pen's location could be tracked.

"Reid, wait." Catching up to Reid, Eldridge shuffled out to the sidewalk.

"Save it, old man. I have an emergency," he said in a rush even as the next message started. "Penelope's compromised her location, and Barrington's men will have a head start in finding her."

He ran to the Range Rover with the phone pressed to his ear. He didn't recognize the wheezing voice at first, but the words sent ice to his core. He stumbled to a stop, checked his phone for the list of calls received and spotted Fowler's number. Fowler—who had agreed to approach Barrington in an attempt to extract a confession from Barrington. Fowler—his hotheaded, self-righteous half brother who had about as much tact as a warthog.

He replayed the message, his anxiety ratcheting up. Fowler had been shot. Barrington was on the run. And Hugh's thugs had Penelope.

"Hell!" he bit out as he whipped out of the parking lot and raced to save the woman he loved.

Numb with shock, Zane tapped the disconnect icon on his phone and lifted a stunned gaze to Mirabella, who sat on the edge of their bed.

His wife's face was drawn and pale. "What did he say? Zane?"

"Reid found Eldridge. He's alive."

She flashed a tremulous smile. "But that's good, right? Why are you—?"

"There's more." Shaking himself from his daze, he told her everything Reid had said in the brief call as he shoved his feet in his boots and found his gun.

Barrington. Fowler. Penelope.

She pressed a hand to her mouth in dismay. "Good Lord, Zane. What if—"

He pressed a kiss to her mouth and turned to leave. "Stay here. You don't need the stress on the baby. Call Alanna and get her to the hospital to find Fowler. I'm going to help T.C. catch Barrington before he leaves the country."

During his years as a detective with the police department, Reid had faced numerous emergency situations. He'd been trained to detach his emotions and apply his training to every crisis. But he'd never had high personal stakes at risk during those events.

He did now. The very thought of Nicholas and Penelope in the hands of hired killers made his blood run cold. He had to fight the panic roiling inside him as he drove, scrambling mentally for his plan of action. All he knew was that Fowler claimed Hugh's men had her. But where?

Pen's message had said she was taking Nicholas to the doctor. Had she made it to the doctor? Had the men intercepted her at the lake house? Had…?

His heartbeat tripped. The lake house. The safe place he'd set up for emergencies…had security cameras throughout.

He pulled to the side of the road and, with hands shaking from adrenaline, dug out his cell phone and brought up the application that gave him access to the cameras at the lake house.

He opened the window for the black-and-white images of the camera feed and swiped from one view to the next. Nothing outside, nothing in the master bedroom, nothing in the garage…

His chest constricted and a four-letter word wheezed from his lungs when he opened the first living-room view. Pen sat on the couch holding Nicholas, while two— no, *three* men—stood around her in various positions in the room.

He tossed the phone aside and pulled back on the highway. Well, at least he knew where he was going. He placed a call to 911 and gave them the address of the lake house, describing the landmarks for the obscure dirt road that led to his property. Then disconnecting, he punched the gas pedal and raced toward his breached hideaway.

Penelope swayed as she sat on the edge of the couch, rocking Nicholas, whose forehead had grown clammy.

She prayed that meant that, since his eardrum had apparently burst, maybe the fever had broken, as well. He still needed a doctor, but at least he seemed to be in less pain. Now he drooped listlessly in her arms, blinking groggily at the scary men.

"My son needs rest. If you won't let me take him to the hospital, can I at least put him to bed?" she asked the driver, who seemed the most rational and whom she'd deciphered was named Greg. Tattoo was Lenny, and the guy with the buzz cut was Marcus. If by some miracle she survived this debacle, she wanted to remember the names to give the police.

Greg narrowed his eyes on her, considering. "All right."

When his about-face and scoff made it clear Marcus disliked that decision, Greg added, "But after that, you come back out here where we can watch you."

Pen's gut flip-flopped. While she was relieved to be getting her son out of the main room, away from the most immediate danger should bullets start flying, she hated, *hated*, the idea of leaving him in the guest room alone. Lucky, who'd been shut in the guest room until she opened the door to carry Nicholas in, scampered out to the hall. "No, Lucky!" she whispered harshly to the escaping kitten, her heart sinking. "Come back!"

But with her hands full with her sick toddler and gunmen waiting in the living room, the kitten was not her priority. Heartsick over the hard choices the men were forcing her to make, she watched the kitten gambol down the hall toward the front room.

In the end, she made the tough call to comply, to tuck Nicholas into his bed with a tearful kiss, and pray that by cooperating with the gunmen, she could buy time for Reid or the police to rescue them.

When she returned to the living room, she swept her gaze around the floor and spotted Lucky quietly bapping a ribbon on a present under the Christmas tree. Rather than call attention to the kitten, she returned to the couch and sat stiffly on the edge of the cushion. Perched. Ready to jump up at a moment's notice. Because if the opportunity presented itself to escape, to disarm one of the men, to do anything to improve her situation, she intended to take it.

Reid checked his phone one last time as he pulled onto the dirt drive leading to the lake house. He needed to know the positions of the men, of Penelope and Nicholas, before he charged in. He took stock of which men had weapons in hand—the one in the living room standing over Pen and the one who'd moved into the kitchen to raid his refrigerator—without assuming that the third guy, standing near the sliding door and looking out at the lake, didn't have a weapon on him somewhere.

After getting the tire iron from the trunk, he abandoned the Range Rover and jogged the rest of the way, staying hidden in the tree line until he got close enough to dart behind the garage. He didn't want the gunmen to hear the motor and give away his approach. His plan depended on the element of surprise. On stealth.

Tire iron clutched in his hand, he crept along the back wall of the garage, then peered carefully around the corner. He could see the man in the kitchen through the glass inset of the mudroom door. Moving quickly in a crouch, he repositioned himself just outside that door, his back against the wall. Taking a deep breath and sending up a silent prayer for success, he eased the door open and sneaked inside. Waited for the gunman in the kitchen to turn his back to the door. And swung the tire iron onto the thug's head.

The man dropped like a rock. One down, two to go.

Chapter 19

A loud thump sounded in the kitchen, rousing Pen from her mental strategizing.

Greg, who'd been staring out the plate-glass door to the back patio, whipped his head around and scowled darkly. "What was that?"

Lenny shrugged. "Marcus?" he called to the next room. "What's going on in there?"

Marcus didn't answer.

Pen's pulse picked up, and she scooted farther to the edge of the couch.

Lenny swung his gun toward her. "Where do you think you're going?"

"I—" she swallowed hard "—just wanted to check on my son in the guest room." She spoke as loudly as she dared, not wanting to either wake Nicholas or tip off the men to what she hoped was true. But if Reid had found his way back to the house, in case he didn't know what he was walking into, she wanted to signal him some way. *Please, God*.

Lenny shook his head. "Naw. Sit your ass back down."

Then quietly to Greg, "Watch her. I'm going to check the kitchen."

After giving the lawn and outbuildings a more careful scrutiny, Greg moved away from the window and withdrew a small gun from his boot.

Pen hovered on the edge of the sofa. Waiting. Listening. Preparing.

In the tense silence, as Lenny sidled toward the kitchen, the boughs of the Christmas tree swayed and the metal ornaments and bell decorations tinkled quietly.

Lenny shot a confused glance at the tree. "Who's there?"

Penelope searched deep in the branches and spied the orange kitten climbing from one limb to another, swatting dangling lights and glittery balls.

And in her next breath, Reid was there, surging out of the kitchen and wrapping an arm around Lenny's neck.

Reid seized the split second of distraction to put the nearest gunman in a wrestler's hold. With a sweep of his leg against his opponent's, he brought the man down on the floor. Before he could aim the weapon he'd lifted from the now-unconscious man in the kitchen, the guy's cohort countered Reid's leg sweep. The man's move dragged Reid off balance and flipped him to the floor, as well. The impact as he landed forced the air from his lungs, and the gun was jarred from his grip. He gasped for a breath, while scrambling to right himself, trying to disarm the thug.

"Reid!" Pen cried.

His opponent wrenched free, and as Reid climbed to his feet, the gunman grabbed Reid's arm and thrust him against the wall. He felt the cool muzzle jam into one ear while the thug's warm breath hissed in his other. "Well, looky what we have here. We've been waiting for you, Colton."

As soon as Reid burst into the room, Penelope had surged to her feet. Only to be met by Greg's gun in her face and his steely hand banding her upper arm.

"Don't," he warned in a low but menacing tone.

While her initial kidnapping and the danger to Nicholas had shocked and chilled her to the bone, Penelope had since had time to stew on the situation, and anger simmered just beneath the surface. How dare these punks put her son in danger? How dare her father be so callous as to sign off on her execution for his own selfish gain?

But watching Reid—a man who'd gone out of his way to help her, a man who'd given years to the Dallas PD to protect and serve…a man she *loved*—slammed against the wall and held at gunpoint made her see red.

Gritting her teeth, she snarled at Greg, "Get your hands *off* me."

He narrowed his eyes. "Shut up."

"You'll pay for this. There's no way you walk away from this free and clear."

His expression faltered for a split second, then hardened. His grip tightened on her arm, and pain slithered down her arm and to her shoulder. "Shut. The hell. Up."

"Do as he says, Pen," Reid said, and stunned at his defeatist suggestion, she angled a look across the room. But the look he gave her was anything but defeated. He might be shoved up to the wall with a gun at his head, but she knew Reid was far from finished with these thugs.

"On your knees, rich boy," the jerk behind Reid growled.

"Bite me," he returned. No way in hell would he bend

to these SOBs. He would spend his last breath fighting to save Pen and Nicholas.

The retort earned him a smack to the side of the head, and Penelope gasped her outrage.

Reid shook off the ear-ringing blow and waited. At any time, an opportunity, a distraction, a split second shift in advantage could come, and he intended to be ready.

Thanks to Pen's comment about checking on Nicholas, he knew the little boy was in the room down the hall. But that could change if Nicholas woke up and wandered into the living room looking for his mother. The sooner they ended this standoff the better.

From his peripheral view, he registered where his dropped weapon had landed. If he could get free…

"What did my father promise you? How much is he paying you for my murder?" Pen asked, her tone full of hurt and bitterness.

"Sit down, and *shut up*," the man holding Pen's arm grated.

"Pen," Reid said, her name a warning not to push the man to rash action.

And then an orange blur at the edge of his vision caught his attention. The kitten. He'd almost forgotten the furball Pen had rescued. Not that a kitten could save them from two gunmen bent on killing them.

And then…

Lucky trotted closer to Reid and the gunman. The kitten jumped and latched onto the thug's leg with twenty razor claws.

"Ow!" The gunman flinched. "What the hell?"

And Reid seized his chance.

With an elbow in the gunman's gut and a quick twist, he freed himself from the thug's grip. He wrapped both hands around the man's gun hand and shoved the weapon into the air. He fought for possession of the handgun, bending the man's wrist to an unnatural angle. But the man fought on. He seemed to have a countermove for every tactic Reid tried. The man was well trained.

A stinging blow landed on Reid's jaw, and he stumbled back a step, his vision blurring. Reid regained his balance, lowered his head...and charged.

When Greg's attention shifted to the struggle between Reid and Lenny, Pen acted. Just as Andrew had taught her, she smashed her forehead into Greg's nose, followed immediately by a hard knee to his groin.

Her guard doubled over, groaning, and she snatched up the stone horse sculpture from the coffee table and swung it down on Greg's head. He crumpled on the floor. His hand went limp around his gun, and Pen wrested it away.

Spinning toward Reid and Lenny, she aimed the weapon at Lenny and shouted, "Freeze, you bastard!"

But he didn't freeze. Instead, Lenny made a move for the gun Reid had knocked from his grip.

Penelope fired. Lenny collapsed, and blood bloomed on the man's shirt. Hearing a grunt and scuffle behind her, she spun back to Greg and fired again.

Greg gave a shout of pain and dropped to the ground, clutching his thigh. He spat invectives that sounded hollow against the ringing in her ears from the gun blasts, the buzz of adrenaline...and the frightened crying of her son from down the hall.

She stood shaking, numb with shock, and stuttered, "N-Nicholas."

Reid appeared at her side, and he eased the gun from her hands. "Well done."

She hiccuped a nervous laugh. "T-told you I could shoot."

He kissed her temple, and hitched his head toward the hall. "Go take care of our boy. I'll secure these SOBs until backup arrives."

Chapter 20

An hour later, after Reid and Pen had given preliminary statements to the police, they were allowed to leave the scene to take Nicholas to the emergency room. The three gunmen, in varying states of injury and under guard, were taken by ambulance to the nearest hospital. Pen and Reid opted to go to a different urgent-care center, one where Pen's pediatrician could meet them and treat her son's infected ear and ruptured eardrum.

Reid's cell phone rang as they sped down the highway. He had Pen answer and put it on speakerphone.

"It's Zane," his half brother said. "We went to Barrington's, but we were too late. The staff said he was there long enough to clean out his safe and throw a few things in a suitcase before he took off again. My guess is he's headed for the airport."

"Damn it." Reid thought a moment. "DFW is too public. Too slow. My guess is he'll have a plane waiting at a private airstrip."

"Yeah. But which one? There are more than a few of those within 100 miles," Zane said.

After a bit of discussion, Zane and T.C. were dispatched to different small airports deemed likely candidates, and Reid promised to check a third after dropping Pen and Nicholas at the urgent-care center.

Pen disconnected the call and sat in silence for a moment before saying, "Harvey Freeland has a plane in the hangar at the airstrip just east of Fort Worth."

Reid cut a side gaze toward her. "You think this Freeland guy would fly your father to Mexico?"

"Harvey would fly him to the moon if he could. My father saved him from going to jail on money-laundering charges ten years ago."

Reid's pulse spiked, and he gripped the steering wheel tighter. "What's the name of the airport?"

She bit her bottom lip and shook her head. "I don't remember, but I know how to get there."

"But Nicholas—"

She turned to look back at her son, asleep in the car seat. "I don't like the delay, but…I hate the idea of my father skipping town. Of escaping justice."

Reid tapped his thump on the steering wheel. "Are you sure?"

She furrowed her brow and met his concerned stare. "His fever has broken, and the eardrum is draining. Dr. Shaw said he'd need to start antibiotics today, but it was too late to do more than that. A short delay won't hurt him." She sighed. "Go to the airstrip."

As they bumped up the pothole-riddled road to the remote airstrip, Penelope spotted her father's Lincoln Continental. "There," she said, pointing it out to Reid.

"All right." He whipped his Range Rover into the parking lot and jammed it into Park. "You stay in the car. Let me handle this."

"He's my father. I—"

"All the more reason for you to stay put."

She started to argue, but knew someone had to stay in the car with Nicholas. And Reid was the ex-cop. He'd know better how to handle her fleeing father. Assuming they weren't too late.

She grabbed Reid's sleeve as he shouldered open the driver's door. When he faced her, she leaned across the center console and gave him a deep kiss. He returned the kiss, cupping her cheek in his palm before climbing out of the vehicle.

"Be careful, Reid."

He jerked a tight nod. "When this is over," he said, his expression grim, "we need to talk."

The car door slammed shut as he rushed off, sending a shudder of dread to her core. Not only was Reid headed toward a confrontation with her father, but the look in his eyes as he'd issued his parting comment boded ill. *We need to talk.* Had anything good ever followed that statement?

While she agreed they had things to discuss, she feared the track his conversation would go down would be much different than hers.

Reid pulled his handgun from his waistband at the small of his back and ran around the side of the airport office to the hangar. He spotted Hugh at the side of a small twin-engine plane talking loudly to a man in coveralls and gesturing with his hands.

The plane's propellers were already spinning, and the engines idled with a rumbling purr.

"Barrington!" Reid leveled his weapon at the lawyer who'd done so much to hurt Pen through the years. Coldness, distance...conspiring to murder Andrew. If he hadn't once sworn an oath to uphold the law, he might have put a bullet in Hugh then and there. But murdering her father in cold blood was hardly the start to the life he hoped to build with Pen. Instead he worked to keep the calm professionalism he'd need to bring the man in.

Hugh spun to face him, and Reid saw Pen's father grimace. Reach in his coat pocket. Extract a gun.

Reid stopped in his tracks, holding his weapon still poised toward Hugh with one hand and raising his other hand palm out. "Easy, man. No one has to die today."

"I shot Fowler. Don't think I won't shoot you if I have to!" Hugh shouted.

The man in the coveralls scuttled away, pulling out a phone as he hurried to safety.

Reid sidestepped behind a pickup truck parked on the tarmac for protection in case Hugh opened fire.

"Fowler survived." At least he hoped his half brother was still alive. "If you surrender now, maybe you can still work out a plea. But if you kill me, my family will see you put away for life."

Hugh shook his head, and Reid could see him perspiring, despite the December chill. "I can't go to jail. I won't. I'm getting in that plane and getting out of here. Don't try to stop me!"

"Too much has happened, Hugh," Reid said evenly, despite the fury that churned inside him. "I can't let you walk away."

"I didn't kill Eldridge! I swear to you I don't know where he is!" A tenor of panic and desperation filled Barrington's voice.

"I know that. I found Eldridge today. Alive. He's been living in downtown Dallas the whole time."

Hugh stiffened. "He what?"

"It was a ploy to see who in the family he could trust. To see Whitney's true colors. And to root out any traitors in his inner circle." Reid paused, watching Barrington's body wilt, though the lawyer still held the gun aimed with a trembling hand.

"Did you tell him...what you found in my office?"

Reid drew a slow breath. "Yes."

Hugh's jaw tightened. "I wanted only what I'd earned. I helped make your father what he became. I saved his ass over and again. I deserved my fair share of his company!"

Reid wasn't going to haggle the right and wrong of what Hugh had done, but he did need one point clarified. For closure. "And Andrew? Did you put the potassium in his insulin vial?"

Hugh hiked up his chin and his face grew florid. "Yes, damn it! I knew he was trying to build a case against me. I didn't mean for you to be the one who gave him the fatal dose. I thought he'd do it to himself one day. But even that was a last-ditch effort, when framing him for stealing drugs from the evidence room didn't get him to back off. I told him I'd clear his name if he'd abandon his witch hunt against me, but he refused."

"Wait...you *framed* him for taking the stolen evidence? I thought he—" Reid's gut pitched. Andrew was innocent. He'd never been a crooked cop. Andrew had tried to defend his honor and reputation when they'd argued that last morning, but all Reid had seen was the circumstantial evidence...

Hugh took a backward step toward the steps of the small plane, and Reid yanked himself from his reflection. "Hugh, stop!"

"No! I'm leaving. I'd die in prison. I refuse to suffer the humiliation of a trial and a jail cell and..."

Reid darted from behind the truck to the door of the hangar, staying behind the wall, but nearer to Hugh. He could almost reach him. Could almost dash out and tackle him during a distraction... "Barrington, I will shoot you to keep you from getting on that plane. Don't put me in that position. I love Penelope, and I don't want to be responsible for shooting her father."

That made him stop. He regarded Reid with a sadness in his eyes. "Penelope." He heaved a deep sigh. "She hates me. She'd be better off without me."

"You've hurt her. You ignored her for years. Her and her mother. Then you took Andrew from her. Can you blame her for being angry?"

"No." Hugh's gun arm faltered, his hand drooping, and his gaze grew bleary, unfocused. "You...you'll take care of her? And the boy?"

Reid narrowed his gaze, his heart thundering. "If she'll have me, I... I want to marry her. I want to be Nicholas's father."

Hugh took another step backward toward the plane. "Yes, you do that."

Reid tightened his grip on his weapon, his finger curled around the trigger. "Now, you put gun down and step away from it."

Hugh scoffed. "No, Reid. I told you I can't go to jail. I won't..."

Then Barrington raised the gun to his own chin... and fired.

Chapter 21

The next day, Penelope stood in the door to Andrew's man cave/office and stared numbly at the half-packed boxes she'd abandoned close to three weeks earlier. Before…

She choked back tears thinking of all that had changed in those weeks, all the ways she'd lost her father. First when she'd learned of his crimes, then when she'd learned of her adoption and finally when she'd learned of his death.

With a deep breath to steel herself, she walked in and sat behind Andrew's desk. Lucky was curled up asleep in one of the boxes, and the evidence of the kitten's last escapade, a scattered and partially shredded stack of magazines lay next to the box.

Penelope swept her gaze around the rest of the clutter. Finishing the cleanup of Andrew's things would keep her busy, her hands occupied if not her mind. She grieved the loss of Hugh Barrington, but in a much different way than she'd have imagined. She mourned the loss of what he could have been. The relationship they'd never repair, the brilliant career he'd ruined for greed, the potential he'd squandered on jealousy. Her chest ached with a hollowness she knew might never be whole again. A gaping wound of disappointment and unfinished business.

Reid Colton was another case of unfinished business. She hadn't seen much of Reid in the last twenty-four hours. After her father killed himself, Reid had stayed to work with the police while she took Nicholas to the doctor. When she'd heard the gunshot from the Range Rover, her heart had stilled, fearing Reid had been the one killed. Even now, thinking back on that moment, her insides seesawed and bile collected in her throat.

A deputy from the sheriff's department had stopped by to quiz her about all of the events of the past several days, starting with the day she'd found Andrew's cubbyhole in the wall. The day she and Reid had launched their investigation of her father, been shot at, and gone into hiding at Reid's lake house. The day her feelings for Reid Colton had turned the corner from bitterness to gratitude. The beginning of her journey to falling in love with him.

But where would that road lead?

We need to talk. That conversation still hadn't happened. He'd been busy with police matters, crime scenes, his family's reactions to the news of Hugh's death…while she'd been busy with Nicholas. Already, only three doses into his antibiotic, her boy was clearly feeling better. She had to keep a sterile earplug in his ear for a few more days, a challenge with a toddler, but Nicholas would make a full recovery.

And wasn't that just the story of their lives? Reid, the skilled crime fighter, the protector and defender, the billionaire playboy with the large blended family to contend with. Her, the single mother, whose sole focus was her son. They were so different. They'd always been different. Why did she think they could possibly make a life together work?

The chiming of her doorbell roused her from her maudlin musing. When she opened her front door to Reid, her tension mounted. His face looked haggard, the cuts and bruises from his fight with Lenny more pronounced today. His mouth was set in a thin line of despondency, and that frightened her the most.

"Reid? What's happened? What's wrong?" she asked as she stood back to let him enter her living room.

He gave her a half smile. "I'm sorry. I didn't mean to alarm you with my glum self." He swiped a hand over his face as he lowered himself onto her couch. "I'm just tired. In addition to all the questions from the police, I've been to the hospital to see Fowler and downtown to talk to my father."

She gave her head a shake and dropped onto the sofa next to him. "Whoa. What? Your father?"

He raised a puzzled glance and then huffed a short laugh. "Oh, that's right. In the midst of all this other insanity I hadn't told you what came of my stakeout. Eldridge is alive and planning to come home tomorrow. He wants it to be a surprise for the family."

He went on to explain all he'd learned about the senior Colton's scheme and how he'd enlisted the butler and his wife to aid and abet his shenanigans.

Penelope rocked back in her seat. "Well, at least your father's story has a happy ending."

Reid covered her hand with his. "Pen, I'm sorry about your dad. I couldn't stop him. I—"

"No, don't blame yourself. I… I'll be fine. It's just a shock. On top of all the other craziness." He squeezed her hand, and she asked, "How was Fowler?"

"Fowler was…Fowler. Bossing the nurses around,

griping about the hospital food, being a pain in the ass. But his ribs are apparently as hard as his head. The bullet stuck in his rib, saving his lung. So other than a flesh wound and broken rib, Fowler will be back at the helm of Colton Inc. in a couple weeks."

"That's a relief." She tucked her hair behind her ear. "And the three gunmen?"

"Will all live and go straight to jail. With your father gone and those guys off the street, you and Nicholas are completely safe again." He paused and looked around. "I assume the squirt is napping? He's feeling better?"

"He's much better. And he's at Mother's Day Out again. I'd hoped to finish Andrew's office today."

"Hey, don't push it. You need to rest. You've been through a trauma."

"What I need is closure. And to stay busy. If I think too hard about everything, I just..." Her voice cracked, and Reid drew her into his arms.

"Sweetheart, what you need is to mourn. Let it out."

She allowed herself a few moments to weep softly against his chest, but the biggest question that needed resolution in order for her to move forward was still unanswered. Dabbing at her eyes, she raised her head and met the deep watery blue of his eyes. "Yesterday you said we needed to talk. I assume you meant about...us. Where we go from here."

He drew a slow breath, expanding his lungs, and gave her a nod. "Right. So..."

She sat up, angling her body to face him, and Reid rubbed both his hands on the legs of his jeans. His apparent nervousness worried her. She'd known Reid wasn't the commitment and long-term type. But that hadn't stopped her heart from diving in.

"Pen..."

"Look," she said, placing her fingers over his split and swollen lip to stop him. "I know that marriage and raising another man's child is a huge responsibility. You have a good life, your freedom, the money to do whatever makes you happy. I can't ask you to give that up for me. I understand that—"

"Hold on." He grabbed both of her hands and squeezed hard to interrupt her. His face furrowed with consternation. "I don't think you understand. Money doesn't buy happiness."

"I know. What I meant—"

"Marry me." When she stared at him silently for several seconds, he repeated his request. "I've had money and freedom and a huge extended family for my whole life, but I haven't been truly happy. I've been...lonely. I've felt adrift, without purpose or focus. Especially over the past year. But spending the past couple weeks with you and Nicholas made me see what I was really missing, what I really wanted in my life. I want you, Pen. I need you."

Penelope blinked as a fresh rush of tears filled her eyes. His words burrowed down to her most private yearnings, her deepest vulnerability and desire. All her life she'd wanted to be wanted, to feel needed. Her father's distance exacerbated that longing, while her animal rescue efforts only scratched the surface of her desire to have someone to care for, someone to love unconditionally. Someone with whom she could build a life of mutual trust and support with, a healthy give and take. She had a degree of that bond with Andrew, and she'd thought she'd never find that kind of love again. But now warmth bloomed in those cold empty spaces of her soul, and she searched Reid's eyes for any hint of hesitation or reluctance.

"Are you sure? Nicholas is—"

"Great," he finished for her. "Nicholas is precious and exhausting and smart and full of energy and in the throws of the terrible twos, and I love him. I want to be his father and watch him grow up. I want to have more children...with you."

Emotion clogged her throat. "Reid..."

"I know you think I'm a spoiled, snobby, rich SOB who doesn't see the value of what he has, but I see you. I see what a treasure you are, and I want to spend the rest of my life cherishing you and making you happy. You give my life meaning, Pen."

"Yes," she squeaked from her tight throat.

"Yes?" His expression brightening with hope.

"Yes," she said again and wrapped her arms around his neck, laughing. "I will marry you."

He exhaled a deep breath in a rush. "Oh, thank God. You've just made me the happiest man on earth."

Epilogue

Christmas morning

Reid knocked on the door to the Manfreds' suite, and while he waited for the door to be answered, he practiced in his head the best way to express his demands.

When Aaron answered the door, he didn't seem at all surprised to see Reid. "Good morning, Mr. Reid. I was wondering when you'd be by."

"Well, it would have been sooner, but I had quite a bit on my plate the past few days."

"So I understand. Is Mrs. Barrington Clark all right?"

"She will be. In time. She's been through a lot lately, but she's a remarkable woman. Resilient. Loving. Strong to her core."

"And you?" Aaron asked, motioning with a hand that Reid should make himself at home in the small sitting room.

"What about me?" He claimed a straight-backed wing chair and perched on the edge of the seat.

"You're well enough?" The older man motioned to

the scrapes and bruises Reid sported from his scuffle with the gunmen.

He shrugged. "I'll live."

Moira walked into the room then and pulled up short. "Oh, Mr. Reid. I didn't—" She cut herself off, frowning at him. "Good heavens! You're injured!"

"I'm fine," Reid said, again trying to brush off his condition. "I didn't come to talk about me."

"Of course, you didn't." Aaron sank onto the settee across from him and sighed.

"I'm obviously disappointed you two lied to the family and kept us in such a state of turmoil all these months."

Moira bowed her head and pressed a hand to her mouth. "Mr. Reid, I'm so—"

"Let him finish, Moira," her husband said quietly and patted the seat next to him. Once the older woman had taken her seat beside Aaron, Reid continued.

"I also understand and can appreciate your loyalty to my father. Truly I blame him for all of this. He put you in an untenable position, and you followed his instructions and took care of him as thoroughly and faithfully as you always have through the years."

Reid divided a look between the two who over the years had become more than just household staff members to his father. They were Eldridge's friends. Family. Whether the cranky old coot realized it or not, these two were more to Eldridge than his father had any right to claim.

"Thank you," Reid said, his voice cracking.

Aaron raised his gaze, clearly startled, and Moira looked at her husband, then back to Reid as if she'd misunderstood.

"You took care of my father, looked out for him while he indulged his selfish game of 'Who really loves me? Who can I trust?' Our family owes you our appreciation for that." Reid turned up his palm, motioning to the elderly couple. "Whether he realizes it or not, you two proved you are loyal to him and care about him even when he's acting like a snobbish child."

"I only wish it hadn't meant deceiving you and Mrs. Colton. It broke my heart to see her grieve," Moira said, her hand pressed to her chest.

"What's done is done, and I, for one, will not dwell on it any further. I will tell my father that you've earned a sizable Christmas bonus for your loyalty and efforts above and beyond the norm."

"Oh, no, Mr. Reid. I don't expect—"

"Oh, but I do!" he said with a laugh as he headed for the door. "It's the least the old codger can do for you. Merry Christmas, Aaron, Moira. Enjoy your day off."

With that, he left the older couple to rejoin his family. He didn't want to miss the highlight of the family's holiday gathering—the return of their wayward and penitent patriarch.

When Reid joined the Christmas party in progress, Josie Colton Grange, Reid's cousin and new wife of Colton Valley Ranch's former foreman, sat beside Penelope chatting pleasantly while Nicholas played with Josie's almost two-year-old stepdaughters.

"I think Lily and Leigh are smitten with their new playmate," Josie said, beaming at the children as they played with a wooden train set.

"Hey," Tanner Grange said in a gruff tone, belied by the twinkle of affection in his eyes, "don't go playing matchmaker with my girls. They're not allowed to date until they're thirty. And then only if I approve the guy."

Fowler had been released from the hospital the night before with orders to take it easy, and he'd made himself comfortable on a chaise lounge in the corner with Tiffany at his side.

Reid slid onto the crowded sofa, pulling Pen into his lap as he did so. "You may regret saying that later, man. Our boy's gonna have a long line of admirers chasing him. Better that your girls get their bid in early."

Pen blinked at him, clearly startled.

"What? Don't you think Nicholas will have lots of girlfriends?"

"Well, sure… I just… *Our* boy?" Her tone was more touched than accusatory.

"If that's okay with you?" Reid said in a quiet voice. "I don't want him to forget Andrew, and I want him to learn what a great man gave him life, but…I'd like to adopt Nicholas as soon as we're married."

Pen's eyes filled with happy tears, and she gave a small nod as T.C. blustered, "Whoa, whoa, whoa! What did you say? Did you just use the M word?"

Pen ducked her head trying to hide her smile, and Reid raked his hand through his hair. "I was planning to save the announcement for later, after—" He caught himself just before he spoiled the second surprise of the day.

"After what?" T.C. prodded, then with a devilish smirk added in a theatrically loud voice, assuring everyone heard. "Are you saying our confirmed bachelor, the last of the Colton brood, is taking the plunge?"

Reid glared at T.C., who returned an unapologetic grin. Shifting his gaze to Zane, he said, "Punch him for me."

Zane jerked a nod. "Love to." And slugged their brother in the arm, so T.C.'s cranberry martini sloshed from the glass.

Reid helped Penelope to her feet and cleared his throat as he stood next to her. "Well, I guess since The Crawler has spilled the beans," he said using T.C.'s childhood nickname with a touch of growl in his tone, "I'll make it official."

Conversations in the corners of the crowded room quieted. The entire family had gathered in the ranch mansion to celebrate Christmas, a sign of how far the Coltons had come in a year. The Dallas Coltons even opened their doors to their late uncle Matthew's children, who'd all suffered through a tumultuous, tragic, and transformative year themselves. At Colton Valley Ranch, feuds had been put to rest, new love celebrated, old wounds were on the mend, and everyone wanted to mark the changes in their lives with a joyful family celebration and feast. What better time to announce his future plans with Pen and Nicholas?

"Everyone, it gives me great pleasure to introduce you to my fiancée and future son. Pen has agreed to marry me and allow me to adopt Nicholas."

Cheers, catcalls and applause rose in response to his announcement. His brothers slapped him on the back, and the women cooed and hurried to Pen for hugs and private congratulations.

Whitney made her way through the throng to embrace him and kiss his cheek. "Oh, darling, I'm so happy for you. If only my Dridgey—uh, your father—" she quickly corrected, and Reid smiled his thanks "—could be here to share this joy." She gave him a strained smile. "I wish—"

Pressing her lips together and giving her head a melodramatic shake...as if she hadn't over the past few days made it clear to everyone in self-pitying fashion how miserable her Christmas would be without her husband. Even if Reid didn't know the truth, his mother's endless attention-seeking complaints made it hard to be sympathetic to her sadness.

He almost told her the big surprise he was keeping from the family, but a movement at the door to the front foyer drew his attention. And the point became moot.

Placing his hands on Whitney's shoulders, he said, "Mother, I think your wish came true. Merry Christmas."

At her puzzled look, he jerked a nod toward the foyer.

"What's this I hear about an engagement?" Eldridge said in a booming voice above the fray.

"Dridgey-pooh!" Whitney shrieked in glee.

Gasps, glad cries and several outbursts of "Father!" or "Eldridge!" filled the room. Reid cleared a path through the swarm of family so Whitney could fall into her husband's embrace. "Oh, darling! You're alive! You're here, you're—" Whitney paused, blinking at Eldridge.

And slapped him.

The assembled group murmured their shock.

"How dare you leave me alone with no word where you were and whether you were alive or dead!" she shrieked in ear-piercing tones. "I've been worried sick! *Sick*, I say!"

"I'm sorry, baby. I need time to get my head straight. To figure out what—"

"Oh, hush, old man! There'll be time for explanations later." She threw her arms around Eldridge and kissed him. "I'm just so glad you're alive. The rest will sort itself out later."

The rest of the family clustered around Eldridge and welcomed him home, tossing questions at him along with hugs and handshakes.

"I think we've been upstaged," Pen whispered to him.

Reid snorted a laugh. "Typical Eldridge."

Pen laid her head on his shoulder and laced her fingers with his. "Doesn't matter. Besides, I think having Eldridge back is the best Christmas present your family could have asked for."

He nodded his agreement and gave her a wry grin. "And six months ago, who'd have ever thought that?"

* * * * *

Don't miss the previous titles in
THE COLTONS OF TEXAS *series:*

RUNAWAY COLTON
COLTON FAMILY RESCUE
HIGH-STAKES COLTON
THE PREGNANT COLTON BRIDE
COLTON COWBOY HIDEOUT
A BABY FOR AGENT COLTON
HER COLTON P.I.
COLTON'S TEXAS STAKEOUT
COLTON BABY HOMECOMING
COLTON'S SURPRISE HEIR
COLTON COPYCAT KILLER

Available now from Mills & Boon Romantic Suspense!

MILLS & BOON®

INTRIGUE
Romantic Suspense

A SEDUCTIVE COMBINATION OF DANGER AND DESIRE

A sneak peek at next month's titles...

In stores from 15th December 2016:

- **Riding Shotgun** – Joanna Wayne *and*
  Stone Cold Texas Ranger – Nicole Helm
- **One Tough Texan** – Barb Han *and*
  Battle Tested – Janie Crouch
- **Turquoise Guardian** – Jenna Kernan *and*
  San Antonio Secret – Robin Perini

Romantic Suspense

- **Undercover in Conard County** – Rachel Lee
- **Dr. Do-or-Die** – Lara Lacombe

Give a 12 month subscription to a friend today!

Call Customer Services
0844 844 1358*

or visit
hillsandboon.co.uk/subscriptions